FULL SPEED AHEAD

BETH BOLDEN

CHAPTER ONE

Adrenaline surged through Lennox's veins as he pulled up to the house. He stopped at the bottom of the driveway, flicking his lights off.

Two years ago, Lennox had been sure that he'd never feel this particular rush ever again.

Being forced into an early retirement from operating with the rest of his team hadn't felt like a death sentence—but a *boredom* sentence.

How would anything ever feel exciting ever again when he was forced to babysit rich kids and install unnecessary security systems and convince people that their lives weren't *actually* in danger?

It turned out he couldn't have been more wrong.

The house was dark, the clock in his car flashing that it was just past four in the morning, as he turned off the engine and grabbed the revolver he'd tossed on the passenger seat when Landon's emergency call had awakened him fifteen minutes ago.

Creeping quickly up the extensive driveway, Lennox made a note that they needed more lights. Lots more lights. Not only for when he had to intervene—but hopefully to deter anyone that would force him into intervening in the first place.

He skirted around the path lined with billowing ferns, and finally made it to the front door. Keeping his head down low, he rapidly typed in the code he'd programmed himself, only a few months back.

Pushing the door open as quietly as he could, Lennox pulled up the memory of the last time he'd been in their house, and cautiously and carefully made his way through the expansive, shadowy foyer, checking each corner as he headed towards the kitchen.

He heard voices—annoyed but not panicked—and a second later, he was around the last turn, flicking on the safety of his gun as he entered the kitchen. There was the intruder, standing near the sink with an outraged, sulky expression on his face, and Quentin, one of the house's owners, brandishing a shiny silver cleaver, holding him in place.

"Thank *God*," Landon Patton, one of the world's biggest pop stars, said as Lennox walked past him, and even though the intruder tried to wiggle away at the last moment, it was easy enough to pin him against the wall.

For a second, Lennox was almost disappointed at how little effort it required to take him out of play. He hadn't really *wanted* a fight, but with the adrenaline coursing through his veins, that first burst of immediate fear, followed by the way Lennox's focus had narrowed so intently on his target, he'd kind of wanted one.

Maybe he'd only been awake for fifteen minutes, but for fourteen and a half of them, he'd been alert and ready to dismantle the threat.

Except the threat hadn't turned out to be much of a threat at all.

The guy was small, about six inches shorter than Lennox's big six-foot-four frame, and slight, but from the way he kept struggling pointlessly against his own tight grip, he was also determined—and almost definitely crazy.

At least if the way he kept ranting about Landon and how he was the father of Landon's baby was any indication.

"Let go of me," he cried out as Lennox pushed him against the wall, "I want to comfort my husband and our child, he's going to hurt it, he's not going to take care of it." He shook his head fiercely against the restraint of Lennox's arm, surprising Lennox with his fight. "I'm *supposed* to be here."

"Listen," Lennox said, finally giving in and exerting his strength fully and pushing the wiggling fish of a guy back harder against the wall, "I hate to break it to you, but male pregnancy is a few centuries away from being a scientific real-ity."

"And," Landon added with an offended sniff, "it's *really* not nice to break into someone's house just to tell them they're looking *fat*."

Lennox chuckled under his breath, despite the effort it was taking to hold the guy.

"I'm not sure anyone laboring under this kind of delusion needs evidence, babe," Quentin, Landon's *actual* husband, pointed out.

"I'm just really grateful you were able to come on such short notice," Landon said to Lennox. "You got here a lot faster than the cops did."

Lennox muttered under his breath. He'd been here five minutes already, and it was five minutes too long, as far as he was concerned. Thankfully, by the time Landon had managed to get to his phone and dial Lennox's emergency number, Quen had already cornered the intruder in the kitchen with the cleaver.

He didn't want to think what this idiot could have done to Quen or to *Landon*, if they'd had to wait for the police, who had yet to show up.

"We're going to upgrade your security system," Lennox said as he twisted the guy around and, digging around in his pocket for a zip tie, none-too-gently tightened it around his wrists.

"Oh good," Landon said.

"But that means you have to actually *use* it," Quentin pointed out gently.

"Is that how he got in?" Lennox wanted to know. "The system was off?"

"And Landon left a window open, I think," Quen said.

It was only a lifetime of practice that helped Lennox restrain his eye roll. When he'd started his security company in Los Angeles, he'd expected that the only target he'd be fighting was boredom. It turned out that most of his clients were their own worst enemy.

Landon, as much as he liked the guy, definitely had that particular problem. He was one of the biggest pop stars in the world, and he acted like he was never in danger.

"Well, first thing," Lennox said as kindly as he could manage, "you've got to actually *turn* the system *on*."

"I know, I know," Landon said, wringing his hands. "I will now. I just never imagined . . ."

"That I'd come for you and our baby?" the guy squawked before Lennox could pull the duct tape from his pocket and shut up the flow of inanity pouring from his mouth. "I'll always come for you and for our baby!"

"You're going to be waiting a goddamned long time," Landon said.

"Don't engage with him," Lennox warned, even though that was like asking water to stop being wet. He dug the duct tape out and, despite the wiggling, finally managed to get a piece across his mouth.

Not that it stopped the guy from continuing his attempts to speak.

"I just thought he was some crazy guy who sent a lot of fan mail and kept commenting on my social media," Landon said.

"Your manager has been forwarding some of it onto me," Lennox said. "Did you read the threat assessment I did?"

He asked the question, even though he already knew the answer.

"Uh." Landon hesitated.

"No," Quentin finished for him, shooting his husband a worried look. "He didn't, I know he didn't, and he *should* have."

Landon threw up his hands. "Alright, so I suck, and this is my fault."

"Nobody is saying that," Quen said gently, wrapping an arm around Landon's shoulders. "We just want you to be safe, that's all. You said you'd deal with a regular bodyguard while you're out, but maybe we should consider getting one to stay in the house, too." He glanced up at Lennox. "What do you think?"

When he'd started his company, The Protectorate, he hadn't envisioned that he'd spend quite so much time both placating clients and diplomatically trying to suggest the best thing for them in a way that would actually convince them to accept it.

He'd stupidly imagined that he could just say it, and they'd believe it.

That hadn't happened much, despite his lengthy list of qualifications and accomplishments, and it definitely hadn't happened with Landon Patton.

"I know you want to preserve your privacy," Lennox said. "I think if we do a few upgrades, add some lights, and you actually *use* the system I installed, you should be fine without a live-in bodyguard. Of course, all that depends on what shakes out with this dude here." Lennox pointed to the sulking, silent man behind him. "If he starts making more trouble, or continues to ignore the restraining order, we'll have to revisit the conversation. Maybe temporarily station someone here twenty-four seven."

"Alright," Landon said with a resigned sigh. "I think that's fair. I can do that."

"And I want everything he writes to you sent over to me," Lennox said.

"I'll let Paul know," Landon said, just as there was an insistent knock at the front door.

"That must be the police, *finally*," Lennox said. "Quen, can you get it? I don't trust this guy not to try something . . ." The guy in question squirmed angrily again. Probably didn't like that Lennox was talking about him in front of him.

Well, Lennox didn't like that the guy had broken into his clients' house and terrified them half to death.

Quentin nodded and went off to answer the door. A minute later, he was back, with two uniformed LAPD officers.

Lennox went over the situation, including the outstanding restraining order that Lennox had convinced Landon's manager, Paul, that he needed to take out, and after taking his statement, the officers took custody of the intruder and hauled him off.

By that point, it was almost six, and Quentin had started making coffee.

The problem with the adrenaline was that even after it had burned out of him, Lennox was still jittery enough that he wouldn't be able to sleep. So when Quentin offered him coffee, he took it, and sipped it, glad that Quen had made it black as mud. He didn't usually head into the office until eight, but he might as well use this extra time to go over all the material that Paul had already sent over regarding the intruder.

"Thank you again," Landon said as he got ready to leave. Landon threw his arms around him and hugged him hard. "I don't know what we'd have done if you hadn't showed up."

Lennox smiled. "Have to wait for the police?"

"Yeah," Landon said, shooting a look at Quen, "he's not *that* good with a cleaver."

Quentin owned one of the best bakeries in Los Angeles, so he actually was, but Lennox knew he didn't have the killer instinct necessary to use it. Neither of them did. They were just good, kind, surprisingly down-to-earth people, despite Landon's tendency towards melodrama.

But he hadn't been overly dramatic this morning. This morning could have turned out far worse.

"We'll get to the bottom of this, I promise," Lennox said. "Thanks for the coffee. I'll be in touch."

"Thanks again," Quen said as Landon wandered off. "I . . . well, you know I worry about him."

Lennox wanted to pretend that he'd never felt that particular kind of worry, but he was intimately familiar with it, had felt it every day for so many years that it felt like it had become part of his bones and his blood.

"I'll take care of him, I promise," Lennox said.

Before going private, he'd never once promised anyone a positive result. He hadn't been able to. But in this world, where the participants were almost entirely safe *anyway*, it was a lot easier to guarantee. And, Lennox had learned, it meant something that he gave his word.

Quentin shook his hand and Lennox headed down the driveway towards his car.

Lennox had been at his desk for hours when Seth, his second-in-command, arrived, carrying a pair of coffees in his hand from their favorite cafe down the street. When Seth had texted, letting him know that he was on his way to the office after a morning meeting with some of the downtown clubs they provided security for, Lennox had asked him to pick up more coffee.

Better coffee.

"Hey, you look a little fried," Seth said, setting the coffee on the desk. "What happened?"

He was sure the last thing he needed was more caffeine but he picked up the cup anyway and drank deeply, the rich flavor of the roasted beans rolling over his tongue.

"Patton had a break-in early this morning," Lennox said, as Seth sat at his own desk, only a few feet away. They were the only two full-time permanent members of the company at this point—everyone else was temporary, or part-time, usually hired through Lennox's connections to the military community.

Seth had served through three tours in Iraq and had gotten out about four years before Lennox. It wasn't easy to adjust to life on the outside, and when Lennox had showed up in LA, angry and resentful and bitter, struggling to adapt to civilian life, Seth had been instrumental in helping him.

When Lennox had started his company, there had been no better person for him to pick to run it with him than Seth.

"You took care of it?" Seth asked, his tone concerned as he sipped his coffee.

"Landon called me on the emergency number," Lennox said. "It was that crazy stalker guy." He sighed. "Landon admitted he's not using the security system, and he'd left some windows unlocked."

"Ugh," Seth groaned. "Really?"

"The silver lining is that he's been scared silly by this. Quentin managed to corner the stalker with a cleaver, so it was mostly under control before I got there, but I think we won't have a problem getting him to accept more stringent security in the future."

"Well, there's that," Seth said. "Have you been here since the break-in?"

"Yeah," Lennox said, scrubbing a hand over his face. "I stopped upstairs and had a quick shower." He'd bought this building with the small trust his grandmother had left to him when she'd died, that he hadn't touched while he'd been in the military. After he'd gotten out, he'd known he'd wanted to do *something*, and while he hadn't been sure what it was, Seth had persuaded him that security was a great business to be in, especially with his qualifications.

But while he'd still been coming around to the idea, he'd bought the building, with the loft living area upstairs, and the potential office space below, knowing he'd need a home base in the city.

Now he lived upstairs and worked downstairs. Seth didn't exactly approve—he was always complaining that Lennox spent too much time in the office—but the property had come with a huge upside.

A year after he'd moved in, the empty lot a few blocks away had been transformed into a food truck collective, with six restaurants on wheels that convinced Lennox to get out of the office way more often.

He glanced at his watch, noticing it was almost eleven.

"I've been reviewing all the files," Lennox said. "Everything Paul sent us on the stalker. All the letters, the social media comments, everything. Even my security analysis, which Landon admitted this morning that he didn't read."

"But you said it, he's gonna pay a lot better attention from now on," Seth pointed out, as he spun around on his chair to meet Lennox's eyes. "Bet that got the blood pumpin' though."

"I remember when I was convinced this would be a boring-ass job," Lennox said with a dry chuckle. "It was definitely not boring this morning."

"At least it was Quentin with the cleaver and not the stalker," Seth said.

"He's too interested in taking Landon and his baby away and keeping them safe," Lennox said, watching as Seth's eyes grew wider.

"Landon and his . . . *baby*?"

"Don't ask," Lennox said. "But I'm gonna overhaul their security system, install some more lights."

"Not today, I hope," Seth said. He gestured at Lennox's knee. "How'd your knee hold up?"

"It's fine. You *know* it's fine." Lennox grimaced. "It's not like I'm crippled."

He didn't mention that sometimes it still ached. Or maybe that was the physical manifestation of the ache in his chest, the way he still missed his team.

He'd been terrified when the stray bullet had taken out his knee. Not of the searing, exploding pain, but of the consequences. The medical team, one of the best in the Navy, had put his knee back together, and it was perfectly functional, but the problem with perfectly functional was that it wasn't *SEAL Team functional*.

Which had been his fear the whole goddamned time.

"No, I'm not crippled." Once in awhile, when Lennox was feeling particularly sorry for himself, he thought it might be easier if he had been. Instead, he could go for a jog if he liked, or go a few rounds with Seth on the mats, and be none the worse for the wear. But it hadn't been *quite* good enough, no matter how much PT he'd done, and finally, horribly, he'd been forced to face the truth.

He wasn't going to be able to operate again. Not like he had. And not with his team. Not ever again.

The damage had just been too great.

"I mean it with love, but man, you look *rough*. There's nothing else you can do for Landon. Maybe you should take a nap." He paused, a teasing light emerging on his face, and he grinned. "Or maybe we should spar today. You look like I could actually take you."

Seth probably could, today, but there was no way Lennox was going to admit that.

"You wish," he said.

"You know me." Seth rested his hip against the edge of Lennox's desk and raked a hand through his over-long reddish-brown hair. The hair that Lennox kept not-so-subtly suggesting that he get cut. "I'm an eternal optimist."

"Despite everything," Lennox said, rolling his eyes. Neither of their lives had been particularly easy. Especially since leaving the Navy. But Seth wore it so much better than Lennox did. It wasn't like Lennox hadn't *tried* to adjust to civilian life, but he wasn't ever going to be Seth and be comfortable and at ease in every situation. He knew that much.

"Despite everything," Seth agreed. "You know, you should go get something to eat." He plucked Lennox's half-drunk coffee off his desk and took a sip. "Not more caffeine."

"You tryin' to get rid of me?"

"No, I'm trying to get an early lunch," Seth said with a knowing grin. "There's nothing more you can do for Landon right now."

Seth was right. They both knew it. "Maybe not," he said. But he'd be lying if he didn't like Seth's plan. His stomach *was* grumbling. He could do with some food.

He grabbed his coffee out of Seth's hand and poured the rest of it down his throat. It was nearly eleven. Some of the trucks would be open this early. *Ash's* truck would be open, because he was always open by ten.

Usually Lennox tried to resist the temptation to pick Ash's truck over all the others, because nobody with a functioning stomach would prefer a salad over a meatball sub or a grilled cheese or a gyro with all the fixings. But Lennox didn't go to Ash's truck because he loved a salad; he went because, despite all the warning bells blaring in his head, Ash was freaking adorable. All big eyes and cheerful smiles and a body that reminded Lennox that it had been too long since he'd had any company in his bed besides his right hand.

"Seriously, go get some food. And . . ." Seth hesitated, charming smile on his face. "If you go by the food trucks, grab me a wrap, alright?"

"The Thai chicken?" Lennox asked as he grabbed his wallet and his phone from the top drawer of his desk. His fingers hesitated over his gun. If he wore his jacket, he could tuck it into his holster. It was never easy for him to leave the gun behind, even when logically he knew he didn't need it.

The most dangerous weapon in his possession didn't need bullets—the Navy had taught him about a hundred ways to take someone down with just his hands and his strength—but his pistol was a reassurance, especially on a day like today.

Lennox glanced outside. It was beautifully sunny and shaping up to be a warm one. He'd leave it behind, and his jacket too. It was good practice; a reminder that he was, for all intents and purposes, a civilian now.

Seth was always telling him to start acting more like it, but old habits died hard.

"Yeah," Seth said. "The Thai chicken."

"Be back in a few," Lennox said and pushed the front door open, feeling the warmth of the sun already through his shirt.

CHAPTER TWO

It was *him* again.

Ash wiped his damp palms against the towel hanging from his belt loop and the smile that bloomed across his face wasn't even a tiny bit forced.

"Hey," he said, as the dark-haired man approached Ash's food truck. "How's it going?"

Ash had been working in the hospitality industry practically since the cradle, and it had been drilled into his bones to always be friendly, to always ask customers how they were doing, to make sure they not only had a great experience, but a *personal* one.

Yeah, the personal experience that Ash wanted to give this guy was definitely not anything like the one his father had coached him on.

"Hey," the guy said back. Ren, Gabriel's cousin who worked with him on his food truck, had discovered that his name was Lennox—nobody was sure if that was a first or a last name—but he hadn't told Ash himself yet. Maybe that was a good goal for the day. Convince Lennox to give him his name. Coax him, one little tidbit at a time.

It was a little game Ash played sometimes. Each time Lennox came back to the Food Truck Warriors lot, Ash hoped that his smile would be a little wider, a little less restrained. The first time he'd shown up, looking uncertainly around, like he wasn't quite sure he belonged, he hadn't smiled at all.

Now he did, cautiously at first, but when Ash leaned over the counter, and grinned, his smile broke free of its wary constraints.

"You hungry today?" Ash asked.

"Starving," Lennox confided. "It's been a *day*."

Ash thought he looked it. Frazzled, in a way that he'd never seen Lennox before. Circles under his eyes. Lines bracketing his mouth. The mesmerizing dark eyes unusually strained.

He was a big man, tall and broad with the most incredibly wide shoulders that looked like they could hold just about any burden. Close-cropped dark hair, and those eyes that had captured Ash from the first moment he'd seen them. The nose on his handsome, arresting face was not quite straight anymore, but the rakish tilt of it suited him.

Lennox was an eye-catching, attractive, *mysterious* man. Was it any wonder that Ash couldn't quite look away from him?

"If you're so hungry, I'm surprised you weren't over at Gabe's truck, then," Ash teased. "I could smell his meatballs across the lot this morning."

Lennox patted his stomach, over his pressed white shirt. He'd shed his jacket today, and his tie, emerald green, was already loosened. "I had a meatball sub yesterday," he said. "Gotta watch my calories."

He didn't need to. His stomach was flat against his hand, and Ash could see the shadows of his undeniably built body under the white of his dress shirt.

"So you're over here today," Ash said, propping his chin up with his palm, elbow resting on the counter. "What sounds good?"

Lennox smiled again. Wider, this time, and Ash gave himself a mental pat on the back.

Someday, maybe in six or eight months, he might actually be able to flirt with Lennox without him getting flustered and essentially running away.

"How about my usual?" Lennox said.

"The grilled steak. Alright," Ash said, and pulled a biodegradable bowl from the stack next to him, filling it with the fresh spring lettuce mix and then beginning to pile the rest of the veggies that he knew Lennox liked on top of the greens.

"What's this?"

Ash glanced up from making Lennox's food to see him pointing to a notice he'd taped to the front window, just this morning.

"We're closing early this Friday," Ash said as he topped the salad with the crunchy fried tortilla strips that he knew Lennox loved. "It's our six-month anniversary and we're celebrating."

Ash watched as Lennox shoved his hands into his pockets. "I'm surprised it's been six months," he said quietly. "Feels like just yesterday you opened."

Ash wasn't proud of it, but he remembered the exact day that Lennox had wandered onto the lot for the first time. It had been only the second day they'd been open, and Ash had watched as he'd perused every menu carefully, his steps as he moved around in the semicircle deliberately, taking in everything from the stage at the front of the lot, to the picnic tables scattered around the center, to the lights draped across the lot. It had been dusk, and Tony, who not only owned a food truck that parked here, but managed the lot, had already switched the lights on.

They'd been reflected in Lennox's dark eyes as he'd approached Ash's truck.

He'd been close-lipped and almost impossible to engage in a conversation, and completely, utterly irresistible.

Ash had never been particularly attracted to enigmatic guys before, but there was something about Lennox that made him want to *dig* and to *know*.

"Yeah, it's been a fast six months, that's for sure," Ash said. He reached down into the fridge under the counter and pulled out two plastic containers of the garlic peppercorn ranch dressing that he knew Lennox preferred.

The man might not be willing to tell Ash his name yet—Ash was still annoyed that Ren had gotten that info before he had—but he knew exactly how the man liked his salad.

"You know, you spend a lot of time here," Ash said, deciding as he rung up Lennox's salad on his iPad system that there was no time like the present to take a walk on the wild side. "You should come to the party on Friday."

Lennox was in the middle of sticking his credit card into the slot when he froze. "I should come to the party?" he asked, the edge of his voice incredulous, like he couldn't believe that Ash had invited him.

Ash couldn't quite believe that he'd invited him. Wait until the rest of the guys heard about this. They'd never let him live it down.

"Yeah, you should. You hang out a lot, which is super cool. And the guys here? I'm sure they'd love to share a beer with you," Ash said, trying for breezy and casual, but not sure he'd actually arrived there. His fingers were trembling a little, and he pressed them against the stainless steel counter in front of him.

"You think they would?" Lennox looked *and* sounded skeptical.

"I know I would. I'm Ash, by the way," he said, adding a bright smile that wasn't nearly as confident as he felt.

What was wrong with him? He invited guys out all the time. He dated, while not regularly because his schedule sucked, but often enough. But none of those guys had ever made his heart race like this, like he was sixteen again, and the cutest guy in school had just said hi to him in the hall.

"Lennox," he said brusquely. "Nice to meet you."

Like they hadn't met ages ago, months and months back. *Six* months ago, to be precise.

"Well, I'd love you to come," Ash said. "Friday at eight."

Lennox picked up his salad. "Thanks. I . . . uh . . . I'll think about it."

"You do that," Ash said brightly. "And I'll see you Friday."

After Lennox left, Ash felt weirdly jumpy, unable to settle back down into his normal routine.

It was lunchtime and the lot was crowded, or else he might have closed the truck and taken a break himself. But a minute later, just when he was contemplating whether Tony would kill him for doing just that, another customer walked up, joined by a couple, and then another group that he recognized from one of the office buildings a few blocks away.

He was lucky enough to be pretty busy for the next few hours, which meant that he couldn't focus on the thing he'd done until the lunch rush ended.

And then, when the crowd finally dwindled down, and he was alone again, he unsurprisingly freaked out.

The front of Tate's truck was also a ghost town, plus he had his sister working today, so Ash shut his own truck, posted a quick sign in the window that said he'd be back in twenty, and ventured over to grab a grilled cheese as a late lunch.

"Hey," Ash said as he approached, waving to Tate, who was leaning against the counter, scrolling through his phone. "Let's take a break."

Tate glanced up, grinning when he saw Ash. "You wanna sandwich?"

"Yeah," Ash said, and even though it was already over eighty, the sun shining brightly in the sky, he added, "And a cup of the tomato soup, if you don't mind."

"Sure thing. I'll grab something for me too," Tate said.

Ash went and sat down at the picnic table closest to the truck, waiting for Tate to make their lunch.

A few minutes later, he emerged from the truck, balancing everything in his arms.

"Everything alright?" Tate asked as he set the plates and cups down on the table. "You don't usually want comfort food unless it's serious."

"It's . . ." Ash wanted to tell his friend that of course it wasn't serious—he didn't even *know* Lennox, it had taken him six months to even get the guy to tell him his name—but it *felt* serious. Like they'd just turned a corner, and nothing after was going to be the same.

Maybe Lennox wouldn't come on Friday. Maybe he'd never come back, and Ash would never get the chance to make him smile again.

Or maybe Lennox would realize what Ash was offering and realize it was something he wanted too.

"I asked Lennox to come to the party on Friday," Ash said.

"You did *what*," Tate said incredulously, setting his fork down, with its bite of macaroni and cheese uneaten. "How do you even know he's interested in guys?"

"I . . . I don't." Ash had to admit that. "But when he turned Ren down, he got the impression that it wasn't because he was a guy, it was because he wasn't interested in a hookup."

Tate raised an eyebrow. "We're taking Ren's word for this?"

Ash knew they all liked Ren a lot. But he went through hookups like Ash went through lettuce, and it was possible he'd misremembered or misinterpreted.

"Ren's a pretty good judge of this kind of thing," Ash said. And it was undoubtedly the truth. He had enough experience for it to be the truth.

"Alright, well, what did Lennox say? Is he coming?"

"He said he'd think about it," Ash said, scrunching his face. "I think he was honestly more surprised than anything else. I don't think . . . well, I don't think he gets a lot of party invitations."

"He *is* kinda awkward," Tate pointed out.

It wasn't awkwardness, Ash thought, because nobody that confident could be awkward. It was more . . . *closed off*. Lennox didn't let anyone in.

Ash took his sandwich and dipped it in the soup, taking a bite out of the corner and chewing with relish. Nobody did comfort food the way Tate and his sister did. If he could, he'd eat their food every single fucking day.

He'd probably be a hundred pounds overweight, but he'd undoubtedly be the most comforted person in existence.

"He's not awkward, he's . . . well, I think he's shy. Secretive. *Mysterious*," Ash disagreed. "He just needs someone to help him come out of his shell."

Tate shot him a look over his macaroni and cheese. "And you think that's you."

"I mean, I wouldn't exactly complain if it was me," Ash said.

"You don't think he just wants to come here and get lunch and hang out?" Tate wondered.

"If that's all he wants, then he doesn't have to come on Friday." Ash kept his voice casual, but he already knew that if Lennox didn't show on Friday, he'd be disappointed.

Not heartbroken, or anything, because he hardly knew the guy. But disappointed, because he felt the breathless antici-pation of possibilities brewing between them. There was no way Ash was alone because that kind of tug required two people—even if one participant wasn't very happy about it. And Ash definitely got the feeling that if he was right, and Lennox was attracted to him, it was an unwilling attraction.

"I guess we'll just have to see," Tate said, as he finished off his macaroni and cheese. He stood. "I'll be there, but the next morning, I'm leaving early, headed to Dallas for one of the Riptide's preseason games."

"Harmony must be working out, if you're leaving her and Rach for a whole weekend," Ash teased. "Or your boyfriend is irresistible."

Tate flushed. "Both?"

"As if we didn't already know," Ash said. "But seriously . . . Harmony seems great? I know she's been talking about wanting more hours, and I thought I could use her, too."

"Yeah, she's great, and I think she'd love that," Tate said sincerely. Then he pinned Ash with a quick, hard look. "Just don't totally poach her, okay?"

"Scout's honor," Ash said with a grin. "I just want to sleep in some days. Get some help on prep. Maybe take a day off once in awhile."

"She'd be perfect for that," Tate said. "But I'm warning you, once you get her help, you're gonna want it all the time."

Ash sighed, as he finished his sandwich. "It's totally possible," he said.

Tate smiled at him. "Definitely more of a sure thing than this Lennox guy." He hesitated, setting a supportive hand on Ash's shoulder. "Don't get your hopes up, okay? None of us are sure what to make of him."

Ash knew it, and he also knew that his friends basically liked *everyone.*

"You'll see," Ash promised. "He's . . . well, he's a good guy. I know it."

Hoped, as Tate walked away, that he wouldn't regret being so goddamned sure later.

Lennox decided and then changed his mind about the party at least a dozen times between when Ash had asked him on Wednesday, and now.

He still, when he'd thrown on his leather jacket, to better cover his gun since he was technically on call, hadn't been entirely sure that he would end up walking over to the food truck lot.

He *wanted* to. Lennox also knew that if he'd told Seth—which he definitely hadn't—Seth would have told him unapologetically that he needed to grow a pair and just *go*. That it was just a party, and that he was thinking and then *over*thinking it way too much.

He liked Ash, even though he had zero intentions of acting on it, and he was pretty sure Ash liked him back, considering that he'd invited him tonight.

Lennox stopped at the edge of the lot, seeing the extra lights and hearing the music playing, the sound of laughter echoing over to where he stood.

It reminded him, even though he didn't want to be reminded, of how many times he and his team had hung out after a particularly difficult mission, unwinding and shooting the shit. Often they'd end up sitting together and drinking one beer after another, understanding that sometimes, what you really needed was the comforting silence of someone who'd been where you'd been.

He had Seth now, of course, who understood. But he hadn't made any other friends in the area, not unless he counted the guys who ran the food trucks, and Lennox wasn't counting them, not yet, because he could tell, other than Ash, they were still a bit wary around him. Not sure what to make of him, because he shared so little of himself while they shared everything. Laughing, and drinking, and eating, and loving.

If Lennox had ever known how to be that free and easy, he'd long lost the ability.

That was probably why, even though he *wanted* to take those few last steps and walk onto the lot, secure in the knowledge that Ash had invited him, he was still hesitating. He didn't know how to do this, felt painfully out of his depth.

You gonna let a little thing like not knowin' how stop you?

The voice came out of nowhere, a voice that Lennox actively tried *never* to remember. It hurt, still, more than he wanted to admit to.

But even worse, that voice was right.

Before, he'd never let something as inconsequential as not knowing how to do something be enough to stop him. He'd been the definition of unstoppable.

Even after losing everything—his job and his career and his adoptive family and the relationship that had meant the most to him—he'd still pressed on ahead, forcing himself to confront the realities of civilian life. He'd never just taken what was handed to him and let it shape him. He'd taken control, damnit.

That attitude carried him onto the food truck lot, and he crossed over to where a makeshift bar had been set up. Ash was standing there, slim figure dressed in form-fitting jeans and a loose bright yellow tank top, the lights overhead catching the blond highlights in his hair.

"Hey," Lennox said quietly, and Ash turned, the brightest smile Lennox had seen to date on his face.

And suddenly, even though his palms were sweating and he was undeniably a tiny bit terrified and there was a strong chance this was all a huge mistake, Lennox was glad he'd come after all.

"You came," Ash said, voice dropping to a conspiratorial tone, his eyes twinkling.

"Well, you *did* tell me to," Lennox said. It had been so long since he'd flirted. Had he and Marcus ever flirted? Once in awhile, privately, maybe. But never like this, never out in the open, where anyone could hear. It made him a little breathless.

It wasn't that he didn't think he could do it, it was more that he was uneasy with it. *Fuckin' awkward,* that voice said again and this time Lennox pushed it down, so far down that he couldn't hear it again. So he *wouldn't* hear it again.

"I did," Ash said, leaning down and grabbing a pair of beers from the cooler, giving Lennox a heart-stopping view of his perfect ass. It wasn't like he hadn't ever seen it before, but it was different when Ash was in his food truck and Lennox was outside of it. Now, there was nothing between them. Nothing stopping him.

Except, he reminded himself, all the very good reasons he had for not pursuing anything with the guy.

"I still didn't expect you to come," Ash continued, handing one of the beers to Lennox, who used the edge of the table in one swift motion to pop the top off.

Ash, who'd been looking around for an opener, gave him a wide-eyed glance. "You're pretty good at that," he said, sounding impressed, as Lennox took his bottle and did the same thing.

"When you're in the middle of the desert, you might be lucky enough to have a beer, but you gotta get creative to get it open," Lennox said.

"In the desert?" Ash didn't just sound curious, he sounded fascinated.

"I was in the military. Iraq. Afghanistan," Lennox said shortly. Hoping that would be the end of the questions, even though he already knew better. Ash's eyes were overflowing with them.

"How long have you been out?" Ash asked, sipping his beer.

Lennox ignored the way his lips looked around the bottle. But it was *hard*.

"A few years," Lennox said. "My knee got blown out. Couldn't operate any longer, not at the level I needed to, anyway." It was more than he'd told anyone in a long time; frankly, more than he'd intended to tell Ash.

"And now?" Ash asked.

"I run a security company." Tony had managed to finagle that much out of him, during one of the times he'd gone to his truck for the best fish tacos he'd ever eaten. And he knew something about fish tacos; he'd used to live in San Diego.

Tony had been making noise, every time he ran into the guy, about hiring Lennox to make sure that their security measures were solid. It wasn't really the kind of work his company did, but since he was the managing partner, he could be flexible. Besides, he couldn't imagine Seth throwing a fit about having more business.

And there was a part of him, trained for so many years to protect what he cared about, that knew he wasn't going to let anything happen to any of these guys—or their businesses.

"That's really neat," Ash said, sounding like he meant it.

"Our office is only a few blocks from here. Which is why I'm here so much," Lennox said. He realized, only a moment too late, how that sounded. Like he didn't appreciate what they'd built here. That he only came because it was close. "And also because the food is good," he finished lamely.

"Even the salads?" Ash raised an eyebrow, a teasing smile growing on his handsome face. "'Cause it seems like you wander my direction more often than not."

Lennox took a drink of his beer. It wasn't really cold yet, lukewarm liquid fizzing on his tongue, but he didn't give a shit because it might cover his awkwardness.

Ash was definitely flirting with him. Testing him out for his interest. He knew that much. It was different than how that other guy, Lennox thought his name was Ren, had done it, coming right out and asking to have sex.

Like Lennox was the kind of guy who could just drop everything and hop on the next vaguely attractive guy he met.

Even though Ash's teasing inquisition was making him sweat, Lennox found he enjoyed it a lot more. Even if he was going to have to ultimately turn him down.

"I like your salads a lot," Lennox said honestly. "And it's always nice to see a friendly face."

"I must have a really friendly face," Ash said, scrunching that face up. "A little friendlier than Ren's anyway."

So he'd heard about that. Lennox shrugged. "I'm not . . . I'm not one for that kind of thing. And Ren, well, he's a little . . ."

He didn't know how to say that the guy kind of intimidated him, without actually coming out and saying it. Because Marcus would kill him for admitting to a cute guy that he'd found another one intimidating.

"Shark-like?" Ash laughed, and Lennox felt the sound ghost over his skin, prickling every nerve. "He knows what he wants and he usually gets it."

"I bet he does," Lennox said. The way Ren had looked when he'd turned him down had made it clear enough. But he didn't want to talk about Ren. He hadn't come here for Ren. "What about you?" he asked, even though he already knew at least part of this story. "How long have you owned your truck?"

"Five years," Ash said.

That was a lot longer than Lennox had anticipated. "You must've been pretty young when you opened it," he said. "That's an accomplishment."

Ash batted his eyes flirtatiously. "I'm older than I look. It's all the super greens I eat."

"It's definitely something," Lennox muttered, mostly under his breath.

The wild grin Ash flashed him made it clear he'd heard anyway. "Thanks."

"Your father must have helped you get going," Lennox said, and realized, as he watched the light in Ash's eyes dim and then darken, that he'd said precisely the wrong thing.

"What?" Ash demanded. "You know my father?"

"I . . ." Lennox hesitated, not wanting to put his foot in it any further. "I've met him, yes."

"And he mentioned me to you." Ash's fingers clenched around the bottle in his hand, knuckles showing white.

Lennox opened his mouth to try to fix this, when Ash abruptly reached out, grabbed him by the forearm, and proceeded to drag him off, towards one of the many dark corners of the lot.

He could have easily shaken off Ash's grip, even though it was firm. He knew a hundred ways to get out of it, a *thousand*, but he let Ash pull him along, anyway. He was curious, despite the apprehension coalescing in his stomach.

Besides, the way Ash was looking, like a thundercloud, made it clear that he wasn't dragging him over here so they could take advantage of the privacy for the kind of activities that Lennox had heard happened here frequently.

"How do you know him?" Ash hissed, dropping his arm the moment they were essentially alone.

"I do security for some of his restaurants, and his bars and clubs," Lennox said, telling the truth.

"And he told you I had a food truck and where I was parked and you decided you'd come check it out. Or maybe he *insisted* you come here to check it out."

Ash sounded really unhappy about this possibility.

"No, no, no," Lennox stuttered. "I mean, maybe the very *first* time, but then I came back, because like I said, it was convenient and well, I *like* it here." It was more than Lennox had even said to Seth about the food trucks, but he felt the chill of something unpleasant rippling up his spine, and there was that horrible distrust in Ash's eyes, replacing all that sweet, teasing flirtation.

Lennox did not like it at all.

Ash started to pace back and forth. "Didn't you think it was weird that I wasn't using his name? Didn't you think I might want to keep my connection to him under wraps?"

"Your connection to him . . ." Lennox was understandably confused. Ash and his father didn't just have a *connection*—they were related. By blood.

"I don't tell anybody about it," Ash said, his voice suddenly full of steel as he whipped around, pinning Lennox with a hard look that Lennox had never anticipated someone like Ash could possess. "That's why my name is different. Because I don't want anyone to know that he's my father." His lips pursed. "We don't speak. Ever."

"Oh," Lennox said, slowly becoming more aware of just how terribly he had fucked this up.

You can fix it, Marcus said in the back of his head, refusing to stay where Lennox had shoved him, *all you gotta do is lean forward and kiss him and he'll forget it. He'll melt into you like butter on hot toast. You know how to do it right.*

He did, because he and Marcus had always done it together. Until they wouldn't ever again.

Lennox gave his head a sharp shake, trying to clear it. He wasn't going to kiss Ash, not like this, and not at all. And definitely not to try to distract him from the way he'd epically fucked up.

"I hate him," Ash said simply. "And I don't want people to come to my truck because of who I am. Because of *him.*"

"So that's why you go by Ash, then," Lennox said, grasping for rock-solid facts in the sudden morass he'd found himself in. He'd been a little surprised the other day, when Ash had introduced himself. For a moment, he'd almost been sure that he'd gotten it wrong, and Ash wasn't the son of Stephan Atkinson, one of the biggest celebrity chefs in the world.

But then he'd gone back to his office, did a quick Google search and discovered that Stephan Atkinson had one child, a son, and he was named Oliver Ashton Atkinson.

Ash.

It had never occurred to Lennox that Ash wasn't just using a nickname, that he was actively *hiding*.

"Yes," Ash said shortly.

"You mean . . . nobody knows that you're Atkinson's son?"

Ash shook his head. "Nobody here, anyway."

"Shit," Lennox swore.

"Yeah, well, if I'd known . . ." Ash didn't finish that sentence, and Lennox both desperately wanted him to, and dreaded what he would say if he did.

Would Ash tell him that if he'd known that Lennox was connected to his father, he'd never have invited him here tonight? Wouldn't have smiled at him so often? Wouldn't have tried, more than once, to flirt with him?

"I'm sorry," Lennox said, because what else could he say? "I didn't . . ." He took a deep breath. "I did not mean to bring up someone that you'd rather not talk about," he said stiffly.

Ash still looked suspicious. "You haven't told anyone?"

"I don't know if you've noticed, but I'm not the most social person on the planet." Lennox chuckled dryly. "I'm not exactly coming around, making small talk."

And, he added mentally, he'd been pretty sure that everyone had known—they just didn't talk about it. But he didn't mention that part of his thought process to Ash, because that was sure to make him hate him even more.

"He really didn't send you here to check up on me," Ash stated suspiciously.

"*No.* Well, the first time, maybe," Lennox allowed. "I did think it was weird he'd mention that his son was part of a new food truck lot that was just starting." Especially considering that during all the time they'd worked together, Stephan hadn't once mentioned that he had a son. And just like Lennox, Atkinson was more likely to bark orders than make normal chitchat.

Looking back, the truth was staring him in the face and embarrassment bloomed across Lennox's face in a hot flush.

Ash crossed his arms over his chest. "I don't feel comfortable begging anyone for anything," he said, and Lennox had already known him well enough to guess that was true, "but I don't want anyone to know. Please don't say anything."

"I won't, I promise," Lennox said. "I . . ." He wanted to apologize again, but he already had, once before, and one apology per conversation was definitely his normal limit. But there was something about the way that Ash kept looking at him like he'd betray him the first chance he got that really bothered Lennox.

"Good," Ash said, giving a sharp nod, turning and walking away.

Lennox watched him walk away, scrubbing a hand over his face. For a split second, he considered leaving. Ash might have wanted him before, and while he hadn't technically rescinded the invitation, Lennox was no longer sure he was welcome. Even if he *wasn't* here as a representative of Ash's father.

Lennox turned to go, and decided, at the last second, that while he was here and it was dark, he might as well take in some of the improvements that Tony had claimed to make to his security. There were at least half a dozen shadowy corners, even though Tony had said he'd added some additional lights.

He was halfway across the lot, checking out the lights, when he stumbled across a couple, who clearly did not want to be disturbed, using one of the dark corners for their own devices. It was Gabriel, the guy who ran the meatball sandwich truck, and Sean, who did the wraps that Seth loved so much. Lennox was surprised, because he was fairly sure that at least one of them had mentioned that they didn't get along, despite having named their truck the exact same thing.

Now that he thought about it, maybe that was the whole problem.

When he stumbled onto them, Lennox realized he should have known better. How many dark corners had he found with Marcus? Too many to count.

That was how they'd lived, in all those dark corners.

"Tony asked me to check the lighting, to make sure things were bright enough." He hesitated. "I guess we've found a spot where the lighting could be improved." He didn't know what else to say, so like always, he fell back on his training. On his professionalism. Technically, Tony hadn't really *asked*, but he'd been making overtures, and he didn't think Tony would mind if he made a few recommendations.

"Tony asked you to do that tonight?" Gabriel sounded skeptical.

"No," Lennox had to admit. "But he mentioned it the other day and I was here and . . ."

"I'm pretty sure Tony didn't mean *tonight*," Gabriel said, surprising the hell out of Lennox by putting a hand on his shoulder. People didn't usually touch Lennox. He knew he looked tense and standoffish. It helped when they got to know him, but Gabriel didn't really *know* him. "Come on, let's go back to the party."

If he went back to the party, Ash would be there. And his cold shoulder would be obvious. "I don't know. I'm here now."

"Seriously, this is a party, not a security check," Sean said. And then *he* touched him. This was definitely a touchy-feely bunch, Lennox thought as they dragged him back to the party.

They got him another beer, and he was in the middle of having at least a decent conversation with Sean and Gabriel, though he hadn't exactly *relaxed* yet, when of course, Ash showed up.

Flushed, carrying a clear plastic cup, like he'd just been over at the bar, drinking.

"Impression of what?" Ash demanded, like he already suspected that Lennox had told Gabriel and Sean the truth.

Lennox told himself that he shouldn't be annoyed. He and Ash didn't know each other that well, but the distrust in his eyes *hurt*.

More than he'd ever expected that it would.

"That everyone's fine fucking around," Lennox said. Frustrated, because he'd *never* once felt that comfortable. Was he jealous? He might be. He was certainly *something*, itchy right under his skin.

"That's not true," Ash said.

"I just know what I've seen," Lennox said, because he *had* seen it. Maybe he was just calling the shots like he'd seen them, but deep down he knew it was more than that.

Maybe they all thought he was the bad guy, the awkward guy in their midst, but they'd never understand that all Lennox had ever wanted was exactly what they had.

And he'd been forced to realize, over too many years, and one painful heartbreak, that it was never going to be something he was entitled to.

Naturally, this was the moment Tony decided to show up. "You certainly have no issues coming around buying meals from us," he said, his arm draped around his boyfriend's shoulders.

"I don't have any issues," Lennox said. And he didn't. Except from a persistent case of envy. "I apologize if you think I did. You're free to live your lives however you see fit."

"We certainly will." Ash's chin jerked up in a stubborn, implacable angle.

"I guess I'll see you around," Lennox said, because it was high time he left.

His invitation had long since run out.

CHAPTER THREE

It had been a day and a half since Gabriel and Ren had discovered the vandalized picnic table, and Ash still felt vaguely sick to the base of his stomach.

Before he'd seen it with his own two eyes, the purple scrawl brazenly written over the surface, Ash had been fully intending to talk Tony out of hiring Lennox for security. He'd believed that Tony was overreacting and they didn't really have a problem.

But now?

Ash eyed the table, which Lucas had adorned with glitter and rainbows in an attempt to own those scrawled purple letters, and couldn't deny that they had a problem any longer.

Suck a dick had ruined that naive optimism forever.

He still wasn't sure he believed that Lennox would keep his secret, but whether he kept his mouth shut or not, at least he would make sure that this safe place *stayed* safe. He did trust Lennox to do that, because it was his job, and it was clear to everyone on the lot that he was damn good at it.

Ash hadn't been surprised to see that Lennox was here tonight, with the music and the party atmosphere. Hoping, probably, to catch the culprit in the act. If Ash didn't know his habits as well as he did, he'd probably have guessed that was why Lennox was removed from the crowd, all the way at the edge of the party, back stiff and straight, his serious expression inscrutable.

Before he'd seen him, Ash hadn't had any intention of talking to him. But now that he was looking, he couldn't quite look away. Couldn't help thinking of how much more handsome he was when he relaxed and smiled. Couldn't help his own feet from walking over to where Lennox was standing by Gabe's truck.

"Hey," Ash said.

Lennox looked surprised to see him. Which wasn't a shock, considering how he and Ash had left things. How *Ash* had left things.

He'd told himself that he didn't feel guilty for yelling at Lennox like that or for accusing him of spying for his father, but he did anyway.

That must explain why he'd come over here, after all. Not necessarily to *apologize*, but to clear the air.

Lennox cleared his throat and looked out over the crowd. "If you want me to leave, you're going to have to come up with a much better reason."

"Than spying for my father?"

Lennox gave a sharp nod.

Ash sighed. "I don't know what I believe, but if you are, then you must be pretty bored by now. So you might as well protect my friends and their businesses and make sure this place stays safe at the same time."

"I'm not," Lennox said stiffly. "He's never brought you up, except that one time. Never even asked me about you."

"I . . ." Ash hesitated. He realized he'd been about to say, *I believe you*, except what reasons did he have?

Was it the horrible look in Lennox's eyes when he'd seen the table, the way the emotion had flashed over his face, and then he'd covered it up, pushing it away almost immediately?

He was hurting too. Just the same way they were.

"I trust you're going to do the right thing," Ash finished.

Lennox didn't say anything for a long moment. So long that Ash almost thought that he hadn't heard him. Or hadn't *cared* that Ash believed him.

Ash had almost decided that this was a completely fucking useless exercise, when Lennox spoke again, this time his voice lacking his normal confidence.

"I dealt with this all the time, you know," Lennox said. "When I first enlisted, it was nearly constant. My shit would be destroyed, vandalized, people would make nasty comments out in the open. Do you know how many times I got told to suck a dick?"

Swallowing hard, Ash nodded carefully. He didn't know what to say to that. But of course, being queer and in the military must have been a nightmare. And Lennox had not only done it anyway, but he'd *kept* doing it.

"Not in some nice purple paint, anyway," Lennox said wryly. "It did get better, over time. Most guys aren't willing to confront you when you could kick their ass from here to next week. So I became the toughest guy there. Trained the hardest. Was the most valuable member of my team. But every time a new guy would show up, I'd hold my breath because I never knew what they were going to say or what they'd try to do to me."

"I can't imagine living that way," Ash finally said. It didn't feel like enough. He felt lower than low, like the kind of asshole who'd antagonized Lennox just because he could. He and the other guys had never been *that* terrible, but they'd never tried to understand him, either.

"And I can't imagine living like this. All out in the open," Lennox said.

"Why are you telling me this?" Ash asked, realizing that so many things made more sense. The unsettled way that Lennox looked when he came here—even though he always came back. Sometimes every day.

Like he was craving something he'd never experienced before, but when he got it, he didn't know what to do with it.

Lennox glanced over at him. He wasn't smiling, but there was something more open about his face. Less guarded. "I know something about you that you didn't want me to," he said. "It seems only fair that you learn something about me that I don't tell anyone, either."

"Thanks for . . . trusting me *back*. Your secret's safe with me, too," Ash said. He really meant to shut up then, but Lennox was still looking at *him*, not at the other people, and he always seemed to stumble, to hesitate, to lose some of the confidence he'd built up whenever he came face to face with the man. "I'm really sorry I yelled at you that night."

Because he *was* sorry. He'd overreacted, and totally lost his composure. Yeah, he didn't want anyone to know he was related to Stephan Atkinson, but that hadn't been a good reason to destroy a friendship before it had even begun.

Maybe not *just* a friendship.

"I'm sorry, too," Lennox said. The corner of his mouth quirked, and that was *almost* a smile. "I'm not very good at this."

Ash waved a hand. "How were you supposed to know?"

"It's my job to know, Ash," Lennox said in a low, deep voice that resonated with Ash on all kinds of levels.

This, he thought, would be *so* much easier if he didn't want to still climb this man like a fucking tree.

But before he'd even gotten a chance to make that a reality, to wear down all of Lennox's reserve, he'd fucked it up by freaking out.

"I wasn't your job, though, back then," Ash pointed out.

"No, you weren't, you were just the guy who convinced me that I liked to eat salad." There was a *real* smile then. Ash had forgotten just how spectacular they felt—like they were warming him from the inside out.

"Oh, that's *all* I was?" Ash teased.

Another smile. Even brighter than the last. "If only you knew how *actively* I avoided salad before this," Lennox said.

"I'll take your conversion as a compliment, then."

Lennox tilted his head. "You should."

"Well, you're welcome to come by anytime." Ash grinned. "Not that you weren't before . . . but now, I expect you'll be spending more time around . . ." It was funny how just yesterday, he'd been nervous and apprehensive about that particular fact, and now he was still nervous, but it was a bubbly, excited kind of anticipation.

There was no way that Lennox would be an easy guy to befriend—he'd be an even tougher guy to try to date.

But Ash had dated lots of guys who'd made it easy. Easy charm, easy laughter, easy kisses, even easier hookups. Something about the challenge of Lennox, about all the mysteries and secrets he was clearly still hiding in that sharp brain of his, made him irresistible even though Ash should've known better.

"I'll definitely be stopping by," Lennox said. "You make my favorite salad, after all."

"You mean, the only salad you're willing to eat," Ash joked, but from the way Lennox flushed for a split second, he knew he must have accidentally hit on the truth.

And wasn't it a real interesting kind of truth?

Maybe convincing Lennox to explore the obvious chemistry between them wouldn't be as challenging as Ash thought it might be.

But then, Lennox tossed cold water all over that optimistic train of thought.

Pushing away from Gabriel's truck, Lennox said, "I need to do my security pass." In a split second, he'd gone from tentative smiles and *almost* flirting back to stiff awkwardness and duty. Ash barely refrained from making a face in the midst of his disappointment.

"A security pass?" he asked.

Lennox shot him a look. "That's my job," he said quietly. "And I need to do it."

And Ash, despite everything he wanted, let him go, even though he didn't want to, but because he'd gotten the impression that *need* wasn't just because Lennox had promised Tony or because it was written into the contract Ash knew they'd signed.

It was because it was burned into Lennox's blood and bones: it was *his job* to protect. He couldn't live with himself otherwise.

Ash was just going to have to come up with a way to convince him that it was alright to *stop* for a minute. Or an evening.

Lennox tried to ignore the voice in the back of his head that told him he was running away.

He'd been part of an organization and a team that not only refused to ever shirk a fight, but typically dropped everything to run *to* the fight.

But Oliver Ashton Atkinson was an entity that Lennox was having a hard time pinpointing.

He was clearly interested in Lennox, even though he wasn't quite sure if he trusted him yet—and Lennox would be lying if he said he wasn't interested back.

Despite determining that would *never* happen, for many strong and valid reasons, Lennox had come to the party a few weeks back because he'd also determined that it wouldn't compromise either of them in any way if they became friends.

It might not be everything that Ash clearly wanted, or that Lennox himself grappled with, late at night, alone in his bed, but it was *something*. It was definitely more than Lennox had allowed himself in years.

Still—instead of clarifying that what he was after was just friendship or even companionship, he'd fucking *run*.

"Stupid, stupid, stupid," Lennox grumbled under his breath as he went through his security sweep. The band was still playing on the stage at the front of the property, but as it grew later, the crowd was beginning to disperse. And none of them, as far as Lennox could see, were behaving suspiciously or lurking around in a way that pinged any of the many years of training he'd had.

Everyone here, he was fairly certain, was here for the right reasons, and had had nothing to do with the graffiti scrawled across the picnic table.

Which left Lennox nothing to do but make his circular pass, noting that the lights were shining on all the previously dark corners, and checking on his phone that the security feeds were all working properly.

And because everything seemed to be perfectly in order, it also left him with a whole litany of self-recrimination that instead of clarifying with Ash what he was after, he'd . . . *bolted*.

This time he couldn't even blame Marcus' voice in his head; this lecture was all on him and he deserved every second of it.

Ash's truck happened to be the last on his pass, and when he'd designed the route, he'd thought at the time that felt fortuitous. If he wanted to stop and chat at the end, he always could.

When he turned the corner, he saw Ash leaning over, unlocking his bicycle from the heavy-duty stand that Tony had installed for him. "Hey," Lennox said, because he knew how quietly he walked, and he didn't need to scare Ash on top of everything else.

Ash glanced up. "Oh, it's you, again," he said.

He didn't sound displeased to see Lennox, but he wasn't smiling like he usually did, and Lennox would have to be stupid not to understand why.

"Listen," Lennox said. "Remember what I told you earlier?"

Ash nodded slowly as he straightened, one hand on the handlebars of the bike. "Yeah."

"It means I'm really terrible at this," Lennox said. He wasn't proud of how unsteady he sounded, because it went against the grain to admit, to *anyone*, that he wasn't good at something. Especially someone who he liked as much as he liked Ash. Ash, who was terrifyingly competent and could serve a whole line of people by himself without breaking a sweat. Who made everyone feel welcomed, personally, and never like they were bothering him when they dithered over a selection, or like they were just another visitor.

"Terrible at what?" Ash wondered.

Lennox blanched. It was bad enough to admit this. It was so much worse to have to go into detail.

What was he bad at? Being friendly. Smiling. Making small talk. And even worse, flirting. And deflecting flirting. Absolutely fucking terrible at that.

Because he kept *not* doing it, even though he knew better.

"This," Lennox repeated stubbornly, because fuck, he was not going to make this any worse than it already was.

"Being friendly?" Ash wondered. "Yeah, you kinda are."

"And . . . other things, too," Lennox said, embarrassed at his nebulous phrasing and wishing he could take it back from the moment it left his lips. Especially when Ash smiled knowingly like that.

Ash set the bike against the stand again, and walked closer. Lennox forced himself to hold his ground. *You are not gonna run from this guy; not him and not now.*

"That's alright," Ash said, sounding unconcerned. "Because I think I'm pretty good at it. Maybe I could teach you."

"Teach me?"

Suddenly Ash was in his bubble, the space around him that nobody ever seemed to invade because they always sensed it would be a bad idea. But Ash pushed right through it like it didn't exist. Like that invisible wall didn't bother him in the slightest.

Lennox sucked in his breath as Ash leaned in, even closer. "Yeah," he said, still smiling, "*teach* you. For example, when someone flirts with you, and invites you to a party, it's only polite to give them a kiss goodnight."

He had plenty of time to avoid it. To move his head. To turn away. To *walk* away. Ash hadn't exactly made a secret out of the fact that he was going to lean and press his mouth to Lennox's.

But he stayed rooted in place, like his feet—and his heart—knew something that his head didn't yet.

The kiss was soft and gentle, like Ash was worried about scaring him away.

If only Ash knew how insanely difficult he was to scare, and how embarrassingly easy it was, at the exact same time.

Lennox got the briefest impression of Ash. Soft lips. Soft hands. And then he was pulling away, eyes blinking open hazily, like the kiss had shaken him more than he'd expected it to.

It hadn't just shaken Lennox; it had rocked his world to the core.

Lennox opened his mouth to say something—*anything*, he thought desperately—and then snapped it shut again.

"First lesson," Ash said softly.

"I don't know . . ." But before Lennox could continue, Ash had put a finger over his lips, stopping him in his tracks.

"I know," Ash said not unsympathetically. "But that's alright."

And then, like he hadn't just thrown a grenade into Lennox's well-ordered life, he stepped back, and grabbed his bicycle again. "Well," he said, when Lennox still didn't say anything, "I guess I'll see you around."

Lennox watched him go and wondered how this could have gone wrong so quickly and so completely.

He'd fully intended to have a conversation about how they couldn't get involved, but that he wanted to be friends. And then he'd just let Ash go off and kiss him? What had he been thinking?

He *hadn't* been thinking. Or he'd been doing all his thinking with the wrong organ.

He'd promised himself the last time he'd done that and it had all gone to hell that he would never, ever let that happen again.

Maybe, he thought, as he watched Ash gracefully pedal down the street, it was time to remind himself of all the ways this could go wrong.

CHAPTER FOUR

"So," Tony asked as he leaned back in his chair, beer bottle in one hand, "how did the festival treat you?"

It had been a busy two weeks. During the first week, Ash had been trying to forget that he'd kissed Lennox, and then trying to forget that he hadn't come around since. He'd sent that other guy he'd worked with—Ash was pretty sure he'd heard his name was Seth—instead of coming himself. At least while Ash was on the lot.

Ash had been forced to mentally work overtime, convincing himself that he hadn't permanently scared the guy away.

Then, the week after, the lot had closed because there was a big food truck festival downtown and a lot of their trucks, including Ash's, had parked down there for the week.

Maybe, Ash decided, two weeks was long enough for Lennox to get over being kissed.

"Sales were great," Ash said. "I'm glad I went."

"Yeah," Tony said, "same." But he didn't look happy. He looked profoundly *unhappy*.

"What's going on?" Ash asked. He'd have known that Tony wanted advice, even if he hadn't asked him to the Funky Cup specifically. He'd known because Tony had the worst poker face of anyone he'd ever met.

Something was definitely bothering him. Ash hoped he and Lucas weren't having problems, because they'd become the bedrock of the lot. If they broke up . . . *well*, Ash didn't even want to think about it. He liked knowing that there was a couple who'd made it, against the odds.

It helped, whenever he thought resentfully of how he'd kissed Lennox and then he'd run away and *stayed* away.

"Ryan and I have been talking about how to expand the lot," Tony muttered, referring to his brother-in-law, Ryan Flores.

"I thought you'd be happy about that," Ash pointed out. "It's something you've wanted to do forever, right?"

Tony glared at the dancing flames in the firepit in front of them. "Yeah, it is. I just didn't think . . . well, I didn't think it would be like *this*."

Ash took a long drink of his beer. "And what is *this*?" he asked.

"You know Basket," Tony said, referring to the food truck. He made a face, crinkling his nose, like he'd just smelled something really offensive. "Aaron and Ross? Well, those fuckers kept trying to get in, and I kept ignoring them."

"Because they 'stole' your onion dip recipe?" Ash barely refrained from making hand quotes around *stole*. Because he was still not exactly sure that was what happened. It was what *Tony* wanted to believe had happened. But how original was onion dip, anyway?

"Yes," Tony ground out. "But I guess they finally got tired of me stonewalling them, and they went around me. Those shitheads."

"Ah, they went to Wyatt," Ash said. Wyatt was Tony's younger brother, and he knew although they had a history of resentment, they'd set all that aside when they started their first food truck together.

"Nope," Tony said. "Even worse. They went to Ryan."

"Crap," Ash said. Ryan was Wyatt's husband, and a rich and successful professional baseball player. He'd been the one to bankroll the food truck lot, and though Ash knew Tony had been making payments to slowly buy it from him, he was pretty sure Ryan still had a managing percentage of ownership.

AKA he could make the decision to allow the Basket guys to join Food Truck Warriors.

"He didn't understand why I wouldn't let them in. They're . . . well, you know how popular they are." Tony's voice went acid and bitter. "He said I was making it personal, and I needed to be thinking about what was best for the business."

Ryan was not wrong. He was both smart and savvy, which Ash had seen right away the first time they'd met. It was one of the reasons he'd always been on board with Tony's idea to form a collective.

"Did you explain about the onion dip?"

"I did," Tony said despondently. "No dice."

"Why do they even want to join? They're pretty successful all on their own."

"Yeah, but it's way more work to have to arrange everything and drive *to* the customers," Tony said. "Here, the customers come to *us*." He paused. "Basically, I think they're lazy as fuck."

Ash shot his friend a look. "You do realize you're saying that we're *all* lazy as fuck, right?"

Tony shrugged, still staring moodily into the fire. "I just don't want to share this with them."

"They're . . ." Ash hesitated. "They're really not so bad. A little egotistical, maybe, but they're formally trained chefs. That's more the norm than the exception. You know that."

"I just wish they'd take their ego someplace else," Tony said.

"That's why you wanted to talk to me, isn't it," Ash said. "Because I know them."

And he had no intention of saying *how* he knew them. Because originally, they'd worked for his father, in his flagship restaurant.

Tony might be acting like this was the worst thing to ever happen to him, but it wasn't great for Ash either. If he wanted to keep his family a secret, the last thing he needed was to bring more people around who knew.

Lennox had been bad enough.

"Yeah, you know them. I know you've even defended them before," Tony said. Didn't sound very pleased about this par-ticular fact.

"I don't know if I would go as far as to call it *defending* them," Ash said. "But yeah, we've chatted. They're not *all* bad, Tony. They're not going to destroy anything. And hey, they might bring a lot more business in. That's never a bad thing."

"Yeah, but it feels a little like making a deal with the devil," Tony complained.

"Then make a deal of your own," Ash said. "Tell them they're welcome, but they're not welcome to sell the onion dip here."

"You really think they'd agree to that?"

Ash didn't really think so. The onion dip with assorted dippers—veggies and homemade cracked pepper parmesan crackers—was a foundation item on their menu. But maybe it would make Tony feel better if he was able to negotiate.

He shrugged. "Maybe. It's worth saying something. Get it out in the open. Also," he added, "if you're going to talk to one of them, Aaron's way more reasonable than Ross."

Please don't ask me how I know that.

Tony's gaze narrowed. "I thought you'd just chatted with them a few times."

"Yeah," Ash said. He knew that was not exactly an answer, but he had no intention of telling Tony how he knew them. It was one thousand percent *not* happening.

It was bad enough Lennox knew the truth.

"Well, thanks for the advice, I guess."

"You guess?" Ash retorted.

"I mean . . . I'm not happy about this. I'm not *gonna* be happy about this. But might as well do what I can to bring them over on my terms, right?"

"Right," Ash said. "It's only fair."

"It kinda feels good, actually, to know they went beggin' to Ryan," Tony said, suddenly grinning. "They must want in bad."

"It's a great situation, and they know it. They're not *dumb*," Ash said. They'd never been dumb. They'd been the smartest guys in his father's kitchen, and that was saying something. Of course, his father had been alternately furious and dumbfounded when they'd quit, probably because he couldn't understand why anyone would want to start a food truck when they could work in a high-end brick-and-mortar kitchen.

After they'd walked away, Aaron and Ross had been one of the first big food trucks in LA, and though Ash would never admit it, their defection had been the final motivation Ash had needed to walk away and do his own thing—which kind of ironically, had *also* been a food truck.

At the time, he hadn't really cared what he was going to do. He hadn't really intended to do anything with food, but that was all he knew, so he'd started working for various trucks around Los Angeles, and then he'd eventually tapped into his trust, using the money to buy a truck of his own.

He'd paid every cent of it back, including interest, and had never touched it again.

"I just wish they would leave me alone," Tony grumbled.

"I doubt this has anything to do with you," Ash teased. He wondered if it had something to do with *him*. But he pushed that thought aside. They'd quit Stephan Atkinson's restaurant and not looked back. Why would they care if his son was running a food truck now? And why would they go out of their way to join him?

"Yeah, well, it *feels* like it does," Tony complained. He drained his beer and stood. "I'm gonna grab another round. Do you want a refill?"

"I'm good, thanks," Ash said.

If he had too much to drink, he wouldn't want to get up early tomorrow and go for his normal jog. And he might, horror upon horror, decide to take a detour on his way home and bang on Lennox's door and demand to know why he'd run after their kiss.

Tony had let slip a week or so back that Lennox not only had an office a few blocks away, but that he lived above it—and Ash really wished that Tony hadn't, because now he felt tempted every single time he rode his bike home.

It was a problem.

"Hey."

Ash glanced up and saw Lucas approaching. "Hey back," he said. "Tony's inside. Grabbing another beer."

"And a beer for me, I hope," Lucas said with a grin. "I texted him and let him know I was on my way over."

"He's pretty upset," Ash said. It was not a wild assumption that Tony had already told his boyfriend about Basket forcing their way into the lot.

"Yeah," Lucas agreed. "Even though I keep tellin' him that it's a good thing."

Ash was not surprised. Lucas was the chiller, more laid-back, more practically minded half of their relationship. He usually balanced out Tony's intensity really well.

At least when Tony chose to listen to him.

"I think it is, too," Ash said. "And I told him that."

"Good," Lucas said, rolling his eyes a bit as he sat down on the bench across from Ash. "Maybe he'll pay attention to what you have to say."

"We'll see." Personally, Ash wasn't going to hold his breath. Tony got real stubborn about some things, digging down deep until nobody could budge him.

If Ryan was forcing him to move on this, it was going to make Sunday brunch a little uncomfortable at the Blake-Flores house for the foreseeable future.

Eventually, Tony would probably come around.

"And you," Lucas said, leaning forward. "You've been quiet. Haven't been here in ages."

Ash hadn't been. It wasn't because he hadn't wanted to. More like, the Funky Cup was only a few blocks away from where Tony had mentioned Lennox's building was. It wouldn't be a huge stretch for Ash to see Lennox here. He'd seen him here before, a handful of times, usually having a beer with that guy he worked with.

It wasn't like Ash was avoiding him.

And even if he was, Lennox had avoided him first.

"I was busy. At the festival," Ash defended. "I saw you down there, too."

"Yeah, I took the vegan truck. I think we're gettin' close to a breakthrough. People were really into it," Lucas said.

"Hey, that is *great,*" Ash said and meant it. He and Lucas had both had some difficulties when they'd started. So many people thought food trucks were reserved for late-night junk food—the kind of food you'd regret eating in the morning.

But Ash had always believed differently, and it was great that Lucas had brought even more attention to the healthier food trucks in their group.

"I saw a huge line at your place, too, a few times."

"Yeah, we were definitely busy."

Lucas raised an eyebrow. "We?"

"Yeah, I'm using Harmony sometimes," Ash said. "You know, she works with Tate and Rach, too, sometimes."

"Oh yeah. That's cool," Lucas said. "That's a big step."

Ash nodded. It was, and even though Harmony was only working a few days a week, it had still put a strain on his budget, even with how well he was doing. But he didn't want to sell *just* salad forever.

Maybe once, when his father had made all kinds of disparaging comments about how assembling raw ingredients wasn't *cooking,* he might have.

But, Ash had learned, living for revenge only felt satisfying for so long.

The blush had begun to go off the rose awhile back, but he hadn't wanted to face it. But realizing that Lennox knew his father, and then coming face-to-face with Aaron and Ross from Basket again? This was all a reminder of why he'd branched out in the first place.

He'd wanted to be different. To be *better*.

At least his own definition of better.

"Maybe we should be the next set of trucks to collaborate," Lucas suggested. "I know Tony hadn't decided on the next pairing yet, but I think we'd work great together."

"Really?" Ash was surprised that Lucas had brought it up. "That wasn't just Tony playing matchmaker?"

"Well, it worked, didn't it?" Lucas said with a chuckle. "And maybe at first, it might have been, though the idea was one we'd been kicking around forever. It worked so well, though, it'd be stupid not to try again."

"True," Ash said. He hadn't considered whether he'd be willing to be part of this new collaboration idea of Tony's. His menu was pretty basic and generally adaptable. Occasionally, he would have a daily special, but it was rare.

"We could do it with Tony's truck, so he wouldn't even be able to bitch," Lucas said with a conspiratorial grin.

Lucas had started working on Tony and Wyatt's truck, What a Catch, originally. But then, after they'd gotten together, he'd mostly transitioned to his own vegan truck. Ash knew sometimes he still moonlighted for Tony, and since Lucas' own truck had yet to join the lot, what he was suggesting made sense.

But Ash wouldn't be Ash if he didn't try to throw a little wrench into things. It was why he'd kissed Lennox, wasn't it? Because he could never quite leave well enough alone. He'd known Lennox was nervous and apprehensive, especially about anything resembling a romantic relationship. And he'd gone ahead and kissed him anyway.

Yes, because he'd wanted to, but also because just like Tony, sometimes he loved to stir the pot.

"Or," Ash suggested, "you could finally convince Tony to let your truck into the lot. If he's giving in to Basket, why not stretch the rules just a little?"

Lucas looked surprised. "You think he would? He wouldn't for Tate and Rachel," he said, referring to the threshold of sales that Tony and Ryan had established every truck needed to be making to be allowed to join the Food Truck Warriors. "Tate even faked a freaking relationship with Chase Riley to generate enough sales."

"Yeah, and we all knew how that was going to turn out," Ash said. "But seriously, you're probably close enough. Pull out your numbers from the festival. I'll be happy to show him how well I'm doing too. We need more than junk food on the lot, no offense to Tate and to Gabe."

"You're right," Lucas said, and there was a determined gleam in his eye that Ash wasn't sure he should entirely take credit for.

At least when Tony demanded to know who had been the one to push Lucas into this.

"You're right about what?" Tony asked, emerging from the bar, carrying two beers in one hand and a plastic basket full of sweet potato fries in the other.

"Oh, we'll talk later," Lucas said, shooting his boyfriend a knowing grin.

Tony sat down, looking slightly apprehensive. "Is this the kind of 'talk' I'm going to enjoy or that I'm going to tolerate so we can get back to the former?"

"The latter," Lucas teased. "Definitely the latter."

"Hell," Tony said. "Nobody's taking it easy on me this week."

"You're the boss," Lucas said. "I don't think we're supposed to."

"You have been hiding in this office for *two* freaking weeks now, and I'm tired of it."

Lennox looked up and Seth was standing in front of his desk, the kind of determined expression on his face that did not bode well for anything in his path.

Especially when the something in his path was Lennox himself.

"I haven't been hiding," Lennox said. It was not *quite* a lie. "I've been busy. Upgrading Landon's security system. Adding lights.

Making sure Landon and Quentin know what to do if the guy ever manages to get in the house again."

Truthfully, he hadn't needed to be quite so hands on, but with Ash's kiss still knocking around in his brain, distracting him at moments when he needed to focus, he'd kept away because that had seemed safer.

Seth rested a hip on the edge of Lennox's desk. "That didn't take twenty-four seven of your energy these last two weeks. I know it. You know it. The stalker guy hasn't even shown his face since he broke in. So tell me, what's going on?"

"I don't want to talk about it," Lennox said.

"I know you don't, but don't you think that means you should?" Seth's expression was concerned.

Lennox sighed. "Not necessarily. It's just . . . a complication."

"It must be. Or you wouldn't have sent *me* to work with Tony over at the food truck place. I know how much you enjoy going there."

"I did. I *do*."

"But something happened," Seth guessed.

Lennox stared at his desk. At the neat pile of plain yellow sticky notes, at the full cup of pens, all emblazoned with the company's logo. Everything was in its place, he had never been more organized—likely because he'd barely left the office, just like Seth had pointed out—but he'd never felt more out of control.

He and Seth had discussed a lot of things about their time in the Navy. Shitty commanders, bad ops, great teammates, but they'd never talked about one of the things that Lennox knew they shared.

"You know . . ." Lennox cleared his throat. "You know those guys down at the food truck lot. They're . . ."

Seth's mouth quirked up in a smile. "They're queer?"

Seth had been out a few years longer than Lennox, but even he wasn't stupid enough to think that was why it was so much easier for him to talk about it.

Because it wasn't like Seth hadn't made it clear they could discuss it, more than once. Lennox had just never taken him up on it. Wasn't sure how he'd even find the words, even now.

Some habits died too hard.

"Yeah, they are." Lennox wanted to hesitate but he forced himself to push through his uneasiness. "There's a guy there. I think he . . . well, I know he . . ."

"Ren?"

"Ren?" Lennox knew who Seth was talking about, but didn't understand why he'd brought up Ren.

"The guy who suggested a hookup. The one who works at the meatball truck. That's Ren."

The dark-haired guy had uncomfortably propositioning him a few months back. Lennox had barely been able to stumble out a response about how he wasn't interested in that. He'd wondered, at the time, if that was something the guy did all the time, and he must have, because he'd asked Seth too.

"Not him."

"I didn't say yes either," Seth said with a grin. "Though I was pretty tempted."

"I wasn't," Lennox could answer honestly. "But this other guy . . . I think he wants . . . more? Maybe?"

He didn't know what Ash wanted. Because he hadn't even had the courage to have the conversation.

"This is the salad guy, isn't it? The friendly, blond one?"

Lennox did a double take. "Yeah, but how did you know?"

Seth laughed. "You've never volunteered to eat salad in your whole life, and now you're eating it three times a week. It wasn't hard to figure out why. So you like him. And he likes you. I don't see the issue."

"You wouldn't," Lennox grumbled.

Seth stood and walked over to the coffee pot, pouring himself a cup, taking his time to doctor it with sugar and creamer he pulled from the mini fridge underneath the counter. "You know, you and Marcus weren't exactly a secret."

Lennox clamped his lips tightly together. "Wasn't that the whole point? *Don't ask, don't tell.*"

Except that the Don't Ask Don't Tell program had officially ended by the time he'd begun his military career. Of course, it wasn't like that had really mattered. Some habits died hard, and some ideas were too entrenched to leave behind.

Seth's expression was thoughtful when he turned back. "Nobody really cared. You guys handled your shit."

"Tell him and his *wife* that," Lennox said, surprising himself with how viciously bitter his voice sounded. He thought he'd gotten over that ages ago. He'd told himself he'd gotten over that ages ago.

"Everyone thought that was a shitty thing to do, to him, to you, to that poor girl who had no idea what she was gettin' into."

Lennox swallowed the bitterness back. "It wasn't her fault. She didn't know anything. He made sure to tell me that."

"Fuck, that's even worse," Seth said sympathetically. "And what, he thought you two could just continue same as before? Hiding in closets, literally and metaphorically?"

"Something like that."

"He was an asshole. A selfish coward. You can't let his stupid ass change what you're doing *now*."

"I just . . ." Lennox took a deep breath. "I'm not. I just can't get used to the way they are, you know? All open and free and shit. Ash looks at me, and flirts with me, and my first instinct is to drag him into some dark corner. The darker the better."

"And you don't think Ash wants some frantic hookup in the dark," Seth stated.

"Why would he?" Lennox heard the frustration rising in his voice. "He's not in the closet."

"Neither are you," Seth retorted, "except the one you keep putting yourself into. You know, I wanted to have this conversation when you first got to LA. Take you to Temple, that club I was tellin' you about. Get a few hookups, maybe a relationship under your belt, so you understood what it was like out here. How open it is. How you don't have to hide it anymore."

"But I wouldn't go." Lennox remembered all too well how fiercely he had resisted any of Seth's attempts to help him find romantic or sexual partners in the aftermath of his discharge.

"I let it go, because I thought you weren't ready. Because of Marcus."

"I wasn't," Lennox said bleakly. "I'm not sure I am now."

"But you want to be," Seth said, coming over and putting a reassuring hand on Lennox's shoulder. But Lennox shucked it off in a quick shrug.

"What I really need to do is go to him and tell him the fucking truth. That I can't do this."

Seth looked at him steadily. "You really think you can't?"

"I do," Lennox said with a sharp decisive nod. Way more decisive than he actually felt. Whenever he thought about going back to the lot and telling Ash to forget everything, especially to forget that kiss? He felt *sick*.

It was stupid. It was weak. And yet he couldn't quite seem to conquer the feeling.

He'd forcibly put Marcus and that whole sordid affair behind him, but he couldn't quite seem to do the same thing with Oliver Ashton Atkinson.

"I definitely think you should talk," Seth said. "But you should listen to him, too. He's a grown man. He's got opinions, too. I really don't think he'd take it too well if you just up and told him it wasn't happening and refused to give him a reason why."

"What?" Lennox was surprised despite himself. "Why do you think I'd do that?"

Seth shot him a wry look. "Because I know you."

"I was going to tell him I'm a terrible idea. I'm . . . well, I'm fucked up." Lennox knew it was true, but it hurt to voice it out loud. Like now that particular fact was concrete and immutable.

Unchangeable.

"You really think he's gonna buy that?"

A dozen different Ashes filtered through his mind, one after the other.

Smiling Ash. Laughing Ash. Flirting Ash. Ash, when someone had tried to cut in line, once. The unexpected steel in his voice when Ash had insisted Lennox not tell anyone about his father. The gumption it must have taken to walk away from Stephan Atkinson in the first place.

Lennox already knew he wasn't going to buy it.

He'd see through it in a second and call it the bullshit it was.

But he didn't know what else he could do.

Which was why he'd been sitting in this goddamned office for the last two weeks, doing *nothing*.

"I thought so," Seth said. He began to turn to go back to his own desk, but paused. "You should've just said yes to Ren."

"What?" Lennox couldn't believe *that* was Seth's parting advice.

Seth shrugged, as he grinned. "He'd have forcibly fucked all this shit out of you, long ago. And then one of us would at least know what he was like in bed."

CHAPTER FIVE

On Friday mornings, Ash liked to get to his truck early, and do a ton of prep for the busy weekend. Even though he had Harmony working during some of the busier shifts, he still liked to do all the prep himself.

There was something incredibly reassuring and very peaceful about sharpening his favorite knife and then tearing through a whole delivery's worth of fresh produce, packing the freshly chopped vegetables neatly into clear containers and then stacking them in the fridge behind him.

This Friday, he unlocked the back door of his truck with slightly less verve than he normally did.

This Lennox thing was fucking him up. He'd tried to pretend it wasn't. That he didn't give a shit that he'd kissed the guy—the barest kiss, only a brush of his lips on Lennox's—and the guy had spent the last two weeks avoiding him.

Logically, he knew there was nothing wrong with *him*, but it still stung.

After climbing into the truck, Ash set his coffee on the counter and checked his watch. His delivery should be here any moment, if they were on time, which . . . Ash had learned practically from the cradle what to do with suppliers who wouldn't keep to their timelines or couldn't be relied upon.

They really didn't want to be late today.

Ash wasn't in the mood for it.

He glanced out the front window, and froze.

There was a piece of paper taped to it—something that had definitely not been there when he'd closed up last night.

Ash stared at the words, printed in damning black and white.

It was an interview that his father had done—likely one of hundreds, if not thousands, he'd done over the course of his illustrious career. But in this one, he had mentioned his son, Oliver. Who Stephan Atkinson had said with some humor, liked to be called Ash.

A silly affectation, his father told the interviewer, that he would grow out of.

Ash had been . . . maybe thirteen or fourteen if he remembered correctly, when this article had come out, and he'd been furious. It had been one of the many things he'd been pissed at his father for.

Now someone had found it, dredged it out of the bowels of magazine hell, had photocopied it, and taped it to his window. Not facing outwards, so anyone could see it, but *inwards*, so only Ash could.

Fury flashed with a frightening power through him. He didn't hesitate. He grabbed his keys, and with shaking fingers, locked up behind him. Walked around to the front of his truck, tore the paper off, leaving the edges trapped by the neatly placed tape fluttering in the early morning breeze, and forgoing his bicycle, took off for the one place that he'd told himself he would not go.

Who else could have done this? Ash thought angrily as he stormed towards his destination. It was still so early the streets were essentially empty. *He's the only one who knows.*

The building that Tony had described was only a few blocks away.

It had been remodeled, with a glass-front office on the lower level, and a living space on the top. There were a separate set of stairs leading to a discreet door on a wrought iron landing.

A discreet black-lettered sign, matching the wrought iron of the stairs and contrasting with the freshly painted taupe stucco of the building itself, indicated that this was the offices of Protectorate.

It might be early, but Ash could see a figure already in the office below.

Tony had mentioned offhandedly that Lennox was a workaholic, always in the office, so it was not a huge stretch to imagine that it was him, up early, and already working.

Ash walked over to the door, and pulled it, fully expecting it to be locked, but to his surprise it opened easily.

Even though he must have been the one to unlock it, Lennox looked up with shock as he walked in.

Ash imagined they probably didn't get much foot traffic.

He stomped over to where Lennox sat at a desk, and slapped the paper down in front of him.

"What the *fuck* is this?" he demanded to know.

Lennox stared at the writing. He took his time answering, clearly reading through the words on the page once, and maybe even twice. Finally he looked up. "It looks like an interview that your father did, talking about his restaurants, and also his son." He hesitated. "You."

"Yes, thank you, I can read just as well as you can," Ash bit off. "What I mean is *why* was it taped to my truck's front window this morning?"

"Taped to your . . ."

"And not facing out, but facing *in*," Ash interrupted. "So I would see it, but nobody else. Someone wants me to know they've figured out who my father is."

"And you think that's me."

Ash gestured wildly, pacing between Lennox's desk, and the other, currently unoccupied. "Who else could it be?"

"Do you really think I needed to do this to get your attention?" Lennox asked, his tone dry.

Ash whirled around. "Nobody else knows. Just you. Maybe you're trying to scare me off . . . you didn't like that I kissed you or . . . or something. I don't know. But this is bullshit."

"I think . . ." Lennox hesitated. "I think it's more than just bullshit. It's concerning."

"Don't want to touch *that* accusation with a ten-foot pole, do you?" Ash knew how bitter he sounded. He'd never wanted Lennox to know how pissed off he'd been that after the kiss, he'd avoided him. If Lennox didn't give a shit, then Ash had wanted him to think he didn't give a shit either.

Well, that ship had sailed. Rather spectacularly.

Ash regretted it, but with the anger still flowing through him, it didn't last very long.

"We need to talk about *this*," Lennox said, pointing to the paper in front of him. "We probably should also talk about . . . the other thing, but right now? *This* is what I'm worried about."

"So you didn't do it, then," Ash said.

Lennox made a frustrated noise, pushing himself away from his desk and standing up, walking over to the coffee station in the corner. "I can't believe you'd assume I would," he said.

"Well, it wasn't a big stretch," Ash said, even though it had been, and he saw that now that he was a little calmer, and thinking more clearly. Lennox *had* been avoiding him. Why would he come back to the lot, only to tape that interview to Ash's food truck? And why would he bother, since Ash already knew that he knew the truth?

It didn't make logical sense that it was Lennox.

The bottom dropped out of Ash's stomach.

"Someone else knows," Ash said uncertainly.

"Someone else knows," Lennox agreed. "Do you know who it might be?"

Ash sat down heavily in the chair in front of the unoccupied desk. To his surprise, Lennox brought him a steaming cup of coffee. Smelled good even. Smelled *strong*.

"I know you don't usually take sugar with your coffee," Lennox said as he watched Ash take a sip, "but it's good for the shock."

"The shock?" Ash repeated dumbly, but of course he was in shock.

Someone *knew* about him, and instead of coming to him themselves, they had dredged up this years-old magazine article and posted it so only he could see it.

Ash felt sick to his stomach, and kept sipping his coffee.

"So, do you know anyone it could be?"

"No," Ash said. "Well, the guys from Basket, but why would they? They want to get into the lot."

"Basket?"

"It's a food truck, a pretty famous one, actually. It's picnic-themed," Ash said. "They've been on the circuit for some time, and now I guess they want Tony to let them join us. The two guys who run it used to work for my father."

"So they know who you are," Lennox said, and to Ash's surprise, he had pulled out a pad of sticky notes, and was making notes on it with a pen.

"What are you doing?" Ash asked.

"Taking notes, so I can assemble a security report," Lennox said in a clipped voice. "Why do you think it couldn't be them?"

Ash stared at him. "A security report?"

"Yes, a security report," Lennox said. "Have you forgotten that Tony hired me to secure your lot? Your businesses?"

"No," Ash said. "But this . . . this wasn't even *inside* my truck."

"I got shot," Lennox said out of the blue, surprising both of them, if the astonishment on Lennox's face as the words came out of his mouth were any indication. "I got shot and I wasn't there to protect the people I cared about. I . . . that's never going to happen again. I won't let it. So let me do my job, okay?"

Ash opened his mouth and then shut it again. He wondered if Lennox had registered that he'd said the phrase *people I cared about*, and if he'd realized that he'd equated his old team to the guys at the food truck lot.

But Lennox shot him a look and kept going. "Is it any less of an invasion of your privacy because they taped it outside instead of inside?"

Ash sipped his coffee. And how *had* Lennox known he liked black coffee, no sugar? Ash didn't know. Wasn't quite sure he wanted to ask. "No," he finally said. "No, it wasn't."

"Someone wants you to know *they* know. But they don't want to reveal who they are, which means they might not have your best intentions at heart. I . . . this is what I was worried about."

"I'm not sure I'm following."

Lennox sighed heavily. "The table. Someone started big, got a lot of attention. And then lay low for a few weeks. Now, they're possibly back, and they're back with this."

"Wait, *what*?" Ash couldn't quite believe what he was saying. He stood again, and began to pace. "I thought that was just some random homophobic asshole who vandalized the table."

"I *never* thought that," Lennox said.

"Really?"

"Think about it. Couldn't they have used much worse words? I know they could have. I heard them all the time. I'm sure you have, too. And the color? They picked purple. Not black. Not red. *Purple*. Does that seem like a homophobic asshole to you? *Suck a dick,* written in purple paint."

"I . . ." Ash sat down again, feeling his legs wobble underneath him. "I guess not."

"Right. I've been waiting to see what would happen. If they'd come back. What they would do if they did. If they would indicate who the message was for. Because I also never believed it was for all of you. I thought it was for one person, specifically."

Panic rose in Ash's throat, clawing at it, like the very worst kind of heartburn. "You think because of that"—he pointed to the paper on Lennox's desk—"it's *me*."

"You're the one with a big secret. And they just informed you that they know it, too."

"Lots of guys there have secrets," Ash pointed out. "We just found out that Sean was married before he came to LA. And his husband died, in a car crash."

Lennox's expression was unrelenting. "Do you really think that has the same kind of impact that your parentage has? You're connected to a very rich, famous, and well-known person. That's quite a bit different than having a past relationship that you didn't disclose."

"Fuck," Ash hissed vehemently. "Fuck, fuck, fuck."

"We don't know for sure. It could be silly, like someone playing a practical joke on you."

Ash shot Lennox a look. "Do you really believe that?"

"You already know what I believe," Lennox said. "The only question is, what are we going to do about it?"

"I don't know," Ash said. "I guess I could . . ." He stopped. He'd always sworn to himself that he wouldn't take this step unless he *had* to, and this wasn't worst-case-scenario territory. *Yet*, anyway, Ash thought.

Lennox raised an eyebrow.

"I'm not going to see my father," Ash said. "I thought I could, but I won't. Not unless I have to."

"I don't think you do," Lennox said. "I was going to say, what *you* have to do is go back to the lot and continue on with your day like nothing's happened."

"What?"

"I know," Lennox said, and his expression had morphed into something far more sympathetic. "It's gonna be tough, I'm sure."

"Tough?" Ash took a deep breath. "More like impossible. Every single person I talk to today, I'm gonna be wondering if it's them. If they've . . . got a problem with me, or something."

"We don't know that the person who left this"—Lennox paused, tapping the paper on his desk—"has a problem with you."

"What else could it be?"

"Your father, for one," Lennox said.

"Ugh," Ash groaned.

"Let's get back to this list. Tell me about these Basket guys."

"Ross Stanton and Aaron Bolton," Ash said. "They worked for my father, for a little while."

"And?" Lennox raised an eyebrow.

"And they left and started Basket. I don't know much else."

"Were you friendly with them?"

"I was still, well, I was still mostly a kid. Not that this fact ever stopped my father from bringing me to whatever restaurant he wanted to personally victimize that day. But they were chefs, employees, you know, so it wasn't like we spent a lot of time making small talk."

"What happened when they left?"

Ash shrugged. "I don't know. They just left. Started Basket. Were really successful with their truck right out of the gate."

"Do you know if they were fired or they quit?"

"Pretty sure they quit," Ash said. "Not that I would know, because it wasn't like my father typically confided in me. But usually when someone got fired, it was pretty fucking spectacular."

"Right," Lennox said, continuing to make notes. "And what has your relationship with them been like after that?"

"We smile and nod, and chat occasionally, whenever we run into each other. But we haven't, not for awhile anyway, because I've been parked at the lot, and they've still been on the circuit."

"But you said they were trying to get into the lot."

"Tony doesn't like them. I guess he was stonewalling their requests, because of that, so they went to his brother-in-law, who financed the lot in the first place, and I guess, still technically owns it."

Lennox tilted his, head contemplatively. "Is there an issue there?"

"Between Tony and Ryan? No way. I mean, Tony's not happy about this, because he has a real ax to grind with Ross and Aaron, but it'll pass. He and his brother, Wyatt, have a strong relationship, and I know Tony's always really liked Ryan, too."

"So no issues there."

"Nope. And like I said, Ross and Aaron aren't going to antagonize anyone right now, because it's hardly going to get them what they want. Tony already doesn't like them. I'm the one person who knows them who's probably willing to give them a chance." Ash finished off his coffee. "Do you need anything else from me?"

Lennox tapped the pen on the desk, his expression contemplative. "I'm assuming you don't want me to tell Tony about this."

It had never occurred to Ash that he would tell Tony. Dread coalesced in his stomach. It was not going to be pretty when Tony found out that he'd been lying by omission for years.

"I . . . don't you *have* to?" Ash wondered.

"I really should." Lennox flashed him an unexpectedly warm smile. "But I think I can keep it under wraps for a bit longer."

"Alright. I'm grateful for it." Ash sighed. "I'm going to have to tell him at some point, but honestly? He's already in a bad mood because of Aaron and Ross strong-arming him into accepting them. I'd rather wait a few days. A week, maybe."

"It's going to depend on whether things escalate," Lennox said gently. "But I'm going to take some time to do some research, first. Look into the magazine this article is from. The distribution. Look over some of the camera footage from last night. See if they captured who taped that to your window, and if they did, we'll run it through our facial recognition program."

"You can do that?" Ash asked, surprised.

"Oh yeah. But . . ." Lennox hesitated. "My guess is this person is too smart to get their face captured on the security feed. But it's always worth looking."

"Alright." Ash stood up. "Thanks . . . for the coffee, and the help."

"It's my job, Ash," Lennox said. He stood up too, and walked with Ash towards the front door. "About the rest . . ."

Ash held up a hand. "If I have to deal with the fact that *someone* knows about me, someone I probably don't want to know my secret, and I have to pretend nothing is wrong, then I'm gonna be honest. I can't deal with the rest. Not right now."

He hated to see it, but the overriding expression on Lennox's face was relief.

"I didn't say *forever*," Ash said, hand on the door. "I said *right now*."

"Okay," Lennox said. "I'll keep you posted, alright?"

"Sounds good," Ash said, and before he did something he'd regret, pushed the door open and walked back out into the Los Angeles sunshine.

No matter how hard Ash tried to dismiss what had happened that morning from his head, he couldn't.

The smiles and friendly chatter he always shared with his customers were second nature to him, but they were still hard to pull off when his mind was racing every time a new person appeared in front of his truck. Maybe each one of his welcoming grins was a tiny bit forced, and maybe his small talk was less creative than usual, and maybe he kept having to force his distraction away, but Ash hoped that nobody noticed.

Still, for a Friday, business was steady. He made it through the lunch hour, and was just trying to decide if he wanted to grab a quick salad to eat or if he wanted something more substantial when Tony appeared in the front window.

"Hey," Ash said, pushing it open. "What's up?"

"Just breaking for lunch," Tony said. "You wanna share some tacos?"

"Sure," Ash said. "Give me a second to put my sign out. Harmony won't be working for a few hours." He reached down and pulled it out, adjusting the little clock hands to read half an hour from now.

"Oh, you nabbed her for the dinner hour, that was smart," Tony said. "I assume it's 'cause we've got that new band coming tonight."

"Yep," Ash said as he put the sign up in the window, trying very hard not to think of the last thing that had been posted in his window. When he'd gotten back from Lennox's office, he'd pulled out a bench scraper and got every last bit of tape off the window. There wasn't a scrap of evidence left that the paper had ever hung there at all.

"I'll be over grabbing our tacos. Is fish okay?" Tony asked.

"Shrimp, if you have it," Ash said, because if he was going to have tacos, he might as well go wild. It had been that kind of day.

"You got it," Tony said, and took off, back in the direction he'd come from.

Ash walked down the back steps and locked the door behind him since Harmony wasn't expected for another hour and a half, and with whoever it was roaming around unchecked, he wasn't going to take any chances.

He picked an unoccupied picnic table near Tony and Wyatt's food truck, and while he was waiting for Tony to appear with lunch, pulled his phone out of his pocket. He hoped that while he'd been working, Lennox might have sent an update. But no dice.

Then, Ash realized belatedly that Lennox didn't even have his phone number. He'd been too upset and then too preoccupied this morning to leave it for him.

Except, Ash thought, he *might,* because he was pretty sure Tony had given him *all* their phone numbers, and this was business, right? It wouldn't be weird to text Ash an update on what he'd found. If he'd found anything at all.

That was what freaked Ash out the most, he realized. That whoever had posted that piece of paper on Ash's window had been smart and clever enough to fool Lennox and to leave both of them guessing.

Leave Ash wondering when they were going to strike next.

"Here we go," Tony said, walking over to the table with his arms full of paper plates. "Shrimp for you, blackened mahi for me. And," he added with an extra flourish and a smile, "plenty of chips and salsa to share."

Ash shot his friend a look. "Are you trying to suck up or something?"

"Can't a guy get his friend lunch without there being an ulterior motive?" Tony asked innocently.

"Yes, but *no.* Not when it's you, Tony," Ash said, spooning pico onto his shrimp taco and taking his first, entirely succulent bite.

"Truthfully, I need some advice," Tony said. "*Again.*"

"Oh, Ross and Aaron?" Ash asked after he'd chewed and swallowed. "How are the negotiations going?"

"Not too bad," Tony said, not looking as glum as he had the last time he and Ash had discussed the Basket truck owners. "Actually, I think they might be joining us in a few weeks."

"That's good, right?"

"I guess so," Tony said, sighing. "I'm still not happy about it, but you were right. They're going to bring us a lot of business, and I need to figure out how to see that as a positive."

"I think it *is* a positive, no matter if you choose to see it that way or not, Tony," Ash said. "I mean, this was always going to happen, right? People were always going to join the lot that you weren't close friends with."

Tony put down his taco. "That was what I was going to ask you about," he said. "I just feel . . . weird about it, you know? I thought maybe I would ask another few people to join us, so it wouldn't feel just like . . . us versus them."

"I think that's a good idea," Ash said. "We've got the space. We've got the foundation already built here. I'm sure that lots of other trucks would be interested in joining."

"Do you know of any that you might recommend?" Tony asked around a bite of mahi mahi. "I know you've got all kinds of connections."

Ash wondered what Tony would say if—*when*, he corrected, *when*—he found out partially why that was.

Almost nobody knew about his father and who he was, but Ash still had all the lessons that Stephan Atkinson taught him over the years. Even the ones that he'd wanted to ignore, the ones he'd been sure wouldn't ever sink in. They were all there, up in his head. He knew how to network, how to find the best suppliers, how to interview to find the most dedicated employees. How to construct an attractive menu. How to get customers, and then keep them coming back. He knew all of that, and more. If he had any connections, it was because of that.

Not, Ash reminded himself, because of who he was.

"I'll think about it and email you a list," Ash said. He did know of a few truck owners that might be interested in the lot. He'd just have to decide if they would fit in here—because nobody who was on the circuit wouldn't jump at an opportunity like this one.

"Great," Tony said.

For a minute or so, there was just quiet, as they sat there and ate. Then Tony wiped his hands on a napkin and dug something out of his pocket.

"Look at this," he said, "someone left some weird-ass photo-copied interview with Stephan Atkinson on the side of our truck."

Ash choked on his shrimp taco.

There were no other words to describe it. The food turned to ash in his mouth, he couldn't swallow, he couldn't chew, he just sat there and *choked* on it.

Tony reached over and thumped him hard on the back, and finally Ash had the sense to open up his water bottle and take a long drink, washing the rest of the food down, even though it tasted sour and suddenly rancid.

"What?" he finally said. "Someone did what?"

If they had left the same photocopied interview that they'd left for Ash, then it wouldn't take Tony very long to put two and two together. And if they'd left them anywhere else? By the time the band showed up tonight, everyone on the lot would know.

"They put this up," Tony said, putting the crumpled-up paper on the table in between them. "Are you sure you're okay?"

"I'm fine," Ash said absently as he scanned the paper. Almost immediately he saw it was a different interview than the one from this morning. Still with his father, of course, and he was still a superior asshole through all of it, and even though there was a brief mention of Ash, he was referred to only as "Atkinson's son."

Ash let out the breath he hadn't been aware he was holding.

"Atkinson is such a dick," Tony said as he stuck a chip into the plastic tub of pico de gallo sitting between them. "All that shit about how 'real restaurants' are the only ones that can serve 'real food'? Ugh, what a tool. I wish someone would shut him up. Or at least stop going to his restaurants."

"Yeah," Ash said. "He's not very nice about it."

"Kinda makes you wonder how horrible he'd be to work for," Tony continued, even though the last subject that Ash *ever* wanted to talk about with Tony was his father. "I mean, Wyatt worked for Bastian Aquino for years, and from what he's said and things I hear, that was a walk in the park comparatively."

"I hear he and Aquino are similar though," Ash said. He had already decided, when he'd been prepping this morning, that if for some bizarre reason, Stephan Atkinson came up in a conversation *before* Ash could tell Tony or any of the rest of his friends the truth, he was not going to outright lie. It was bad enough to lie by omission. They might never forgive him for that, but he certainly wasn't going to make it any worse.

"Aquino's not so bad," Tony said. "He settled down and married that guy he was working with. I think he's mellowed a lot. I'm not sure Atkinson knows what the meaning of the word is." He chuckled lightly, like they were gossiping about some random person in the LA restaurant community and not Ash's *father*, who had made his life a living hell from almost the first moment.

And, Ash realized, Tony thought they *were* only gossiping. He had no idea. He couldn't know how each thing he said felt like another nail in the coffin.

"Is that what marriage does, Tony?" Ash asked, digging down deep and finding a teasing tone of voice to use. Hoping against hope that he could change the subject. "You gonna settle down and mellow out anytime soon? I bet Lucas would look *real good* in white."

Tony flushed, and Ash couldn't help but think, *success!* with a whole lot of exclamation points after. "We've talked about a longer-term commitment," he admitted. "But it's a big step. And I'm not sure we're ready for that."

Ash rolled his eyes. "That means *you're* not sure you're ready for that. I think Lucas would marry you tomorrow if you asked nicely."

"Maybe," Tony said. "I'm still stuck on the 'asking nicely' part, honestly."

"You'll figure it out," Ash said, picking up his taco again. Now that Tony was derailed from talking about Stephan Atkinson, eating was officially safe again.

"I'm sure I will." Tony nudged the paper between them with a fingertip. "You really don't think this is weird?"

Ash swallowed his last bite of taco. "What's weird?"

"That someone went through the lot and hung up photo-copied interviews with Stephan Atkinson?"

"There . . ." Ash's heart was in his throat. "There was more than just this one?"

"Oh, a handful of them. Lucas was on trash duty this morn-ing and noticed. Threw a bunch of them away."

"Ah," Ash said. "That *is* weird." What else could he say? It was super fucking weird. So weird he was having real difficulty not freaking out right now.

He wished he could call Lennox and freak out. But the last thing he was going to do right now was pique Tony's interest by asking for his number.

"Well, what can we do about it, if people think we aren't real dining?" Tony shrugged and reached for the paper, crumpling it up. But before Tony could toss it into the nearby trash can, Ash motioned.

"Can I . . . can I keep that?" he asked. He knew Lennox would want to see it. Would be disappointed to hear that Lucas had thrown the others away.

"Sure, but *why*?" Tony asked, crinkling his nose. "You don't have the hots for Atkinson, do you? I guess he's kinda hot, in a sort of intense controlling Daddy way."

Worse words could not have come out of Tony's mouth.

"Ew, *no*," Ash said. "I'm just . . . I'm curious. I don't know much about him." Technically, that was not really the truth, but he *could not* continue listening to how Tony thought his father might be considered attractive—or *why*.

Because as bad as the beginning of that statement had been, the end had been so much worse.

Tony shrugged. "Alright," he said, and pushed the paper over towards Ash. "But I'm not sure what you're gonna learn, except that he's a patronizing asshole. Especially in this interview."

"Well, it's a start, right?" Ash said, trying to sound optimistic—and like he actually *wanted* to learn more about Stephan Atkinson, when actually the opposite was true.

If whoever was doing this wanted Ash to sweat it out, it was working way too fucking well, because as he walked back to his truck, he felt hot and cold all over, prickly with anxiety.

After unlocking the door, climbing back into his truck, and taking the "temporarily closed" sign off the front window, he pulled out his phone and did a quick Google search for the name of Lennox's company.

He didn't have to ask Tony for the number, or wait for Lennox to show up. He could call him *right now*, if he wanted to. Ash stared at the number for a long second, feeling his heart rate finally begin to decelerate and logic begin to seep through the panic cresting in his brain.

What was Lennox going to do anyway? Tell him to calm down? He could do that for himself. And he'd already said he would swing by at some point today. When he did, Ash could give him the second photocopied interview. He didn't need to call him down here right now, like a child in the throes of a meltdown.

He could handle his shit.

He'd told his father ages ago that he could, and Ash remembered the disbelief distinctly etched on his father's face when he'd said it.

No matter who was fucking with him, Ash told himself with a deep breath, he was going to prove him wrong. He'd been doing it for years. He just had to keep doing it.

But of course that was not where things ended, or where Ash's challenging day suddenly got easier.

Nope, it got harder, when midway through the afternoon, he looked up from the weekly produce ordering he was doing on his iPad, and his mother was standing there, right in front of his truck window.

It occurred to him then that it *might* have been her leaving the interview taped to his window this morning.

But then, he couldn't think of a good reason why she would.

It wasn't entirely unusual for her to show up mid-afternoon like this, to check in, or to text him occasionally. Usually when she knew his father was busy and wouldn't realize that she'd headed over to the enemy camp.

"Hey, Mom," he said.

She nodded. Natasha Atkinson was elegant and slender, her white slacks and lemon-colored silk shell looking out of place in the food truck lot. He knew he'd gotten his fairly good looks from her—and his more even temperament.

He'd known, from a very young age, that Natasha could never hold her own with his father. But unlike Ash, who'd learned to fight back, and then learned that fighting was never going to get him anywhere and *stopped* fighting, over time she'd been flattened by her husband's attacks.

He could see it in her now, the clear exhaustion in her blue eyes.

"Oliver," she said, tilting her head. "It's good to see you."

"Would you like something to eat?" he asked. He'd rather ask her why she stayed with Stephan. Why she tolerated his bullshit. But he'd asked those questions too many times already and had never been remotely satisfied with any of her answers. So he'd stopped. Maybe it was cowardly to pretend that everything was normal when she appeared like this, but it was easier. For both of them.

"No, thank you," she said politely. "I just wanted to stop by and see how you were doing."

"Fine," Ash said. "No complaints here."

"Business seems steady," she said.

"Can't complain there, either," Ash said. He leaned over the counter further. If he reached out, she'd be just close enough to touch.

He could walk out and stand next to her, but she seemed easier, somehow, and more comfortable when he was in his truck. Like she could pretend that she hadn't come here with the express purpose of seeing her son, but had decided on a whim that she might be interested in a chopped salad for lunch.

"How are you?" he asked, even though he had a feeling that the answer would only frustrate him. He still asked because as difficult as it had been to leave, she *still* hadn't left.

He'd woken up on the morning of his twenty-first birthday, dreading going downstairs, dreading what his father was going to say, dreading what his father was going to *do*, and he'd realized then that he'd felt that way almost every morning for every year of his life.

If he didn't do something about it, he'd never leave. Just like Natasha.

So he'd left. He'd waited, throughout the whole painfully interminable day, throughout all the birthday celebrations, during which his father had made it clear, more than once, that he was expected to follow in exactly his footsteps, with no deviations, and then he'd gone up to his room and packed everything he'd owned.

He'd left a very specific, very explicit note on his desk.

He was done being an Atkinson.

It hadn't taken right away. It had been *years* before his father had finally really, truly washed his hands of him. But every single ounce of that fight had been worth it.

Ash had his own life now. And he was *Ash*. Not Oliver Ashton Atkinson, a mere vessel for his father's control, his greed, and his ambition.

"We're fine," Natasha said, answering as Ash expected, in the plural, not the singular. Natasha had long since lost the ability to separate herself from her husband. "Your father has been given a very prestigious award, Oliver. And we'd both love it if you came to the ceremony."

"No." The answer was not just habit, but *more* than that.

"Oliver," his mother repeated in a slightly more stringent tone.

"I have made it as clear as I can possibly be," Ash said. Not angrily. He wasn't *angry* with her. He couldn't be. "I don't want to have anything to do with him. But if you won an award, I'd be there. Front row."

But that was the heartbreaking part of it all. Natasha Atkinson wasn't ever going to win any awards, because everything that made her *her* had been sucked away by her emotionally abusive and controlling husband.

Ash had barely escaped. But he *had* escaped.

"Oliver, don't be ridiculous," she said. "It's your father who is up for the award."

"Did he ask you to come see me about it?" Ash asked, not because he actually thought that his father had suggested it, but because he needed to make sure that whatever was going on with the lot—with that horrible interview taped to his truck today—it didn't originate with Stephan.

"No, of course not," Natasha said. "You know . . ." She cleared her throat. Looked away. "You know he is very upset you've wasted your talents here. At this . . . lot."

"Yeah, tough shit," Ash said unapologetically.

"Oliver Ashton," she said rebukingly. "*Language.*"

"Sorry, Mom," he said with a smile. First time he'd been able to really smile today since she'd shown up.

At first he'd been sure that her appearance must be related to what had happened, but now he thought it was more than that. The universe had known, somehow, that he needed to talk to her today. That just seeing her face would make him feel a little lighter. Somehow, impossibly *less* like Oliver Ashton.

It had never made sense to Ash, but he wasn't going to turn it down. Not today.

"I just want the best for you, son," she said.

"I know, Mom," he agreed, gently. "Believe it or not, I think I've got it."

"If you're sure." She looked hesitant, but was already turning to leave. Like she knew, no matter how hard she tried, he wasn't going to listen.

"I am." And the truth was, he'd never been surer of anything in his life.

CHAPTER SIX

Lennox skipped lunch.

When his stomach grumbled, he dug in his desk drawer, pulling out what was likely an old, stale granola bar. Peeling off the label, he shoved it in his mouth, barely tasting it.

Seth was out today, installing a security system with a few of their contractors, and so there was nobody to remind Lennox that he didn't need to solve this *today*.

It wasn't like he actually thought he could figure out who was behind the problems at the food truck lot that quickly. There was a lot more research to do, and the longer the pattern continued, the more likely it was that the perpetrator would end up accidentally revealing himself.

Still, Lennox was going to preemptively do everything he could.

First, he'd reviewed the security footage from the night before, pulling up not only the cameras he thought were most likely to catch anything, but *all* the cameras. Maybe the culprit had gotten lazy or sloppy when they'd first entered the lot or when they'd exited. But all Lennox had ended up with was a shadowy figure, with a dark hoody pulled up and an even darker bandana over most of their face, leaving only the sliver of their eyes.

The figure was also annoyingly androgynous. Lennox's initial impression was it was a man, but the build was slender enough it could have been a woman.

Besides, Lennox thought, this kind of non-violent confrontation spoke less of a man, and more of a woman, potentially. But still, he wasn't able to rule anything out, and that was annoying.

He pulled up his file on Stephan Atkinson, and with some of the background-check sites he used, bulked it up. Still didn't find much that was personal. The man, as Lennox had always assumed, lived to work.

He ended up with a lot more information on the man's various restaurants and business enterprises, even on his successful television show, than he ended up with personal info to add to the file.

Still, he did it anyway, because sitting here and doing nothing when it was possible that Ash was being targeted was unacceptable.

Then Lennox moved on to the other guys that Ash had mentioned—the owners of the Basket food truck. Their histories were frustratingly slim too. Most of the info he found on them was about their shared enterprise and how successful it was.

He found nothing about why Aaron and Ross had left Atkinson's most famous LA restaurant, Hook & Slope.

Lennox made a frustrated noise and closed his browser, leaning back in his chair. His instincts told him that there was something more to that story—if only because Atkinson was notoriously difficult to work with, even as he presented a suave, charming front to the public—because he'd found not a single article or even a *line* in an article that speculated why Atkinson had lost two of his most promising chefs.

All Ross and Aaron had ever said about it was that they'd wanted to branch out, to do something different, and Atkinson had been encouraging.

"Encouraging my ass," Lennox muttered as he pushed himself upright and walked over to the coffee station. His knee was stiff, as it usually was when he spent too much time at his desk, but stretching it was good, even though he didn't really need another cup of coffee.

He'd already had too much caffeine today, but he had to keep his mind sharp to pick up on even the tiniest, most insignificant detail. Anything to keep Ash safe.

He really did not want to go to Atkinson himself. He *could*, but not only would Ash likely kill him, Lennox hadn't been able to completely eliminate that the person behind the issues was Atkinson himself.

The last thing he wanted was to tip the guy off that he was looking into him, if he was actually to blame—though even Lennox could admit that while Atkinson was a pathetic asshole and an absolutely terrible father, it was unlikely he would stoop *this* low.

Still, that left a really slim list of suspects, and Lennox was frustrated that even though he'd worked for *hours*, it wasn't any longer than when he'd started.

Resting a hip against the coffee station, he glanced outside. The shadows were longer, and when he glanced at his watch, he realized with a start that it was almost five.

Had he spent almost eight hours digging?

It seemed that he had.

It was almost embarrassing that he'd spent all this time and felt like he was no closer to uncovering the problem.

Still, he'd promised Ash that he would stop by the food truck lot and update him, and he'd intended to go a lot earlier in the day.

But, he decided, he was stiff and uncomfortable from sitting all day. He'd run upstairs, shed the suit, and take a quick shower before heading over to the lot to grab some dinner and at least give Ash a quick rundown on what he'd learned.

Which, Lennox thought with frustration as he climbed the stairs up to his loft, was a whole lot of fucking nothing.

Twenty minutes later, he was dressed and getting ready to head out the door. He hesitated by the door, looking at his black leather jacket. It *was* warm out today, in the upper eighties, and he really didn't want to wear it, but at the same time, he also wasn't sure he wanted to leave his revolver behind, especially considering the bullshit that had been happening at the lot.

He decided to compromise, heading downstairs and digging through the supply cabinet, pulling out an ankle holster. It wasn't the easiest way to wear his gun, and didn't make it particularly accessible, but it was better than wearing a jacket on a hot summer evening.

By the time he made it to the lot, the sun was beginning to set, and the dinner crowd was converging on the food trucks. Almost everyone had a line, including Ash, so instead of approaching him when he wouldn't have the time to talk, Lennox got in Alexis' line, ordering a roasted chicken pita with extra tahini and an order of his Greek-style fries, piled high with feta cheese and sprinkled with fresh oregano, lemon zest, and red wine vinegar.

He claimed a table with a good view of Ash's truck and ate, watching as the line slowly began to dwindle.

Popping one last fry in his mouth, Lennox cleared his trash and approached Ash's truck.

He could see Ash in the front window. Harmony was next to him, head down, busy prepping some additional vegetables, but Ash was daydreaming, staring out the window, unseeing even as Lennox approached.

"Hey," Lennox said and Ash jumped, clearly not expecting to see him. Or *anyone*.

Ash was not usually so tense, but Lennox couldn't blame him for that.

Anyone would be tense if they were being targeted and they didn't know who or why or what they would do next.

"You hungry?" Ash asked.

"Already ate, actually."

Ash made a face. "Of course you did. I've been . . . well, I've been . . ." He took a deep breath. "It's been a long day."

"I know. I'm sorry. I *was* working, but got kind of caught up," Lennox said. "But then I showed up and you had a huge line, and I didn't think I could steal you away, so I grabbed a pita from Alexis while I waited."

"You know, that's a good idea," Ash said. He turned towards Harmony. "Can you hold the fort down for a few minutes?"

"Sure," she said brightly. "Take your time. I think the dinner rush is mostly over."

"Alright." Ash turned and disappeared from view. In a moment, he was walking around the side of the truck.

"I expected you a lot sooner," Ash said, falling into step beside Lennox as they walked towards Alexis' truck with its distinctive blue and white flag design on the side. "I've kinda been freaking out here."

Lennox hated the pulse of guilt he felt. "I really was working on it all day."

"Did you get anywhere?" Ash asked as he got in line behind a handful of people.

"No," Lennox admitted. "I did a bunch of research. Filled in a lot of blank spots. Reviewed the security footage, but couldn't eliminate anything. So yeah, unfortunately no closer to figuring out who's behind this."

"Well, they didn't just visit my truck last night," Ash said, and dug in his pocket, pulling out a crumpled piece of paper. "They made the rounds."

Lennox took the paper and looked it over. It was very similar to what had been posted on Ash's truck—photocopied interview with Atkinson, but in this one he didn't mention his son by name.

"There were more of them too," Ash added. "Lucas was on trash duty this morning and threw a whole bunch away that were apparently posted all over the lot. Tony and I had lunch and he brought this one and I grabbed it, thought it might help. I wished I could've gotten the others too, but it was hours earlier, and I wasn't going to go digging through the trash."

"So," Lennox said, "this person finds a bunch of interviews that your father has done, and photocopies them. But saves the one where he refers to you not only by name, but by *nickname*, therefore identifying you, for your own truck. But posts the rest, no doubt making everyone wonder what the fuck they're up to."

"Tony thinks it's some kind of pointed comment about how food trucks aren't serving 'real' food," Ash said. "It was uncomfortable as hell. He wouldn't let it go." He sighed.

"You didn't tell him."

"Not yet," Ash admitted. "I . . . if you had heard him, you'd probably understand why."

"You're not going to be able to keep this secret forever," Lennox cautioned. "Especially if there's more escalation."

"I know," Ash said.

"My mother also stopped by today."

"Natasha Atkinson. Housewife." Lennox offered the definition that he had for the woman that Atkinson was married to. There hadn't been much more about her that he could find.

If he had to guess, she'd been swallowed by Atkinson.

The sadness in Ash's eyes seemed to confirm this fact.

"Does she come by a lot?"

"No," Ash said. "But I don't think her coming by today had anything to do with the rest of it."

"You're sure?"

"She had some crazy idea of a family reconciliation." Ash grimaced. "I had to tell her it wasn't going to happen."

"She does this a lot?"

"Every few months or so," Ash said. He sighed.

The person in front of them ordered and Ash approached the truck, Alexis grinning at him.

"Hey," Lennox said, "get me one of those baklava cheesecakes, too, yeah?"

Ash rolled his eyes, but he put in a very similar order to the one that Lennox had enjoyed earlier, adding in the cheesecake. "Which," he said as he turned towards Lennox, and they walked over to the side, waiting for Alexis to prep Ash's food, "we can *share*."

"I don't share," Lennox said.

"You're not going to eat that cheesecake in front of me," Ash said. "I know that much."

"Fine," Lennox grumbled. "I'll share a few bites with you."

"You owe me. It was *not* a fun afternoon," Ash said. "Between wondering what the fuck was going to happen next, and having to dodge Tony's questions . . ."

Lennox felt properly chastised. "Sorry," he apologized again.

"And you've got no idea who's behind this?" Ash said after he grabbed his food from Alexis and they carried it to a table set slightly apart from where the majority of the crowd was settled. "None at all?"

"These things take time," Lennox said. He stuck a fork in the cheesecake and heard the satisfying crunch as it cut through the flaky honey-and-nut-filled layers. "I don't have a lot to go on."

"I've been trying to think of anything else I can tell you that might help," Ash said as he took a big bite of his pita. "But I've got nothing."

"No fights with other food truck owners? No disgruntled customers? No jealous ex-boyfriends?"

Lennox heard how steady his voice was through the recitation, but only he'd know how his pulse accelerated at the thought of ex-boyfriends.

Ash shook his head. "I honestly haven't had a fight with anyone. Even a disagreement. And I've dated in the last few years, but nothing serious. Been too busy."

"Right." Lennox drummed his fingertips on the tabletop. Didn't want to think that he was special, but he felt it anyway. It seemed as if dating hadn't been a priority for Ash, but he'd still tried to date *him*.

Of course, Lennox had immediately ruined that by freaking out and running away and then *staying* away, but Ash had still tried.

Lennox found himself wishing that he hadn't pushed Ash away. That he'd kissed him back. With a *real* kiss. The kind that Ash would remember for a long time, even if things didn't work out.

"I hope you at least eliminated Aaron and Ross," Ash said, digging around in the cardboard container like he was looking for the perfect fry, drenched in vinegar and coated in feta. "'Cause I *know* it's not them."

The problem was, Lennox was not as convinced as Ash. "They're the only ones around who know your secret," he pointed out. "I can't eliminate them."

"Even if it doesn't serve any purpose? They want to get into the food truck lot, and it looks like Tony's gonna relent. Freaking me out isn't going to get them what they want."

"Do you think that this person is that logical?" Lennox asked seriously. "They're digging out really old interviews with your dad. And they're not just doing a Google search. They're finding the actual magazines. That's dedication."

Ash made a face. "Don't remind me. It freaks me out." He shuddered.

"What I'm trying to say is that while, *yeah*, it doesn't make logical sense for Aaron or Ross to be the culprit, that doesn't mean they aren't. It means maybe they've got another reason. A less logical reason, maybe."

"Like what," Ash stated. He did not seem particularly convinced.

Lennox wondered if it would be easier for him if it turned out that this was someone he didn't know. Or at least someone he didn't know very well.

Lennox definitely understood that—but the chances were it *was* someone who knew Ash.

"Like why they left your dad's restaurant," Lennox suggested.

"No way. No freaking way," Ash insisted. "They didn't even argue about it."

"And that was what? Ten years ago? You might not have been around. Your father might have shielded you from knowing the truth."

"Maybe," Ash said dubiously. "It's not like he can't be a stone-cold asshole."

"Exactly," Lennox said.

"But what would going after me accomplish?" Ash wondered. "It's not like I had anything to do with it."

"There you go again, thinking logically," Lennox said.

"Ugh," Ash groaned, setting the rest of his pita down. "I think I just lost my appetite."

"Sorry," Lennox said. He'd apologized more today than he'd apologized in the last year, at least.

"It's not your fault." Ash stared at his plate. "I just . . . this is supposed to be my happy place, my *safe* place, you know? And what am I doing now? I'm staring at every customer. At every person who works here who used to be a friend, and I'm wondering if any of them are to blame. If someone has it out for me, and I don't even know why."

"They didn't *used* to be your friends, past tense," Lennox said gently. Seth would die if he could see him like this—apologizing, not wearing his shoulder holster, and being all gentle and shit. "They *are* your friends. You know that."

"I'm having a hard time remembering that," Ash said.

"Here," Lennox said, sliding the half-eaten cheesecake towards Ash. "You can't eat this and be sad. It's physically impossible."

Ash perked up a little. "You're right," he said as he picked up his fork. He used it to dig into the cheesecake, cutting himself a big piece that he shoved into his mouth hungrily. "Oh yeah," he moaned around the forkful. "Yeah, that's fucking delicious."

Lennox shifted uncomfortably on the wooden bench. "I'm glad you enjoy it," he said. Trying very hard not to think of what Ash would look like with something else in his mouth.

Ash pulled the clean fork out of his mouth. "I never let myself get this," he said. "Because I will demolish the entire piece, and even working hard all day isn't enough to burn all these calories away. Alexis is a closet sadist."

Lennox watched Ash load his fork up again and moan around the bite of cheesecake and thought that Alexis wasn't the only sadist around.

His jeans felt uncomfortably tight and he couldn't look away as Ash's tongue flicked out, licking a bit of honeyed nuts off the end of his fork.

There was a part of him that he'd long forgotten—that he'd been *sure* had died when his relationship with Marcus had ended—that wanted to lean across the table and lick all that honey off Ash's lips.

They were shiny with it, and Lennox dug his fingers into his thigh, trying to keep himself focused. Centered. Narrowed in on the target. Anything but distracted. Which was really tough, because Ash was one of the most distracting people he'd ever met.

"So there's nobody you think could be doing this to you?" he asked, changing the subject before he did anything he'd regret.

Or something he didn't regret at all.

Ash shook his head. "Nobody I can think of. Unless we're talking *everyone*, and trust me, I spent all day imagining crazy-ass reasons why every single person I talked to might want to hurt me." He sighed. "Please don't apologize again," he added when Lennox opened his mouth to do just that. "Somehow it's even worse when you apologize."

"Okay," Lennox said, filing that information away for later. "I'll just say that I'm going to do my best to get to the bottom of this, as quickly as I can. But . . ."

"These things take time?" Ash said wryly, copying the phrase that Lennox had said earlier. "Yeah. I'm beginning to figure that out."

"The good news is now I have this," Lennox said, pointing to the photocopied page he'd smoothed out. "I can cross-reference it with the other one. See if I can get anywhere with that. And . . ." He hesitated, but added anyway, "My guess is there will be more. I'll start my day here tomorrow, see if they come back, maybe I can grab them before the trash collection starts."

"It's Alexis' morning tomorrow," Ash said, standing and gathering his trash. "He'll be here early, because that's the kind of guy he is. And he's *thorough*, if you get my drift."

"I do," Lennox said, resigning himself to a late evening and an early morning—though it wasn't like he hadn't done that plenty of times in the Navy. "I'm going to stick around tonight, though, because I know there's a band playing, and that would be a great cover for the culprit to do something else, while everyone's distracted and there's a crowd."

"Alright," Ash said. "We're going to stay open another few hours, I think. That crowd might get hungry and hopefully some of them aren't just wanting drunk munchies food."

"Probably the safest place for you is in your truck," Lennox admitted. "But I'll be around, and I'll keep an eye out for you."

Ash shot him a grateful smile as they began to walk back to his truck. "You're a good guy," he said.

"Just doing my job," Lennox said, and then when Ash's smile dimmed, just a little, he realized it had been the wrong thing to say.

Seth kept telling him he was terrible at taking compliments, but it seemed he wasn't going to get any better, anytime soon.

"But thanks . . ." Lennox added awkwardly.

"Hey," Ash said, "at least you didn't apologize again." He waved at Harmony as they approached. "How's it going?" he asked her. "You get very busy while I was gone?"

"Not really," she said. "But someone came by, and bought a salad and asked me to give you this."

"What?" Ash questioned and Lennox took a step closer as Harmony slid a piece of folded paper across the counter. He watched as Ash opened it and his face went white and then flushed red.

Ash turned to Lennox, a wordless plea on his face. He plucked the paper out of Ash's fingers and felt his insides ice over.

The message was scrawled in messy capital letters, scribbled in thick black marker.

Did you get my offerings? I hope so. Because there's so much more excitement to come.

"Shit," Ash mumbled under his breath and Lennox could see him about to lose it. And the last thing Ash needed was to freak out, like *really* freak out, especially in front of this crowd. He was a business owner and a leader in this community. Having a meltdown? Ash would never forgive him if Lennox let it happen in public.

He grabbed Ash's hand and shot Harmony a look and she nodded. "We'll be right back," Lennox said and then dragged Ash behind his truck, where he had his bike locked up.

"I need you to keep breathing," Lennox ordered as Ash propped himself against the back of his truck, his eyes wide and panicked, his chest rising and falling way too rapidly.

"I . . ." Ash mumbled. "Oh my fucking God. They were *here*. They talked to Harmony!"

"Yes, though we don't know that for sure. Maybe they sent someone. Maybe they sent someone who didn't even know who they were. We don't know yet. I'll talk to Harmony, and we'll start to put a profile together."

"Not yet," Ash said, and his hand shot out and grabbed Lennox's arm, holding it surprisingly tightly. "Not just yet, okay?"

"I'm not going anywhere," Lennox promised.

Ash closed his eyes. "Someone hates me so much," he said in a small voice. "Why?"

"It might not be hate. But they do seem hung up on you," Lennox said. And then before he could stop himself, he added, "I kinda understand how they feel, sometimes."

Ash's eyes opened even wider and he stared at him unblinking. "What?"

Lennox flushed. He hadn't meant to confess that. He also hadn't meant to make Ash freak out about *him*, but maybe that was the best method to calm Ash down: distract him.

"You know I don't even *like* salad, right?" Lennox said, chuckling, and hoping that the humor and irony would do its job.

"What?" Ash repeated. He was still far too pale, under his summer tan. "What?"

"I've wanted to do this forever," Lennox said and stepped closer, and then closer still. Ash's eyes never left his own, and he didn't move away even a fraction. Just stood there and waited like he'd known this whole time that Lennox would never be able to resist.

Lennox leaned down, and this time when their lips met, it was just as soft and sweet as their first kiss had been, but then Ash moaned, and Lennox just couldn't help it anymore.

He shifted his weight, pushing Ash against the steel side of the truck, and devoured him whole.

Ash tilted his head, hands sliding up Lennox's shoulders, and then even further up, cupping the back of his neck with one warm palm.

It was too much to focus on at once. So much sensation swamping him, Ash's tongue slipping between his lips as their kisses became hotter and wilder. For a brief moment, Lennox almost grasped for control, thinking he should pull back, but then Ash's hips aligned with his own, and pleasure rocketed through him, short-circuiting the thought before he could do anything about it.

Ash might have been shorter and smaller, but despite all the sunny smiles, he'd never been a pushover—one of the things that Lennox had always loved about him. He'd spent so long believing kindness was a sort of weakness that there was something un-deniably attractive about Ash's sweetness *and* his steely spine.

He didn't take shit from anyone and he was one of the genuinely nicest people Lennox had ever met.

And he kissed like a man who was starving, and Lennox was the feast he'd been waiting for—when it *had* to be the opposite.

Lennox hadn't kissed anyone since Marcus, but right now, he couldn't even remember who Marcus was. There was only Ash. Lennox's hands in his hair, sliding down his sleek back, down to the ass that he'd found impossible to ignore, skating right over the curve of it.

"I guess you *are* here."

Lennox sprang back, like a bucket of cold water had been dumped on his head. His fingers trembled and he shoved them in his pockets. His erection throbbed and there was no way it wasn't obvious that he and Ash had been only a minute from straight-up dry humping against the back of his food truck

He looked up and met a pair of kind, dark eyes. Gabriel's expression was wry. Amused.

"Harmony told me Lennox dragged you away and I thought, *no way*, and yet, here you are. With *him*," Gabriel said, pointing to Lennox like he wasn't even there.

Ash took a deep breath. Lennox could feel his chest rising and falling beneath the thin fabric of his t-shirt, with its embroidered logo. "Yeah," he said. Like he didn't have any words left in his head either. Like Lennox had burned them all away, the same way Ash had burned his own. "Yeah, I'm here."

Ash's voice was totally normal, completely unembarrassed, like Gabriel hadn't just caught them making out. Lennox pushed his panic down, pushed it *away*. If Ash could live through this, then so could Lennox. It was hardly the worst thing that had ever happened to him. Yet, he thought back, remembered three years ago, and remembered a time when it *might* have been the worst thing that could've happened to him.

It definitely would have been the worst thing that could have happened to Marcus.

"I was wondering if I could borrow some spring mix?" Gabriel said. "We ran out."

Ash raised an eyebrow. "You ran out of lettuce? I wasn't aware you *used* lettuce?"

"*Old* menu," Gabriel said, his chest puffing out like he was very proud. "Several of the new menu items use that spring mix and I guess I miscalculated how popular they'd be."

"Well, let me go grab a bag for you," Ash said. "I got my delivery this morning. I've got plenty."

"Thanks," Gabriel said, and then grinned. "No need to rush on my account. By all means, finish . . . whatever you were doing."

Ash rolled his eyes. "You know exactly what we were doing. If you need a refresher, though, I'm sure Sean would be happy to conduct one."

"Maybe I'll ask him," Gabriel said and Ash laughed.

"I'll be right back," Ash said. He pushed himself away from the back panel of the truck and opened the door, disappearing from view.

Gabe finally looked at Lennox, shooting him a knowing glance. "I guess it was your turn, huh?"

It had only been a month since he'd caught Sean and Gabe in a similarly compromising situation, and *no*, Lennox knew he hadn't been very nice about it. In fact, he'd been downright awkward about it. As awkward as he was being now?

"I don't know what you're talking about," Lennox said even though he knew exactly what Gabriel meant.

"I knew you'd be back here, eventually." Gabriel chuckled. "It was inevitable."

"Oh?" Lennox kept hoping that Gabriel would be awkward and nervous, the same way he'd felt when he'd interrupted him and Sean. But it seemed that, like he'd guessed before, everyone here was a lot more comfortable with displays of affection. Even when the affection grew a little hotter.

It was completely foreign to Lennox. He couldn't imagine touching a guy in public with something more than friendship.

He couldn't deny it any longer, he felt more than friendship for Ash.

It was a distraction—a terrible, horrible, potentially catastrophic distraction—but he couldn't help it any longer. He'd fought against it as long and as hard as he could.

He was still digesting that state of affairs and dealing with Gabriel's knowing grin, when Ash emerged in the doorway. He tossed Gabe a bag of mixed greens. "Here you go," Ash said.

"What do I owe you?" Gabriel asked.

Ash waved a hand. "I'll swing by in a few days, when you get your veg shipment, and take one of yours, if that's alright."

"Works for me," Gabriel said. Smiled again, even wider this time. "Have fun, you two. And, don't forget to wrap it."

"Oh my God," Ash said, and coming down the stairs, playfully shoved Gabriel. "Get out of here."

Gabriel shot them both one last grin, and then he was gone.

Leaving Ash and Lennox to deal with what had just happened.

"Well, I guess Gabe's right. That *was* inevitable," Ash said, with zero regret in his expression.

Lennox discovered he couldn't disagree. "I guess so," he said slowly.

"It happened," Ash said, "it's fine. We've got . . . well, some chemistry. It's only surprising that it didn't happen earlier." He tilted his head. "Well, maybe it isn't, because you didn't let it."

"I didn't," Lennox agreed. He shoved his hands back in his pockets and began to pace. "I'm . . . I'm still not good at this."

"I know," Ash said honestly. That was another reason why Lennox liked him. He was straightforward without being mean. Realistic without ever being fatalistic.

Not like you, that voice in the back of his head reminded him.

There'd been a time when he hadn't been sure that every romantic entanglement wasn't destined for disaster. There'd been a point when he'd been hopeful and in love and certain that if he and Marcus held on *just long enough,* it would all be worth it.

Instead, he'd learned that they'd been doomed from the beginning.

"I'm not sure how this is going to work," Lennox said.

"I don't know either," Ash said, not sounding particularly perturbed by this. "We'll figure it out."

"It can't be that easy," Lennox said dubiously. "What if . . ."

Ash stepped right into the middle of the track he'd been wearing in the dirt, and put a finger over his mouth. "I never said it would be easy," Ash said. "I said we'd figure it out."

Lennox digested that. "Okay," he finally said. "I just . . . I want to figure out who's doing this to you. That has to be my number one priority."

"I *want* it to be your number one priority," Ash said, shuddering a little. "I can't believe he was *here.*" He seemed still a bit shaken, but nothing like he'd been right after Harmony had given them the note.

"We don't know that he was," Lennox said. "I'll talk to Harmony. Figure out if there's anything we can use that she remembers. My guess is that this person is too smart to expose themselves like that. I bet they just asked someone to give Harmony the note."

Ash sighed. "I hate this."

"I know," Lennox said, and hating how awkward he felt about it, reached for Ash, gathering him into his arms, running a reassuring hand over his back. "I'm gonna fix it."

"Not feeling safe in my own place . . . it's intolerable."

"You'll feel safe again," Lennox vowed.

Ash pulled back, and there was something precious in his expression: *trust*. "I know," he said. "I know you'll do everything you can."

"I should go talk to Harmony, while her memory is still fresh," Lennox said.

"You'll keep me in the loop?" Ash asked.

"Everything I know, you'll know," Lennox promised.

"Good." Ash leaned in and brushed a kiss across his cheek. Like he knew that making out behind Ash's food truck was something Lennox had broken down and had allowed but that he wasn't quite comfortable with yet.

A little corner of Lennox's heart—a part he'd declared dead and buried long ago—began to warm up, all over again.

CHAPTER SEVEN

Lennox worked through the weekend—using all the skills he'd learned in the Navy and from Seth—to filter through the Google results. He hadn't told Ash, because this was just a hunch at this point, but he was fairly certain that this had something to do not with Ash, but his father.

Somehow, Ash had gotten entangled in whatever resentment or feud was happening, even though Lennox believed him when he said he had no idea how or why.

Lennox spent a lot of time on digging through various articles from ten years ago, right when Aaron and Ross had left Atkinson's restaurant and started Basket, but he still came up empty.

"Maybe," he said, rubbing his tired eyes on Sunday afternoon, "I'm imagining things."

"You're doing what?" Seth asked, looking up from his computer.

"It just feels coincidental," Lennox said. "The only two people who know who Ash's father is, who *worked* for him, happen to apply to join the food truck collective he's part of, right before all this shit starts happening."

"Maybe it's coincidence," Seth said, spinning around in his chair to face Lennox. "Maybe it's not. You've got good instincts, though."

Lennox sighed. "So you keep saying. But I've got nothing here."

"Nothing from the security feed? Nothing from the interview with the other employee?"

"Nothing." Lennox knew how frustrated he sounded. "Whoever's doing this isn't stupid. They hid their face, and somehow, they seem to know the weaknesses and the blind gaps of the cameras. Somehow they're getting around most of them. And as for the note, the handwriting's so messy, analysis is a joke. And the paper? All super generic copy paper you can buy at any office supply store by the ream."

"So the only thing you have to go on is your hunch," Seth said.

"Yeah," Lennox said.

"Then explore it," Seth said. "Have you talked to Atkinson about this yet?"

That was a whole kettle of worms that Lennox didn't know how to deal with. Even though they hadn't talked it over, he already knew that Ash would be pissed as hell if Lennox went to his father and told him everything that was happening. Even if he *didn't* tell him everything that was happening.

"No," Lennox admitted. "I want to. I don't think he'd tell me anything about what happened ten years ago with Ross and Aaron, but I do think I might be able to get him to slip up but . . ."

"You don't want to piss off your new boyfriend," Seth finished for him.

"He's not . . ."

"*Yet,*" Seth said. "And it makes sense. You've got to be more cautious here, since he and Ash are estranged."

"Yeah," Lennox said.

"You could talk to him about it."

"I could." Lennox hesitated. "He's pretty certain that it can't be either of the Basket guys, though."

"But you don't think so," Seth said. "Either you've got to convince him, or wait until things get bad enough that he doesn't care what's logical—he just wants it to go away."

Lennox had thought about that.

He'd been sure he'd wake up either Saturday or Sunday morning with a panicked text from Ash.

But instead, he'd woken up to Ash wishing him a good morning and telling him that there was nothing new at the lot. Hoping that he'd have a good day, that he'd uncover something that would solve this whole mystery.

Lennox knew, even though Ash hadn't said it out loud, that he thought maybe the worst of it was over.

But Lennox knew that wasn't true; whoever had done everything wasn't stopping now. They were just biding their time, possibly lulling Ash into a false sense of security before they struck again. Harder, this time, Lennox theorized. It would be a shock, whatever it was.

It was tough enough to brace himself for it, even harder to brace Ash for it, without making him dread going to work each and every morning.

Even if he was incapable of taking all of that away for Ash, he had no intention of making it any worse.

"Take a break," Seth finally said. "Go for a run. You've done everything you can, at least for right now."

"I *know* that, but I also can't help but think, *if I dig a little deeper, a little further . . .*"

"You know better than to believe that," Seth said. "Give it a rest." He stood and stretched. "And I'm off, anyway. I think Landon and Quentin are set up."

"Any sign of the stalker?"

"None," Seth said. "And it seems like they're finally using the system. You were right, getting scared was the best way to convince Landon it was important."

"I'm just happy it didn't turn out worse," Lennox said. For everyone. Including him. If something awful had happened to Landon Patton, his own referrals and contacts would have dried up, because it was *his* responsibility to keep Landon safe.

Just like it was his job—and his *vow*—to keep Ash safe.

Maybe Seth was right, and it was time to take a break.

Clear his mind.

Lennox stood and stretched, heading up to his loft apartment. He changed into running shorts and hooked up his phone to his earbuds, clicking on the newest episode of his favorite podcast.

He ran regularly through the week, but today, he pushed himself until his legs were shaky and sweat was dripping down his forehead.

He didn't feel any better.

There was nobody who could figure this out but him, and the pressure was mounting.

After he got back to his place and showered, he sent Ash a text.

Nothing new here today. I'm striking out everywhere I look. How are things at the lot?

Ash's response was fairly instantaneous, which meant things were slow.

Nothing new here either. There was a pause, and then Ash sent a second text. **I'm bored as hell. I guess that's better than being scared half to death.**

We'll take that, Lennox texted back. **Take care of yourself.**

You mean, don't take any unnecessary risks?

Lennox could nearly *hear* the wryness of Ash's voice even over text.

Yes, that's what I meant, he replied.

You'd come down here and escort me home if I asked, wouldn't you?

Ash's response was quick, like he'd been thinking about it and had only needed the opening to say it.

I would. Do you want me to?

There was a part of Lennox that wanted to, very much, but there was another part of him—the scared-as-shit part—that didn't know what would happen if he escorted Ash home.

Would Ash invite him in?

Would they kiss again?

Would they get carried away again?

This time, they'd be in private—at Ash's house. They could do whatever they wanted.

Lennox wasn't quite sure he trusted himself to be alone with Ash. He already had a feeling that desire was going to overwhelm every bit of good sense, and he wouldn't be even the tiniest bit surprised if Ash helped it along in his own way.

Frankly, Ash had the ability to destroy all of Lennox's common sense with a single touch, and they both knew it.

Ash took his time responding. Lennox got up, got some water, paced around his apartment a little. Half-ready to head down to the food lot if Ash said that *yes*, he wanted Lennox to come take him home.

No, the text said when it finally came through. **I'll be fine. But I appreciate the offer.**

Lennox fought back a wave of disappointment. He didn't know why Ash had decided against it, even though he knew it was for the better.

Instead of getting his shoes on, he flipped the TV on and watched, barely listening or seeing, until he got another text from Ash, letting him know that he'd gotten home safe.

Only then did he drag himself to bed, and then instead of falling asleep right away, he stared at the ceiling for a long hour.

Thinking about everything and nothing all at the same time.

About what had happened with Marcus. When he was going to have to be honest with Ash about that whole fucking mess.

About this annoying-as-hell stalker, and why he wouldn't leave Ash alone—and what he hoped he wouldn't have to do about it.

And how pissed off Ash was gonna be if he had to talk to his father.

Lennox woke up with a phone call.

It was never good when his phone woke him up before his alarm.

"Lennox," he said after snatching it off the nightstand next to him.

"Hey. We were doing our patrol, and you said you wanted to hear if there was anything going on at that food truck lot?" It was Adam, one of the security guys that did rounds at night between all the properties that Lennox provided security for downtown. He'd added the food truck lot to the list the other day because he'd wanted to have a set of real eyes on it at least once a night.

Or, in this case, early in the morning.

Lennox blearily stared at the phone. It was just after five AM.

"Yes," he said. "What's going on?"

"You'd better get down here," Adam said, and the concern in his voice had Lennox's stomach sinking to his knees.

"What is it?" Lennox was already sliding out of bed, quickly pulling on jeans and grabbing a t-shirt from one of his dresser drawers. "Is it the salad truck?"

"No," Adam said. "It's one with a big Greek flag on it?"

Lennox stopped in his tracks, he was so surprised. "What? Alexis' truck? Are you sure?"

"It's hard to miss, sir." Adam's voice was wry. "We'll be around when you get down here."

"Alright," Lennox said. "See you in a few."

He grabbed his holster, strapped it on, put his gun in it, and threw a hoody over it, then was out the door, more jogging than walking as he headed towards the food truck lot.

A few minutes later, he was on the property, and first thing, before he headed to Alexis' truck, he checked Ash's.

The security lights were bright in his eyes as he checked the door and the lock, and then made his way around the front. There was nothing, not even a piece of paper taped to the window like last time.

Lennox let out a little of the breath he'd been holding since Adam called.

Then he headed towards Alexis' truck.

The moment it came into view, the issue was obvious.

Bright purple paint was scrawled across the distinctive blue and white flag that decorated the front of the truck.

Did you enjoy his food?

Lennox sucked in a breath. Whoever was doing this had been there on Friday night, when he and Ash had sat at the table only a few feet away, and Ash had enjoyed his chicken pita and they'd shared Alexis' baklava cheesecake.

Ash was going to lose his fucking mind when he found out about this.

If it had been his own truck, it would have been bad enough—but for someone to do this to the truck of a friend of his? Whose only crime had been to serve Ash food?

Lennox felt his stomach cramp at the thought of how much Ash was going to blame himself.

But first, before he talked to Ash about this, he was going to have to call Tony, and Tony was going to have to call Alexis. And when Tony showed up, Lennox was going to have to explain to him, somehow, why he hadn't made a bigger deal about any of this. Why he hadn't looped Tony in on any of the new things that were happening.

Ash reluctantly holding out on telling Tony the truth and Lennox giving him that option had just made his job a hell of a lot tougher.

Lennox rubbed a hand across his face. "Is it still fresh?" he asked, directing the question towards Adam.

"Paint's gone a little tacky," Adam said as he approached Lennox, "but still pretty fresh, yeah. You've got cameras on this place, right?"

"Yes," Lennox said, "but I think our culprit knows it. I doubt I'll find anything useful."

But that wouldn't mean he wouldn't look. First thing he'd do when he got back to the office after dealing with Tony and Alexis, would be to scan through the footage and see if this asshole had gotten any sloppier since last time they'd come around.

He pulled his phone out and dialed Tony's number.

It rang and rang and rang some more, and just when he'd assumed that Tony had set his phone on silent or *do not disturb* overnight, he answered in a bleary, exhausted voice. "Yeah?" he said.

"It's Lennox," he replied in a clipped voice. "We've got a problem down at the lot. You should come down here."

He heard Tony fumble around. "But . . ." he complained, "but it's not even six in the morning."

"You want to get this cleaned up before you open, you're going to want to get down here." Lennox paused. "And you should call Alexis, as well."

"Alexis?"

For the last two years, Lennox had dealt with myriad situations, some more treacherous and dangerous than others. But he'd never been this close to a client before, and he'd underestimated how difficult it would be to tell Tony what had been happening, and what had *just* happened.

"Alexis' truck has been vandalized."

Lennox heard Tony's breath catch, and the muttered oath. "What happened?" he demanded.

"More paint," Lennox said shortly. "I think you'll be able to clean it up."

"Shit," Tony said. "I'll call Alexis, and we'll meet you at the lot. Give me . . . twenty minutes?"

"Sure," Lennox said and Tony ended the call.

While he was waiting for Tony, Lennox was tempted to call the police—not because they could do his job better than he was doing it, but because sometimes it came in handy to have an official record of any incidents that had happened. But before he did, he wanted to discuss it with both Tony and Alexis, face-to-face.

In the meantime, he opened the recorder app on his phone and began making notes, examining the paint and noting that it looked very similar to the purple paint that had been used to vandalize the picnic table a month back. Similar handwriting, too, to the note that had been delivered to Ash's truck on Friday night—the same messy capital letters, like whoever it was had attempted to use the scrawl to disguise their real handwriting.

Adam had taken a few pictures, but Lennox had him take quite a few more, sending them to the folder that he could access from his computer in the office.

He wanted to get all his first impressions out of the way, and a solid recording of the scene, before Tony and Alexis showed up—because no doubt their first instinct would be to want to clean it up as quickly as possible.

He'd just finished recording his impressions, when he heard a commotion and saw Tony and Lucas approaching.

"What the fuck," Tony spit out, coming to a stop right in front of the dripping purple paint. "What does this even mean?"

Lennox sighed. "It's . . . complicated. But I'm fairly certain it's directed towards Ash."

"Ash?" Lucas questioned. "But this is Alexis' truck?"

"Yeah, but Ash ate Alexis' food on Friday. And," Lennox added, mentally preparing for Tony to get pretty fucking pissed off, "there's been a few other incidents pinpointing Ash."

"You think this is all about him? Why? And why am I just now finding out about this?" Tony's brows slammed together and he didn't look very happy about being kept in the dark, but he also didn't look angry enough to punch Lennox in the face either. He was gonna take that as a win.

"Honestly, I wasn't entirely sure yet. I was still doing some digging. And up til now, it's been fairly innocuous incidents that I didn't think would escalate this fast to property damage."

"But you were wrong," Tony countered.

"I was wrong," Lennox said in a flat voice.

He didn't need Tony to see his guilt. Or how terrified he was becoming for Ash.

"I guess you were," Tony said. "You wanna tell me about what's going on?"

"You know about the picnic table, obviously," Lennox said. "And then there were the photocopied interview pages that have been floating around."

"Why do you think that either of those things have anything to do with Ash?"

And this was the problem.

"I wish . . ." Lennox cleared his throat. "I really wish I could tell you, but I've promised Ash that I wouldn't. But I have made *him* promise to tell you the truth, himself."

"What?" Tony looked stunned. Maybe just as stunned as he'd looked when he'd walked onto the lot and seen the purple paint scrawled across Alexis' food truck.

"He's going to have to talk to you about it," Lennox repeated. "I can't betray his confidence."

"But I'm the one who's paying you," Tony said, crossing his arms over his chest.

"I can tell you that I'm doing everything I can to prevent this kind of thing," Lennox said. "I've been working on these issues nonstop since they began. I'm hoping I can find some more information to give you in a few days. And I hope Ash will talk to you."

"He'd better," Tony said, his jaw clenching.

"I think you should encourage him," Lennox said, hoping that Ash wouldn't be pissed that he'd said as much to Tony.

"I will," Tony promised. "So, what can we do about this?" He gestured to the ugly dripping letters on Alexis' truck. "What can we do to make sure this doesn't happen again?"

"I'm going to increase security," Lennox said. "That's the first thing. And I'm also promising to get to the bottom of this. As quickly as possible."

"What about cleaning this up? Can we start right away?" Lucas asked. "I don't want Alexis to see this."

"Too late."

All three of them turned towards the voice, which of course belonged to Alexis. He was staring at what had previously been his pristine food truck.

"Oh, God, Alexis," Tony said, and even though Alexis was a member of their circle—Lennox knew it, he'd seen it during the few times he'd seen them all together at the Funky Cup—he was still surprised when Tony and Lucas immediately went over to him and wrapped him in a big bear hug.

For a moment, they just stood there, supporting their friend, and then they moved away from each other. Lennox could see the pain on Alexis' face. Couldn't imagine how hard it would be to build something, only to see some stranger try to tear it down.

You know exactly what that feels like, that annoying voice in the back of his head reminded him. *You know because something like that happened to you. Except it was worse; it destroyed your entire career. One bullet, in exactly the wrong place, and you were done. And after, you didn't even have your team to lean on.*

Because that was what these guys were to each other; Lennox could see it now, clearly. They had each other's backs, the same way his team had had his. No wonder when he'd started coming here, it had felt like coming home.

"I can't believe someone would do this," Alexis said, staring at his truck, rubbing a hand across his face. "What does it even mean?"

"Lennox thinks it's about Ash," Tony said.

"What?" Alexis sounded even more baffled.

"Ash and I both ate at your truck on Friday," Lennox said.

"Lots of people ate at my truck on Friday. And Saturday. And Sunday," Alexis pointed out.

"Apparently it's because this person is targeting Ash," Tony said. "Or else that's what Lennox thinks, anyway."

"Really? Ash? What would Ash have done to ask for this?"

There was no part of this conversation that was going to be easy. That much was clear. "Ash is going to have to tell you that," Lennox said. "It's not my story to tell, but suffice it to say, he's clearly the target here."

"I guess we're gonna have to take your word for it, until Ash shows up and decides to tell us what's going on," Tony said, his voice frustrated. "Which I hope will be soon."

"It's his day off," Lucas pointed out.

"It *was* his day off," Tony said. "We'll have a meeting tonight, after close. An emergency staff meeting."

"Sounds like a good plan," Lennox said. "Do you want to call the police?" he asked, directing the question towards Alexis.

"Should I?"

Lennox shrugged. "We still don't know who's done it, and if I can't figure it out, no offense to the LAPD, but *they're* not going to be able to figure it out either. Best scenario, they ask for the security footage, which based on what I got from the last few incidents, isn't going to tell them much of anything."

"So you don't think it's a good idea, then," Alexis said.

"I think it would only be a good idea if we wanted to make sure there's a record of what's happened," Lennox said, "but we didn't call them for the picnic table, and with the other incidents, the culprit wasn't exactly breaking the law, so there was no reason to call them then."

"If we don't, then can I clean this off right now?" Alexis asked, gesturing to the paint scrawled on his truck.

"Yes," Lennox said, nodding. "I've got what I need. Plenty of record of what happened. We've been over the scene. No reason you can't get started on cleaning it up."

"Great," Tony said. "We've got some stuff in the storage shed but . . ."

"I'm on it," Lucas said. "I think there's a hardware store down the street that's open twenty-four seven."

"You guys don't have to . . ." Alexis said and then stopped when Tony shot him a look.

"Hell yes we do," Tony said.

"I'll stay and help," Lennox said. It was the least he could do, when he'd been the one to stay quiet about what was really going on. The guilt of that wouldn't be fading, not anytime soon.

"That'd be great," Tony said, clapping a hand on Lennox's back. "Help me get the stuff out of the shed."

"I'll be there in a second." He went over to Adam and Jon, giving them a final set of instructions, before sending them on their way.

When he got to the storage shed, Tony was digging out some cleaning supplies, piling everything in a spare bin.

"Hey, please don't let Ash know about this," Lennox said, bending down and helping Tony. "After we're done here, I'm going to head over to his place, tell him in person."

"Alright," Tony said. He straightened and swiped hair out of his eyes. "You really aren't going to tell me what the hell is going on with him?"

"I wish I could," Lennox said, and meant it. "But they're Ash's secrets to tell."

"And you don't want to piss Ash off, not when you're this close to winning him over," Tony said wryly. "I get it. I'm not trying to fuck this up for you. But . . . *God,* I really thought we were safe here. I guess that was ego talking."

"If it makes you feel any better," Lennox said, tossing a bag of sponges into a bucket, "I don't think you're *unsafe* here. This is one person, and they've got an ax to grind with Ash. Not with the rest of you."

"Tell that to Alexis," Tony said, hefting the bin up on his shoulder. They headed back towards Alexis' truck.

"I really didn't think there'd be any collateral damage," Lennox said, meaning it. "The person has been super focused on Ash so far."

"I believe you," Tony said, setting the bin down and facing him. "But don't keep me in the dark again, okay?"

"I won't," Lennox promised.

A few minutes later, Lucas appeared, holding a plastic bag. He set it on the nearest picnic table, unloading several different kinds of cleaners. "I got everything I thought might work," Lucas said. "Alexis went to go get coffee."

"God bless Alexis," Tony said fervently. "It is way too fucking early for this."

"It's never a good time for this," Lennox said, pulling the hose out of his bucket.

"Water hookup's around the back," Tony said, gesturing.

After Lennox found the water, attached the hose, and got the bucket filled, Alexis was back, holding a paper bag in one hand and a cardboard drink holder in the other.

"Coffee," Tony exhaled happily.

"It's the least I can do," Alexis said as Lennox grabbed one of the cups from the holder. "You guys didn't have to help me clean this up."

"Yes, we did," Tony said. "You're fucking family, Alexis. And we're not gonna stand for this."

"Still means a lot," Alexis said, ducking his chin bashfully.

For the next hour, they scrubbed away at the drying purple paint, racing against time as the sun rose, the temperature went up, and the paint got even harder to remove.

By the time the neighborhood was beginning to stir, a few curious people walking by as they started their shifts at the lot for the day, the four of them had scrubbed away almost all of the purple.

"Well, I think that's just about as good as it's gonna be," Alexis said wryly. "I was thinking of changing up my branding, so maybe that's something I'll look into sooner rather than later."

"If you do, let me know," Tony said. "You shouldn't have to pay to fix this by yourself."

Alexis looked critically at the faded shadow of the letters. It was hard to even make them out anymore. From a few more feet away, it might just look like a shadow, overlaid over the Greek flag. "I was going to do it anyway, sooner or later," he said. "It's fine that it's sooner."

"Are you sure?" Tony asked.

"You're not going to pay for this." Alexis sounded very firm. Lennox had considered opening his own mouth and adding his promise to Tony's, but he also understood pride.

And Alexis definitely had his fair share.

"I'll file a claim with my insurance," Alexis said. "I bet they'd consider this covered."

"Good idea," Lucas said.

Lennox stayed, helping Tony put away the cleaning supplies back in the shed, and it wasn't until he and Lucas headed off to their respective food trucks that he walked off the lot—after checking Ash's truck one last time, in the daylight—and went back home.

He decided he'd take a quick shower, and as the water was getting hot, he shot Ash a text message.

Want to check in this morning, Lennox texted. **Are you at home?**

When he got out of the shower, a response was waiting for him.

At the big farmer's market downtown, Ash said, **can you meet me down here?** He'd also included the address, even though Lennox could've done a quick Google search to look it up.

He dressed quickly, hesitating as his fingers brushed over the ankle holster sitting on his dresser. The forecast was calling for it to be way too hot for his shoulder holster and the jacket he'd have to wear with it.

He *could* go unarmed. It wasn't like he couldn't easily overpower anyone with his strength and skill alone. And the farmer's market? It *should* be fine, Lennox told himself. He didn't need a gun to defend Ash—or himself.

It was still weird to step downstairs, and into the little garage where he kept his bike, without carrying.

When he'd first been discharged, it had been really difficult for him to go out anywhere without carrying a gun. He'd been seeing ghosts and dangers everywhere. Slowly, Seth had helped him conquer those fears. But now, with these threats against Ash, it seemed they'd returned.

He was going to have to fight them back, the same way he'd done the others—not only with intent, but with confidence in his own skill and ability to keep himself and others safe.

The drive down to the farmer's market was refreshing, waking him up the last little bit from his early morning. He didn't get to take his bike out enough, and even though the weather was supposed to be hot today, especially warm for September, it was still cool enough that the breeze on his face felt wonderful.

He parked and only had to go a short distance before he found Ash, crouched over some bins of zucchini and squash.

"Hey," he said, taking in the big basket of produce at Ash's feet. "Busy day off so far?"

Ash glanced up. "Yeah, I was going to work on some new recipes."

Lennox hesitated. He'd been thinking about anything else but this conversation, but now there was nothing else but to confront it.

"Hopefully nothing that takes too long," Lennox said, finally. Maybe he could start with the emergency staff meeting that Tony had decided was necessary tonight.

"Why?" Ash wondered. "Is everything alright?"

"Tony's called a staff meeting tonight," Lennox said.

Ash groaned. "You know, I thought when I worked for my-self that there would be a lot less meetings. But Tony especially loves them. I really don't get it."

It made sense; Tony didn't really strike Lennox on the sur-face as a meeting kind of guy.

Digging money out of his pocket, Ash paid for his squash and they moved over to an empty bench, one of many lining the permanently closed street that the farmer's market now lived on.

"Well, this one is probably more important than usual," Lennox said.

Ash glanced up at him. "You gonna tell me what happened?"

There was no putting it off any longer. "I've been having my normal patrol crew run by the food truck lot the last few days," Lennox said. "Usually on their way back to the office to put in their report for the night. It's been quiet the last couple of nights."

"And nothing going on at the lot either, Saturday or Sun-day," Ash pointed out.

"But last night, the person decided to graduate from leaving photocopied notes, and left something a little . . . more per-manent."

Ash looked apprehensive. "Oh God, what happened? Did something happen to my truck?"

"Not yours," Lennox said. "It was Alexis. Remember how we ate there Friday?"

"I do," Ash said, and then hesitated. An awful look washed over his face. "Oh no, they didn't do something to Alexis' truck, did they?"

"Same paint as the table. They wrote, *did you enjoy their food?*"

"Fuck." Ash put his head in his hands. "They were talking about *me*, weren't they?"

"That is the current assumption," Lennox said. Hesitated. He wanted to comfort Ash, because this was just as terrible as he'd worried it would be, but he didn't know what to do. He was never comfortable touching in public, even if it was plenty platonic—probably because his own feelings were *not* platonic.

But Ash needed it, and besides, Lennox told himself firmly, he needed to get out of his own way.

Instead of keeping his hands to himself, he rested one palm on Ash's back, cotton t-shirt warm from the morning sun, and rubbed up and down, reassuringly. "It's not your fault," he said, even though he knew better than to believe that the words would be enough for Ash to avoid blaming himself.

"It sure feels like my fault," Ash said in a muffled voice. "Is it terrible? What did Alexis say?"

"Alexis wasn't happy about it, but he got it cleaned up. Tony, Lucas, and I helped him."

Ash looked up at him. His blue eyes were teary. "You helped?"

"Well, of course I did," Lennox said. "I'm not a heartless monster."

"I know you aren't," Ash said reproachfully. "I was just saying it because that was really nice of you. You weren't hired to do that."

"Well, I haven't been very good at what I *have* been hired to do," Lennox admitted. "But I'm working on it. The more things this person does, hopefully the better I can get at targeting him."

"Hopefully," Ash said. "So . . . Alexis isn't angry with me?"

"Why would he be?" Lennox questioned. "Though, you really need to tell Tony what's going on. He kept asking, and I *know* he's not very happy that I couldn't tell him why this person is targeting you."

Ash sighed. "I'm going to have to tell him the truth, aren't I?"

"Yes," Lennox said.

"I probably made it harder for you to do *your* job, too, didn't I?" Ash sounded distraught again. "By asking you not to tell Tony the truth."

Yes, Lennox thought, *but I understood.*

He'd met Stephan Atkinson a dozen times, at least, and each time had been more unpleasant than the last. He couldn't imagine having a father who was that much of a self-absorbed asshole.

"Until today, nothing really terrible had happened that could have impacted the lot," Lennox said carefully. "But yeah, I should have kept him more in the loop."

"I'm sorry," Ash said wetly. "I'm so sorry. I never meant . . . I just didn't want people to judge me."

"Those guys all love you. There's no way they were gonna judge." Lennox slipped his arm over Ash's body, and pulled him tightly against him. It was only after he'd already moved that he realized what he'd done—and how good it felt.

"I know, but . . . *ugh*, I just never wanted anyone to know. It's just annoying, you know, to constantly have to answer questions about it. It's why I changed my last name. It's why I started going by Ash. It was easier to do that than to keep having to explain that my father was a total asshole and I didn't want anything to do with him even though he was rich and successful."

"I know what that feels like," Lennox said. "It's why I left San Diego and came here." Not *entirely* why, but that had been a big part of the reason. "I kept getting asked why I left my team. Why I was discharged early. Explaining a dozen times, then two dozen times, and then *three* dozen times, that I got shot in the knee and they couldn't repair it well enough that I could operate again. Not something I enjoyed."

"Is that why you aren't in the military anymore?" Ash asked and then flushed, like he realized he was just as guilty of it as everyone else had been. "Sorry," he mumbled. "*Obviously* that's why you're not in the military anymore."

"It's alright. It helps when the question comes from a cute guy," Lennox teased, surprising himself, and clearly Ash too, who smiled for the first time since he'd told him about the vandalism.

"Oh my God," Ash exclaimed, in a faux shocked voice, laying a hand across his heart. "He *can* flirt."

He knew a few years back he wouldn't have, but today, without even thinking about it, he laughed.

"I never said I was very good at it, but once in awhile . . ."

"That's all I need," Ash said. "Once in awhile." His voice suddenly turned serious as he laid his head on Lennox's shoulder. Just like that, they were nearly cuddling in public, and two-years-ago Lennox would have absolutely had a fucking heart attack, but today? He just leaned in, discovering that he enjoyed the simple warmth of Ash's body against his, and also that genuinely, not a single person passing by them gave a shit.

"What are your plans for the rest of the day?" Lennox asked.

"Trying some new things," Ash said, nudging his basket of produce with his sneaker-clad foot. "Apparently going to a staff meeting. And now telling Tony the thing I swore I would never tell him."

"You know, he's not going to be pissed. He might be a little annoyed you didn't tell him, but I think, if I know Tony at all, he's going to understand."

"You really think so?" Ash sighed.

"I don't know what happened between you and your dad," Lennox said, "but I don't need to know. You said you couldn't talk to him or be close to him anymore, and I believe you, because I know *you*."

Ash didn't say anything for a long moment, just sat there, snuggled up against him. It felt so good that Lennox wondered if they ever had to move.

"There's really not much to tell," Ash admitted. "He was always critical. Both me and my mom never could do anything right.

But it wasn't so bad when I was younger, he basically forgot I existed. Then when I turned thirteen, he remembered and it was worse. But he never really wanted *me*, Ash. He wanted Oliver Ashton Atkinson, who would follow in his footsteps and run his restaurants and be an extension of him. I couldn't ever be that. I didn't *want* to be that."

"I can see him not taking that very well," Lennox said.

"He didn't. We fought all the time. If it wasn't one of his ideas, it was a bad idea." Ash sighed. "You've met him. There's no *bend* in him, and I don't expect that to change anytime soon. Or ever. It was just better for us to go our separate ways."

"What about your mother?"

Ash shrugged. "I'm sure you can imagine what being married to Stephan Atkinson is like. She did whatever he said. She's just as much his creation as he wanted me to be. We do text occasionally, and once in awhile she'll come see me. But I'm not sure *he* knows that she does it."

"I'm sorry," Lennox said. What else could he say? But the words didn't feel adequate.

"Don't be," Ash said, the corner of his mouth quirking up. "I *have* a family. A fucking amazing family. I just really hope that the one I avoid won't ruin the one I actually care about."

"They won't. I won't let them," Lennox said. "You guys . . . I know I wasn't always as friendly as I could be, but . . . you've created something special there. Nothing is going to destroy that. As far as I'm concerned, nothing *could*."

"Not even my secrets?" Ash wondered.

"You're not *that* important," Lennox teased.

"I think you might be right. You're going to come to the meeting though, right?"

Tony had already asked him to come—so he could give a report on what was currently on his security plan and what he hoped to add to beef it up—but he was touched that Ash wanted him there, too.

"Of course," Lennox said. "I'll be there."

"I'm sure you've got lots of stuff you need to do today, so if you need to rush off . . ." Ash sounded reluctant, like he didn't want Lennox to leave.

Truthfully, Lennox didn't *want* to leave. Were there things that he could do? Absolutely. But he'd have time this afternoon. For the first time in a very long time, there was something else he wanted to do that *wasn't* work, and he was going to do it.

"Actually, I was hoping I could tag along with you for a little bit," Lennox said.

"Really?" Ash sounded surprised—but in a very good way. "I'd love to have you tag along. Like a date?" His smile glimmered with mischief, and Lennox felt his heartbeat begin to accelerate. What he'd had with Marcus had been nothing like this, and he felt unexpectedly young and green and new at this.

Had he ever been on a date? He and Marcus had certainly never dated.

He would have never dared to even suggest it.

"Yeah," Lennox said, surprising even himself. "Yeah, like a date. You know anywhere around here we could get a cup of coffee and something to eat for breakfast? I'm starving." He was, he realized, his stomach rumbling.

Ash smiled, practically glowed with happiness.

It was unbelievable to Lennox that it was *so* simple to make him happy, so unbelievably easy, and his father had made such a complete hash of it. But then Lennox was sure that his father had never bothered trying to understand Ash either.

"Yeah, I've got just the place," Ash said, and to Lennox's disappointment, he stood up. He immediately missed the press of Ash's body against his, but maybe . . . maybe this was something they could do more often. Maybe this wasn't the only taste of closeness that Lennox would get.

If they were dating . . .

Lennox cut that thought off hard and fast. They weren't really *dating*, yet. They were trying it out. Maybe Ash would get tired of him. He *wasn't* good at this, just like he'd said, and while Ash claimed he was fine with it, Lennox had to wonder if his inexperience would get annoying.

"There's a great little cafe just down the street. Best coffee in the neighborhood," Ash said as Lennox joined him, picking up his basket of vegetables before Ash could protest. "I always stop there on my way out, after I visit the market."

"Sounds great," Lennox said as they headed out past the market, turning onto a side street. "I could use some more coffee, honestly. It was an early morning."

"How early?" Ash wondered as they approached a brick building, painted sunny yellow, with a sign that proclaimed it the "Sunshine Cafe."

"It was just after five when my security team called me," Lennox said.

"Ugh," Ash groaned. "That is insanely early. And you're still on your feet! I'd be napping if I was you." They walked inside the propped-open door, and after Ash indicated there was two of them, the hostess grabbed menus and told them to follow her.

"I'm used to long hours, honestly," Lennox admitted. "I probably shouldn't tell you that. You're going to think I'm some kind of crazed workaholic."

"What? *You*?" Ash teased again as they took their seats on the patio in the back of the restaurant. "I can't believe that."

"Remind me never to introduce you to Seth," Lennox said, opening his menu.

"Who's Seth?"

"My second-in-command. I run Protectorate with him," Lennox explained. "He's been out of the military longer than I have, and when I came to LA, a friend of mine recommended I look him up. He hadn't started a company or anything, but he was doing some freelance security. We met and hit it off, and now we work together."

"And he's a friend," Ash said, stating rather than asking. Trust Ash to get right down to the truth of the matter, quickly and easily.

"Yeah. Yeah, he is."

Ash nudged Lennox under the table. "That's okay, you know, to have friends, and to *admit* you have friends. Especially on a date."

Lennox laughed. "You gonna give me dating lessons? I probably need them."

"You might, but you're doing okay so far," Ash said.

"Good to know."

The waitress approached, and they ordered, Ash ordering not only the coconut banana pancakes, but a chai vanilla whipped coffee concoction.

When the coffee arrived—Lennox's black and plain, and Ash's towering with whipped cream and chocolate shavings—he had to ask, "You got a sweet tooth today?"

"It's so sweet, but I try not to indulge too much," Ash confessed. "I know so much sugar is bad for me, but it's so good . . ."

"Probably not as good as this real strong coffee," Lennox said.

"What about you?" Ash asked as he watched Lennox across his coffee cup.

"What about me?" Lennox asked, raising an eyebrow.

CHAPTER EIGHT

Ash wondered if this was the moment when Lennox was going to freak out.

He'd been waiting for it, a little bit, since the first kiss, and definitely since the second.

It was clear that Lennox, based on what he'd been through in the military, was not used to dating so openly. Ash had to wonder if he was even used to dating at all.

"What about you," Ash repeated. "We've spent so much time talking about my father, that we haven't talked about yours, at all."

"He's back in Ohio, still, with my mom. I've got a younger brother, who still lives by them. Dad's a cop, Mom works as a nurse. There's . . . not much to tell," Lennox said.

"Not much to tell?" Ash repeated. "I think there's a lot to tell, and I don't know anything. Like . . . why did you go into the military instead of becoming a cop?"

"9/11," Lennox answered succinctly. "I wanted to protect our country."

"Dang, I can't tease you about that," Ash said. "You know you're a hero, right?"

"I don't think so, not particularly," Lennox said flatly.

It was clear he believed that, even though Ash knew he couldn't be more wrong. He'd known Lennox long enough to see just how fiercely dedicated he was, and before Tony had hired him, he'd rhapsodized more than once over how amazing his credentials were.

Truthfully, that was one of the reasons why Ash had always been attracted to him. Sure, he'd been a little awkward and mysterious, nearly impenetrable at points, but competence and confidence radiated off of him, and there was nothing sexier than that. At least to Ash.

Now that he was finally opening up? Ash knew he was more interested than ever.

"Does your family know that you're . . ." Ash hesitated. Lennox had never specified if it was just men he was interested in, but he took a chance anyway. "Gay?"

"Yes," Lennox said shortly. He clearly did not want to talk about this.

"After this, I swear I'll ask something stupid and silly," Ash said, reaching out and squeezing Lennox's hand quickly, "but I want to know *you*. And this is part of who you are."

The waitress arrived then, setting their food down—the pancakes for Ash, and a huge meat-laden breakfast skillet, with potatoes and eggs and cheese, for Lennox.

He'd always suspected that eating so many vegetable-filled salads hadn't been Lennox's normal MO, but now he knew it, and he was touched. Lennox *had* been coming by his truck for *him*.

After the waitress left, Lennox continued.

"I did tell them, but not right away, not until I'd been in the Navy for years," Lennox admitted. "They . . . well, they didn't know how to deal with it. My mom doesn't care much, and I don't think my brother does either, but my dad was real uncomfortable with it. He didn't want it to impact my career, and in that, he was right."

"But you told them anyway."

"I . . . it wasn't some big brave gesture," Lennox said wryly, "not like I think you're building up in your mind. I thought, well, I really stupidly fucking thought that a guy and I might have a future together, and so I told them, thinking that they'd have some time to get used to it, and it turned out . . ." Lennox stared behind Ash's head, like he wasn't even seeing him in that moment. "It turned out that I was wrong," he finally said.

"That's kind of unfair," Ash said. "Especially when I promised to ask about something stupid and silly next."

"Well," Lennox said, unexpectedly cracking a smile, "the reason why was fairly stupid, so I think it counts. It didn't work out because he decided to get married."

Ash tried very hard to keep his jaw from falling open. "He *what*? To someone else?"

"To a very nice lady." Lennox pursed his lips. "Too nice of a lady, all things considered."

"Oh my God," Ash said, shocked, setting his fork down with a click. "He . . . when you guys were together?"

"It turns out that the only one who thought we were something was me," Lennox said. "But to answer the question I know you're dying to ask, yes, some men in the military still feel like they have to hide. Even now."

"That's . . . really fucking sad."

Lennox nodded, digging through his skillet. "I'm not going to disagree."

"How long were you together?"

"Friends and teammates for a dozen years," Lennox said, "and 'involved,' I guess I could say, for half of that."

"And he went off and married a woman." Ash couldn't believe it. He'd essentially abandoned his pancakes because he couldn't bring himself to eat. It felt *rude* to not give proper attention and respect to this horror story that Lennox was in the middle of confessing.

"While suggesting to me that we could continue our 'arrangement,' yes," Lennox said. "I'd just been shot, was recovering in the hospital, away from the team, and away from him, and I thought when I came back, because back then I thought I *would* come back, and he finally came to see me in the hospital." His voice went wry and Ash knew he was covering up the pain. "Thought

I'd want to wish him a very happy life, while still fucking him on the regular."

"That's . . ." Ash couldn't find the words for it. "Horrifying." It didn't feel bad enough. He couldn't imagine what Lennox had been through. Suddenly so much of his reticence about dating made sense.

"Obviously I was not going to do that. To her. Or to myself."

"So when you said you weren't good at dating . . ."

"I meant it?" Lennox cracked a smile. "I've never really been on a date."

"Well, if this is your first date, it's gonna have to be pretty fucking awesome," Ash declared, because he literally could not imagine how painful and shitty that situation had been for Lennox. He'd always suspected he was one of the strongest, most committed people he knew, but now? There was no denying it.

"Technically," Lennox corrected, gesturing with his fork, "this is date number two."

Ash raised an eyebrow. "Did we have a date I hallucinated through?"

"You invited me to the anniversary party," Lennox said. "It might not have ended the way I hoped it would, but it still happened."

This was intriguing. "How did you wish it had ended?" Ash wondered, even though he had a few suspicions of what Lennox might say.

Lennox's dark eyes somehow grew even impossibly darker. "Why don't we try a do-over?" he suggested.

"When?" Ash asked, knowing he sounded eager and not giving a fuck. He wanted this man, and he was fairly sure Lennox wanted him just as much. He just kept all of that locked down tight, letting only tantalizing clues slip.

"Tonight?" Lennox asked. "After the meeting?"

"You're saying you're gonna walk me home after?" Ash teased.

"I'd be honored," Lennox said.

If any other guy had said that to Ash, he'd have been tempted to laugh in their face. But with Lennox? Honor was something that wasn't just a meaningless, obscure concept. Honor was a central tenet of how he'd lived his life.

"I promise to not end this date with accusations of you working with my father," Ash said, trying to lighten the mood, because even when Lennox had been talking about his ex, he hadn't looked nearly this serious.

Ash could only assume it was because Lennox wanted him to know he *was* serious.

With someone like Lennox, there wouldn't be just a few silly dates and a quick fuck, and then a half-hearted debate about whether Ash would call him again.

This was a guy who had likely only been with one other man, and that had been for six years—and Lennox had approached their relationship like he was in it for the long haul.

If he got involved with Ash, it was because he was equally as committed.

Ash hadn't taken many—or *any*—of his relationships this seriously. But this one? It didn't feel weird or scary to think about it in those terms.

Maybe he hadn't at first, but now, Ash would trust Lennox with his life.

Even with his heart.

"Sounds good," Lennox said, smiling. "And I could hardly blame you for that. I'm the one who stuck my foot in my mouth. First date ever, and I fuck it up."

"You didn't fuck it up. Or else I wouldn't be here today."

They finished eating, keeping the talk light, until after Lennox paid the bill—which he'd insisted on doing, despite Ash's protests.

"Tonight you can buy me a beer," Lennox said, looking so pleased about this that Ash had shut right up.

With Ash's basket of produce, they'd headed out of the cafe.

"I'm parked just down the street," Ash said, as they emerged onto the street. It was mid-morning now, and after the farmer's market had closed up, the sidewalks were empty.

"I'm the opposite way." Lennox sounded like he really regretted this.

"Well, I guess I'll see you tonight," Ash said, juggling the basket of vegetables. "At the Funky Cup, right?"

"Yeah, after closing. So nine-ish, I'd assume?" Lennox said.

"Right." Ash looked up and down the street, and decided that even though they were technically out in the open, Lennox couldn't protest because there was nobody around to see. So he set his basket down and leaned in.

"Thank God," Lennox murmured right before they kissed, and Ash felt like his heart was going to break apart like a coconut, falling from a tree. It was too sweet that Lennox wanted this just as much as he did.

And he *really* wanted it.

Ash had kissed him almost hesitantly, because he hadn't wanted Lennox to feel uncomfortable, but the moment their lips touched, he'd groaned into Ash's mouth and then his hands were all over him, running down his arms, his torso, his back, his questing fingers pausing and digging into the hair at the back of his neck as he tilted Ash's head, tongue moving eagerly against Ash's own.

It was a pretty hot kiss, Ash thought dimly, considering that they were mostly exposed, and Lennox had said he wasn't always comfortable with public displays of affection.

After Lennox pulled away, licking his lips as he lifted his head, Ash had to wonder what would happen when they were finally, *really*, alone. Tonight. His blood heated and his cock grew harder, just at the thought.

At all the possibilities.

"Tonight?" Lennox repeated, his voice gravelly around the edges. Ash didn't think it was possible to be even more turned on, just by a kiss and a promise, but he wanted this man. *Badly.*

"Tonight," Ash said.

Ash usually really enjoyed his days off. Not that he didn't love his job—because he *did*—but he typically spent his days off experimenting with new ideas, with the kind of cooking that he loved but that never seemed to fit with the theme of his truck.

He didn't want to change it, necessarily, but once a week, it was fun and a nice change to do something different.

But after his meetup and his date with Lennox, Ash couldn't seem to relax into his regular habits.

He got the vegetables home from the market, and cleaned and prepped them, but he felt distracted, and anxious.

Not necessarily about seeing Lennox after the meeting—*that* was a kind of nervous excitement, too—but the idea of telling Tony, and likely the rest of the guys at the lot, the truth, made him feel sick inside.

He'd never wanted them to know, because he'd never wanted them to treat him differently. Not only was that a possibility, but there was an even stronger chance that they'd be pissed that he'd lied for so long about who he was.

He almost texted Sean and asked him how hard it had been to confess his own big secret, but that would mean telling Sean the truth first, and if anyone found out before Tony did, Ash knew there'd be hell to pay.

There was no question about it: he was going to have to pull Tony aside first, before the meeting began, and confess.

Tony was a good guy—one of the best, as far as Ash was concerned—but they'd also known each other for *years* at this point, and there was no way it wouldn't sting when Tony found out that he'd never mentioned that he was related to one of the most famous chefs in Los Angeles.

One of the most famous chefs *in the world*.

Instead of cooking, Ash ended up cleaning, airing out his room, changing his sheets, making sure that nothing was dusty or cluttered. He had a feeling that Lennox would want to go back to his own place, because that was where he was most comfortable, but on the slim chance they didn't, and they came to his place instead, Ash didn't want to have to worry about anything.

Finally, he ate a quick dinner, barely tasting it, and headed out for the Funky Cup early, hoping to catch Tony before the meeting started.

Shaw was behind the long hardwood bar tonight, a bright smile on his face as he traded quips with his brother, whom he owned the Funky Cup with.

Ash approached the bar just as Jackson ducked back into his office.

It was cowardly, but Ash was glad, because Jackson was dating Alexis, and he still wasn't sure how he was going to face him. Or anyone who loved him.

"Hey, I hear there's a meeting tonight," Shaw said as he reached down to grab Ash his standard light beer.

"Something stronger, actually," Ash said, and Shaw straightened, a glimmer of surprise on his face.

"Everything okay?" he asked. "I heard something went down at the lot this morning. Jackson certainly wasn't happy."

Guilt swamped Ash again. Why had this person stopped targeting him and gone after Alexis? Alexis hadn't done anything wrong.

"Yeah, there's some weird shit going on," Ash said nebulously. He was pretty sure that Shaw knew what had happened—his brother was dating Alexis, after all—and he was trying to get Ash to open up about it, and normally it might have worked.

But not tonight.

"Seems to be," Shaw said, leaning over the shiny hardwood of the bar. "What can I getcha instead?"

"Gin and tonic," Ash said.

Shaw raised an eyebrow but began to mix the drink, loading a glass with ice and pouring in a hefty measure of gin, and topping it with tonic and a few slices of lime.

He slid the glass over the bar towards Ash. "I'll add it to your tab?" Shaw questioned.

Ash nodded, swirling the liquid in the glass to mix it. "Is anyone here yet?" he asked.

"Nope, you're the first," Shaw said.

Ash reached into his pocket and pulled out his phone, shooting Tony a quick text, asking him to come early, if he could. Ash knew Tony well enough to know that even if he *couldn't*, he'd still show, because his curiosity was a powerful thing, and Lennox had obviously already piqued it earlier today by refusing to add context to what had happened to Alexis.

Ten minutes and a half of his gin and tonic later, Ash was feeling not necessarily any calmer, but at least more resigned to the conversation he was about to have, and then the door opened and closed. The moment he heard Tony's voice, he wanted to turn and run.

But he didn't, because he was a grownup and grownups didn't run at the first sign of adversity. Well, *most* grownups didn't run, and if Ash could give his father credit for anything, it was at least instilling a sense of responsibility in him.

At the time, he'd loathed every minute of it, but now? He supposed he was grateful for every lesson.

"Hey," Tony said, sliding onto the barstool next to Ash's. "I got your text."

The Funky Cup was just about a ten-minute walk, so the moment he'd received it, he must have dropped everything he was doing.

"Yeah, I wanted to talk to you before the meeting. Before . . ." Ash took a big swallow of his drink. *Before I have to tell everyone else.* "I know you talked to Lennox this morning."

"Yeah," Tony said, gesturing towards Shaw, who grabbed him a beer. His fingers hesitated over the condensation-covered bottle. "Wait, am I gonna need something stronger for this?" he wondered, nodding towards Ash's glass.

Ash shrugged. "It's been a long day."

"Tell me about it," Tony said. "I got woken up at ass o'clock by your boyfriend."

"He's not . . ." Ash hesitated. Sure, they'd been on a date, and from the confessions Lennox had made today, it was clear he did not date often, so a date was big news in Lennox's world. A serious declaration of intent. "I'm not sure what he is," Ash finished. "But yeah, I heard about that. About Alexis' truck."

"It was rotten," Tony said. "But we got it mostly cleaned up. Cleaned up enough, anyway." He raised an eyebrow. "You gonna tell me what all this is about?"

There was no way to do it except quick and fast, like ripping off a Band-Aid.

"My father is Stephan Atkinson," Ash said.

Tony just stared, shocked, finally, for the first time in the many years they'd known each other, into speechlessness.

"I know I didn't tell you," Ash said, pressing on, because he couldn't quite meet Tony's incredulous gaze, and because it was easier if he just got all this out at once. "I didn't tell you because I didn't want you to know. I didn't want *anyone* to know."

"So you . . . *what*, changed your name?" Tony didn't sound angry, but he sounded . . . *hurt*, Ash realized. Which was way fucking worse.

"Yeah, I did. I'd broken ties with him before we met, and I started going by an abbreviated version of my middle name and my mom's maiden name. I just . . . I didn't want anyone to think I was like him, and I didn't want anyone to think he was helping me. Because he wasn't. Not back then, and definitely not now."

"So you just . . . left the fold? The famous Hook & Slope fold?"

"Yeah," Ash said. He turned his glass in his hand. "I couldn't be what he wanted me to be, which was a clone of him."

Tony cracked a little bit of a smile, which Ash took as a positive sign. "You couldn't ever be a clone of that asshole," he said. Then hesitated, the smile growing wider. "Shit, he's your dad. I probably shouldn't call him an asshole."

"Be my guest," Ash said. "Won't hurt my feelings. He *is* an asshole."

"He didn't help you at all?" Tony wondered.

"I have a trust," Ash admitted. "I used it to help pay for my truck. And then I paid it back, with interest. Haven't touched a dime of it since."

Tony's forehead crinkled. "How does this have anything to do with Lennox and with the vandalism?" He suddenly smacked his hand on the bar. "The photocopies everywhere. Someone wanted you to know that *they* knew."

"And they wanted others to suspect, I guess," Ash said. "But as to why they went after Alexis? I've got no fucking clue."

"Lennox said he thought that was a message to you. *Did you like his food?*" Tony repeated what Lennox had told him had been scrawled across the front of Alexis' truck. "And he said that you ate there Friday. With him."

"Yeah, we did," Ash said ruefully. "I wish now that we hadn't."

Tony shot him a reproachful look. "It's not your fault. You know that, right?"

"If I hadn't kept this a secret, he wouldn't have a leg to stand on," Ash said.

"It doesn't seem to me like he cares if people find out the truth or not. He's got an issue with you regardless." Tony hesitated. "Could it be your dad? Atkinson?"

Ash just laughed. "No. This isn't his type of thing at all. He'd order me to come visit him at one of his restaurants or his office and expect that I'd just come."

"Would you?" Tony lifted the bottle of beer to his mouth and drank.

"Hell no," Ash said.

"Then, that's what I mean. Maybe you've forced him to try . . . unconventional methods."

"Honestly, I don't know who it is or what they want," Ash said. "Lennox keeps focusing on Aaron and Ross, because they know, but why would they do this? Right when they've gotten what they wanted?"

"Wait," Tony said. "Aaron and Ross *know*?"

"They worked for my father, a long time ago, before they started Basket," Ash explained. "I ran into them in his kitchens plenty of times."

Tony leaned back on his barstool. "I'm with Lennox on this one."

"That's just because you always want them to be the bad guys," Ash said, rolling his eyes. "They're not villains."

"Just because you knew them way back when, doesn't mean you *know* them," Tony argued.

"It's not them," Ash insisted. "I know you're angry because you think they stole your dip recipe, and maybe they did, maybe because that backstabbing asshole Jeremy sold it to them, but I don't think they'd have any reason to go after me."

"Why, because you're *friends*?" Tony wondered, the edge of his voice going hard.

"I wouldn't call us friends," Ash said. "But Lennox isn't ruling out anything right now."

Tony sighed. "Are you going to tell anyone else? Or do I have to try to keep this a secret?"

Ash shook his head. "I'm done keeping secrets. I'd rather not . . . anyone talk about it? You know? With other people? I don't really want to be *found*, but I don't want to lie about who I am anymore. I have to trust that you guys won't believe that I'm like him. At least that's what Lennox says."

"Lennox is not stupid," Tony said.

"No, he's not." Lennox was a lot of things, but stupid was not one of them.

"He didn't want to order me to tell everyone, but I think it'll help him if the other owners know," Ash said. "That's why I'm doing it. And because it's the right thing to do."

"But not easy," Tony said. He clapped Ash on the shoulder. "I should probably be pissed. We've known each other for *years*, and I had no idea, but you know what? It was your secret to keep and I understand why you didn't tell me."

"Thanks." Ash felt humbled and grateful. It had definitely been within Tony's rights to be angry. "It means a lot."

"I said it before, and I'll say it again," Tony said. "That guy is an asshole, and he definitely doesn't deserve you."

Ash raised his glass and tipped the rest of the drink into his mouth. It was either that, or burst into relieved tears. *Grateful* tears.

"And if anyone says anything to you," Tony added, "I'm gonna kick their ass."

Ash laughed. "Really?"

"Okay, well, not really. I'll send Lucas to kick their ass," Tony admitted with a bright grin.

"That's what I thought. But really, it's the thought that counts. Thanks, Tony," Ash said. "It means a lot."

"Of course," Tony said. "You're a friend. And a partner. We're gonna support you."

Even though Tony had said unequivocally that everyone supported him and cared about him, it was still difficult to get up in front of so many people he considered friends and admit that all this time, he'd been lying.

Even though it didn't seem like anyone blamed him, it still sucked. No matter how many understanding nods he received, no matter how much he apologized to Alexis, he wasn't sure he'd ever be able to fully expunge the remnants of guilt.

Lennox spoke after him, going through everything that had happened. The picnic table, outlining the factors about the incident that had convinced him it wasn't a random homophobic incident, then he went on to the photocopied interviews, and ended the recap with the overview of what had happened to Alexis' truck today.

"I'm also going to be setting a patrol up at the lot," Lennox said in conclusion. "The person who's doing this is smart. They've been able to get around our security measures, but that won't always be the case. I'm convinced they're going to mess up at some point."

"I just hope they do it before anything else bad happens," Gabriel said, sounding unusually serious. The whole evening had a pall over it, unlike their normal staff meetings.

Everyone had been understandably horrified at what had happened to Alexis.

But Alexis? He wasn't the kind of guy to be cowed by it. He'd accepted everyone's sympathy with an unexpected smile on his face, repeating over and over again that he'd been planning to rebrand anyway, with a new wrap for his truck, and he hoped that the insurance would pay for it.

"How often are they going to be patrolling?" Tony wanted to know.

"Three times a night," Lennox said.

Tony didn't look too thrilled with that. Maybe he'd been hoping that Lennox would set a patrol there for the entire night, but with the damage so far mostly superficial, it made sense not to go overboard. And Ash knew that this would already put a strain on Lennox's resources. He didn't have a ton of employees, and Ash assumed the kind of people that Lennox hired didn't exactly grow on trees.

"I'm also asking everyone to not stay alone, or to walk home alone, if you're walking."

"You gonna escort Ash home on his bike?" Lucas wondered, a sly look flashing across his face.

"I am," Lennox said seriously. "Ash isn't going to be here by himself, or on the way from his house to the lot by himself, until this is over."

"Is that really necessary?" Ash wondered. "They haven't really done anything to me."

"Yet," Lennox added.

Ash hated the shiver that ran up his spine at the thought that things could—and probably *would*—get worse.

That he might actually *need* Lennox's protection, and not just because it felt reassuring to know that someone so completely capable and competent was looking out for him.

"We'll all watch out for him," Lucas promised.

"Thanks," Lennox said. "And if anyone sees *anything* not just suspicious, but out of the ordinary, please let me know immediately." He handed out business cards to each and every truck owner.

Tony took the floor next.

"One last thing," Tony said, "we have two new trucks joining us. Lucas' vegan truck, the Good & Planty, will be taking up the spot next to Gabe and Ren's truck, and Basket will be parked next to Alexis."

"That's awesome," Sean said, leaning over and giving Lucas a quick hug. "We're all super proud of you."

"The festival really brought it home for you," Tony said, the pride on his face and the love in his eyes unmistakable. "He earned it. And we all know Basket is undeniably popular." Tony's expression went sour as he said it, but everyone knew it was true. "And that brings me to the last thing I wanted to mention. Sean and Gabe's collaboration dish was so popular, it's ended up on Gabe's menu permanently, and I want to do another one, right away." Tony's gaze locked onto Ash. "Since you already know the Basket guys, I think you'd be a great partner for them to have, to help introduce them to the rest of our customer base."

Ash couldn't say he was *happy* about it. Tony liked to meddle, that was undeniable, and he wasn't entirely sure if Tony was meddling now. It was possible he'd already decided who the next collaboration team was going to be, and it made sense to have an established truck pair up with one that was new to the lot. But Ash wasn't completely convinced that Tony hadn't just come up with this idea on the spot, after Ash had told him the truth earlier about how long he'd known those guys for.

If Ash wasn't happy about it, then Lennox looked positively murderous about it, his brows slamming together, and shooting Tony a look that promised that they'd be having words after the meeting.

It broke up a few minutes later, and sure enough, Ash watched as Lennox immediately went over to Tony and began to discuss something. Loudly. With gestures.

Ash sighed and got up, deciding if he was ever going to get out of here with Lennox tonight, he was going to need to do something to diffuse the situation.

"What's up?" Ash said as he walked over. "Everything okay?"

Lennox glowered. "No," he said. "Tony keeps trying to meddle."

"I'm not meddling," Tony insisted, putting his hands up in a completely meaningless gesture of mock innocence.

They all *knew* he wasn't innocent.

"So you starting the collaboration project last month didn't have anything to do with Sean and Gabriel," Ash said, raising his eyebrow. "Nothing whatsoever."

"Pairing you with Aaron and Ross makes a lot of good sense," Tony said stubbornly.

"Yeah, it does. They also happen to be my number one set of suspects for all the shit that keeps getting aimed at Ash," Lennox said.

If anyone could match Tony in stubbornness, Ash would bet on Lennox.

"And?" Ash asked. "I already told you, about a thousand times, I don't think it's them."

"No offense, Ash, but you think the best of anyone," Tony said. He turned to Lennox. "I paired them together because it makes sense. Ash is a veteran, they're new. Their food will mesh well together."

"I thought you were going to do a pairing with you and Lucas?" Ash asked, because last time he'd talked to Lucas about his vegan truck joining the lot, he'd mentioned that as a possibility.

Tony flushed. And it definitely wasn't because of the beer he'd drunk tonight. "We talked it over, and well, we kinda already *have* about five collaborations, on both our menus. It won't be as exciting and fresh, 'cause we've already done it. But you and Basket? That's new and interesting. Besides, I thought you wanted to try branching out to things that weren't exclusively salads."

Ash sighed. Mention something once or twice and Tony would never leave it alone. Maybe in a head-to-head battle of who was the most stubborn, he *could* best Lennox.

"So the point of this isn't to dangle Ash like bait, to try to lure one of them into showing their hand?" Lennox asked archly.

"Would I do that?" Tony asked, again with all that pointless mock innocence.

Pointless, because they all knew the truth.

"Yes," Ash and Lennox answered simultaneously.

"It makes sense on a lot of levels," Tony said. "But it makes the *most* sense for this lot. Besides, I thought you were going to do everything you could to keep him safe."

Ash frowned. He didn't like being talked about like an object, like he wasn't even there. Like he didn't have his own opinions.

Truthfully, he didn't mind the collaboration idea. Tony was right; from a business perspective it did make sense. And, he *had* been considering moving away from strictly salads for awhile now. The collaboration dish would be a great way to segue into that.

"I'm keeping him safe," Lennox said, his tone brooking no arguments, "but I'm also not putting him into any unnecessary danger, either. We're minimizing risk . . . and this is risky."

"It's my decision," Ash said, before Lennox said anything about wrapping him in cotton wool and putting him away like a favorite toy. That would definitely kill any hot and hungry feelings he had towards the man. "It's my decision, and I want to do it."

Lennox did not look convinced, but thankfully, he didn't argue.

"Great," Tony enthused. "I knew it'd be good for you."

"Good for everyone," Ash agreed.

CHAPTER NINE

OLIVER ASHTON ATKINSON WAS going to be the death of him.

Ash had walked to the Funky Cup, forgoing his bike, no doubt so that whatever they did afterwards, he didn't have to worry about where to stash it.

He'd waited approximately a minute and a half after they'd left the Funky Cup together, Ash nodding briefly when Lennox had suggested they head towards his place, before bringing up Tony's suggestion.

"You really want to do this," he stated, didn't ask.

The corner of Ash's mouth quirked up as they passed under a streetlight.

They weren't touching—Lennox couldn't imagine holding hands—but they were walking close enough that every once in awhile their hands and shoulders brushed. It wasn't nearly enough, but it would have to be, for the next seven minutes, until they got to Lennox's loft.

"Have sex with you?" Ash asked, eyes twinkling with mischief.

"No, uh, *no*, well, *yes*," Lennox stammered. "That's not what I meant."

"I know," Ash said, "but it's hard to resist teasing you sometimes."

"I meant . . . you really want to do this collaboration thing, with Aaron and Ross," Lennox said.

"Yes, I want to have sex with you," Ash said seriously, causing his heartbeat to accelerate. "And yes, I want to do the collaboration. Tony was right, as much as I hate to admit it. It's a good idea. Good for them, and actually, something I *have* been wanting to do."

Lennox sighed. "I was afraid you were gonna say that."

"Why?"

Ash always asked the simplest questions, with the most complicated answers.

"Because I don't ever want to stop you from doing something you want to do, even if it's not necessarily the safest idea."

Ash stopped in his tracks, right under a pool of light. Lennox's fingers itched to touch him, to pull him closer. *We're only a few blocks away*, he reminded himself, *and then you can really be alone.*

Of course they were alone on the street now. But the thought of being so exposed and of exposing his intentions . . . Lennox didn't like how anxious even the thought made him.

"You really mean that," Ash said, sounding surprised.

"I do." He always wanted Ash to be safe, but he also wanted him to have a life. And if that life included working with Aaron and Ross, then Lennox would work harder to make sure he could have both.

It seemed like a very small price to pay if he could make Ash smile.

One moment, he was standing there, a little uneasily, and the next, he had an armful of Ash.

He'd made a career out of not being surprised, but Ash could still do it. Could shock him to his bones, could strip him down to his barest parts. Lennox relaxed, enjoying the feeling of Ash pressed against him. Wishing they could teleport the rest of the way to his house and they could finally be *really* alone.

Reluctantly, Ash moved away from him, even though Lennox really did not want to let go. "Thanks," Ash said, "here I was all worried, you were going to go caveman on me, and lock me up and keep me away from everything I wanted."

"Never," Lennox answered honestly. "That'd be counterproductive, anyway."

"It would," Ash agreed as they started walking again.

Five minutes later, they arrived at Lennox's building. He bypassed the downstairs office, and instead, led Ash up the staircase to his door. Typing in the code, he pushed the door open, and they walked inside.

Alone. Finally.

Ash turned towards him, hair gilded by the lamp he'd left on in the corner. He put a hand on Lennox's chest, and he felt the impact of every one of his fingers, and the heat of his palm.

"You alright?" Ash asked, probably because he could feel the way Lennox's heart was beating so fast—*too* fast. It had been a long time for him, but it wasn't entirely because of how many years it had been since he'd been this close to another man.

It was because the man was Ash.

"I've never been better," Lennox said, and meant it.

He leaned down and caught Ash's lips with his own. It was still a wonder and a fucking revelation that he could do this and Ash wouldn't stop him. Would *lean* into it, fingers hungrily running across his back and his shoulders, up his neck, digging into the short hair there. Would kiss him and kiss him and kiss him until he was gasping for air. Like he couldn't possibly get enough.

That's me, Lennox thought dimly, *I'm the one who can't get enough.* They stumbled over to the couch, only pausing their kisses to catch their breath. He collapsed onto the cushion, and Ash immediately scrambled on top of him, fingertips digging into his shoulders as they kissed deeply, intensely. Lennox's blood heated as Ash did something clever with his hips and aligned his crotch with his hardening cock, sending a rush of pleasure through him.

He tore his mouth off Ash's, digging his own hands deep into the couch cushions, trying to get ahold of himself. He wanted more than a quick dry hump session to get off. He wanted to spin this pleasure out and make sure that Ash knew just how precious he was to him.

Because he *was* precious. Lennox didn't do half measures. He never had. He was all in, even if he hadn't been sure of it himself only a few days before. But today, he'd told Ash all his secrets—or most of them, anyway—and he knew now that they'd been heading to this place not just for the last few weeks, but the last few months.

Every single time Ash had flirted with him, and he'd told himself that he was too awkward, too out of practice (had he ever been *in* practice?) and he should just leave the guy alone—but then he'd gone back the next day. And the next day after that.

He'd never been able to resist the teasing light in Ash's eyes, or the kindness in his smile.

"Wait," Lennox said, but before he could stop him, Ash was sliding down off his lap, and his palm was hot and sweet against his hard dick. It strained against the fabric of his boxer briefs and his jeans, wanting to be closer, to feel more.

"Wait," Lennox repeated, even though it nearly killed him. If it felt this good, and he was still completely clothed, he couldn't imagine how incredible it was gonna feel when it was bare skin against bare skin.

But Ash didn't wait, he reached up and was undoing the button of his jeans, and then the zipper, flashing Lennox this flirtatious, teasing little smile that practically screamed, *I know you said to wait, but I know you want this bad enough that you really can't, after all.*

But he could, and he would.

He reached down and caught Ash's wrist in his hand. "What are you doing?" he asked, a little embarrassed at how gravelly his voice was. How needy he sounded.

Ash waggled his eyebrows. "I think you know," he said. "I wanna take care of you."

He got it, because his overwhelming need was held in check by an even more overwhelming compulsion to take care of Ash, too. But there was something about this that didn't ring true.

"You don't think . . ." He was probably going to ruin everything with the question, but he was going to ask it anyway. "You think I'm not comfortable doing this, right?"

Ash shot him a look. "I don't know what you mean."

But he did believe that. Lennox was convinced of it.

"You think I'm not comfortable having sex with men. So you're just gonna blow me and then I help you get off, and that's it, then?"

"Uh," Ash said.

"Trust me," Lennox said, reaching down and lifting Ash up. He wasn't that heavy, and the way Ash melted at his touch was so goddamn hot. He settled him back in his lap. "Trust me, I'm comfortable with this. I did it for a long time, didn't I?"

"In the *dark*."

"You mean, *in the closet*," Lennox corrected gently.

Ash squirmed a little. "Yeah," he said.

"Doesn't mean I don't like it. Doesn't mean I don't love it. Doesn't mean . . ." Lennox took a deep breath. "Doesn't mean I don't want you to fuck me so good I scream."

Ash's mouth dropped open in surprise. "You'd . . . you'd want that?"

"Hell yes I would. I was hoping you'd be into that, too," he said.

"You surprise me," Ash said wryly, setting a hand against Lennox's chest. "I didn't think you'd be into that."

Lennox felt the edge of his mouth quirk up. "I'm into more stuff than you'd probably suspect."

"Well, you can't say that and not tell me." Ash hesitated. "Or *show* me."

"I'd much rather show you," Lennox said, leaning in and brushing a slow, sweet, hot kiss across Ash's mouth. "Let's go to the bedroom, alright?"

Lennox didn't wait for Ash to respond, just wrapped his arms around him and picked him up, surprised at how little he weighed. He always seemed so certain and strong and sure, with a spine of steel that surely must weigh more than that. But he carried him easily down the hall and into his bedroom, setting Ash carefully on the bed.

"You are not what I expected," Ash said, eyes big as they followed Lennox's movements. He flicked the lamp on in the corner and returned, cupping Ash's cheeks in his palms.

"Is that a bad thing?" Lennox wondered.

"It wouldn't have been bad if you were exactly what I thought you'd be," Ash said, "but now? You're so much more. Like an iceberg, buried under the sea. I wish you'd show more people who you are."

"I'm working on it," Lennox said, which was *mostly* true. He was. He might not ever be as comfortable in public as Ash was, but he could be better. Not just for Ash, but for *himself*.

"What do you want?" Ash asked. "What you said before? You want me to fuck you til you cry?"

"I think I said scream," Lennox teased.

Ash shot him a look that somehow made his cock even impossibly harder. "You say that now," he said, "but I know what you need."

"Yeah?" Lennox wanted to believe it was true. It had been *so long.*

"Yeah," Ash said with a sharp nod, and then he stood up, and putting a firm hand on Lennox's shoulder, pushed him down.

He watched as Ash pulled his shirt off, and then toed his shoes off, leaving him clad only in a pair of denim cut-off shorts. Lennox swallowed hard, reaching out and trailing his fingertips down Ash's bare chest. "You're goddamn gorgeous," he said. "I'm never . . . I can't . . ."

"Yes, you can," Ash said firmly, reaching in and tugging Lennox's t-shirt over his head. "You can sit there and let me do whatever I want with you, can't you?"

Lennox took a deep breath. "Okay."

Ash didn't answer, just pressed his mouth to Lennox's pectoral muscle. He squeezed his eyes shut, feeling the pulse of his blood echo in his head, his heart, and his cock as Ash spent the next few minutes leisurely exploring his chest and then his abs, mouth skating right down to where he was sensitive.

"God, *you're* gorgeous," Ash murmured into his skin. "I can't believe you hid all of this under those jackets."

Lennox's fingertips dug into the comforter as he hit a particularly pleasurable spot. "If I'd known you'd do this, I'd have stripped down that first day."

Ash chuckled, his palm skating over Lennox's straining hard-on again, fingers nimbly beginning to unbutton and then unzip his jeans. Lennox lifted up as he pulled them off. "Condom?" Ash asked. "And lube?"

"Now you're talking," Lennox said. "Drawer."

His pulse jumped even more with just the words. It had been so long. He hadn't been even able to fuck himself, even though he knew that was something men did, sometimes, because right after Marcus, he hadn't wanted anything that reminded him of the man who'd broken his heart, and then for awhile after that, he hadn't even felt the inclination. And then, he'd met Ash, and he'd wanted it *too much*, so he'd avoided it, afraid that the sexual pull he felt towards the man would overpower all his judgement.

He'd wanted to *know* Ash, before he dragged him off to bed, like some kind of uncontrollable caveman. And now he did, and he wanted him somehow, impossibly, more.

Ash looked over from rummaging in the drawer. "It's been a long time, hasn't it?" he asked casually, but Lennox knew him enough to know his words weren't casual at all.

"A few years," Lennox admitted as Ash turned back towards him.

"Get on the bed," Ash said. "And don't argue. We're gonna go slow, okay?"

"Would I argue?" Lennox asked, doing what he said, but Ash's laugh made it clear he didn't really believe him.

But then Ash was naked, stripping down almost casually, and then he was between Lennox's legs, tugging down his boxer briefs.

Lennox hissed as his cock, so hard and with come pooling in the tip, met the cool air in the room.

Ash gave a happy sigh. "I hope," he said, "you're not against doing the fucking, sometimes."

"I'm not," Lennox said, his voice growing even impossibly deeper. "I'm really not."

"Good. Because I want your cock inside me," Ash said, leaning down and flicking his tongue across the tip. "I want to strip you down and taste you and ride you."

"Fuck," Lennox said, his head hitting the pillow. "You're killin' me."

"I know," Ash said smugly, pushing Lennox's legs apart, like he knew that if he spent much more time teasing, Lennox wouldn't be able to stop himself from coming.

That was probably true, Lennox thought weakly. He felt so close to the edge already, pleasure rocketing through him with every single brush of Ash's fingertips against his skin.

Then, Ash reached down and pushed a slick thumb against his tight hole, nudging him so much closer to that edge.

"Just relax," Ash murmured, and slid in his thumb.

It had been a long time, but he'd done this plenty of times before. Enough to know to do what Ash suggested and just breathe through the inevitable stretch, understanding that when he did, he was going to get rewarded with the kind of pleasure that might make him cry.

"Oh yeah," Ash said, pushing a second finger in, "you love that, don't you?"

Lennox realized then that the little bite of pain had already faded, and he'd started thrusting back against Ash's hand, he was *that* eager, wanted it that badly.

"Yes," Lennox groaned, forcing himself to look at Ash. To see the wonder in his eyes. He'd never expected that Lennox *would* love this. That he'd open himself up this way. But there was nothing he wanted to give Ash more than *him*.

Ash reached over and kissed him, messy and wonderful, as he continued to finger fuck him slow and perfect, the pleasure washing over him in wave after wave, until he didn't know where one ended and the other began.

"One more," Ash murmured into Lennox's mouth. "You can do that, can't you? For me?"

Lennox squeezed his eyes shut. It felt so good already, he felt like he was going to explode, but he'd waited so long, surely he could do this. For him. For *Ash*. He nodded.

"Good boy," Ash said, and slid in another finger, stretching him out for his cock.

He could be good. He could be the best goddamn fuck that Ash had ever had.

But even Ash's fingers trembled on the condom as he tried to unwrap it and he finally ripped it with his teeth, sliding it on with careful movements.

"Goddamn, you are so fucking sexy," Ash groaned as he lined himself up, the blunt tip of his dick pressing in right where Lennox wanted him.

"You feel . . ." Lennox lost his words, every thought in his brain, and probably the very last bit of his self-control as Ash's cock slid inside him.

Then Ash leaned over and kissed him, lips sliding sweet and hot over his own, their limbs sliding slickly against each other as Ash began to thrust.

Maybe it had just been a really fucking long time, but from almost the first slide of Ash's cock against his spot, the one that lit him up from the inside out, Lennox was sure he was going to come.

Then he made the mistake of glancing up, at the blissful expression on Ash's beautiful face, his hair mussed from Lennox's hand, his fingers curled possessively around Lennox's ankle, the other stroking his dick, and he lost every shred of self-control he'd had left.

It was a wonder it hadn't happened that very first time they'd met, when Ash had smiled at him like that, gently teasing him.

But today? Tonight? It was inevitable, and Lennox felt himself begin to spasm, pleasure overtaking him.

"So good," Ash said, his eyes squeezing shut as Lennox clenched around him, and a half an unsteady thrust later, he was coming too, moaning loudly.

It had been years since he'd had an orgasm with another person, but as Lennox slowly came back to reality, the echo of pleasure still working its way through him, he didn't think it had ever felt like this.

He and Marcus had scratched a mutual itch. They'd shared a strong friendship, and Lennox had been undeniably certain that he loved him, that they loved each other, that they were going to spend the rest of their lives together.

But lying here, with Ash collapsing next to him, Lennox wondered if any of that had really been true.

It didn't feel like it had been true.

Because what he was feeling now dwarfed anything he'd ever felt for Marcus.

Ash's legs weren't quite steady underneath him as he stood and walked towards the bathroom that Lennox had just pointed out to him.

He was still in bed, a dreamy, wondrous expression on his face, naked as the day he was born—but he didn't look anything like a baby. He was muscular, but not bulky, every limb in perfect proportion, the hottest guy that Ash had ever slept with, hands down—and he already knew it was going to be more than that.

Lennox trusting him with something he wanted so badly, that he hadn't done since his split with his longtime partner, told Ash that this wasn't just a quick fuck and done.

And the way he'd looked at him? That wasn't just lust.

It hadn't ever been just lust.

Ash's fingers trembled as he pulled off the condom, tying it and tossing it in the trash. He found a washcloth in the cupboard—neatly folded, too, but that didn't surprise Ash, because from everything he'd seen, the guy was absolutely fucking meticulous—and dampened it with some warm water, and walked back out to the bedroom.

Lennox was still lying there, his eyes still unbelievably soft. Nothing like the wary, unsure, apprehensive guy that Ash had met six months back.

He had a feeling that some of the walls would go back up. It was inevitable, because Lennox was a closed-off guy, wary and cautious, but he hoped that when the walls rose back up, he might still be inside.

"Here," Ash said, and Lennox sat up, taking the washcloth and cleaning himself with zero embarrassment.

He felt a little stupid, because he *had* assumed that Lennox not only didn't bottom, but wouldn't even dream of asking for it, even if he wanted it.

But he'd clearly wanted it, and he'd done it lots of times before.

Ash knew lots of guys who weren't part of an institution rife with toxic masculinity who still had trouble asking for it.

But not Lennox.

It was impossible not to feel warmed and honored by his incredible trust.

He lay back down next to him. Lennox wrapped an arm around his shoulders, pulling him in tighter.

"You good?" he asked, his voice deep and rumbling against Ash's skin.

"Never been better," Ash said honestly. "That was . . . well, I hope it was as good for you as it was for me."

"I barely got to touch you," Lennox teased. "How *could* it have been good for you?"

Ash turned his face into Lennox's bicep, reveling in the feel of smooth skin overlaying all that big, beefy muscle. "Trust me, it was definitely that good for me, too."

"Next time," Lennox promised, like it hadn't been that good for Ash. Like he might genuinely need to convince him to stick around.

Ash chuckled. "Trust me, you're not going to have to convince me. I can't wait to get you naked again."

"Still naked now," Lennox pointed out, even as his voice grew sleepier.

"Stay naked, and maybe when we wake up in the morning . . ." Ash trailed off. He'd had an early morning, but he knew Lennox's had been even earlier. He'd been woken up at the ass crack of dawn by his security detail.

"You want to stay?" Lennox asked, sounding so hopeful Ash's heart just melted into jelly.

"I'd love to stay," Ash said.

"Then stay," Lennox said, and yawned. "But I gotta warn you, I'm done for."

"Go to sleep," Ash said, patting his arm. "I'll be here when you wake up."

"Promise?"

"I promise," Ash said.

CHAPTER TEN

The next day, Basket arrived.

Tony had told Ash that they'd be parking the truck the next day, and that it wouldn't be a bad idea to get a head start on their collaboration.

Still, it surprised Ash that they'd arrive so soon, when they weren't officially opening until the weekend. But, as soon as his prep for the morning was done, he headed over to the truck, now parked in the empty spot next to Alexis. As he passed Alexis' truck, Ash could still see the faint purple outline of the graffiti that had marred the front yesterday, but the guys had done a really good job of scrubbing all the paint away.

The back door to Basket was open, and as Ash approached, he could hear voices inside.

He knocked on the stainless steel panel next to the doorway, and walked up the stairs before waiting for an invite.

Aaron Bolton and Ross Stanton were standing in the middle of their kitchen, discussing a shipment of supplies, and even though there wasn't anything in their expression or their tone that would make Ash think that they were arguing, there was a weird, tense feeling in the air as he walked in.

"Hey," Aaron said, glancing over at Ash. "Tony said you might be by this morning."

"Yeah, I figured might as well get started on this, so we're all set by the time you open," Ash said.

"*If* we open," Ross said grumpily. "Tony was already by this morning and I swear if he could get us kicked out for some trumped-up health code violation, he'd do it."

"Well, the truck looks super clean, anyway," Ash said brightly, making a mental note that he was going to have to talk to Tony. Harassing Aaron and Ross wasn't going to improve the situation; they were here now, it was time to just accept it and move on.

"You tell him that," Ross grumbled.

"I will," Ash said. "Sorry that Tony's being a bit of a bear. He'll get over it."

"Will he?" Ross sounded pessimistic and annoyed, and Ash didn't think he could really blame him. Tony had been really painfully stubborn about this whole thing.

"I think he will," Ash said with a confidence he didn't quite feel.

"Did you have any ideas for the dish we're supposed to be working on?" Aaron asked, shooting a glare in Ross' direction, and obviously changing the subject.

"A few," Ash said. "I thought it might be fun to try a few different kinds of salad. I know you guys are famous for your fried chicken, and I thought about doing a variation on the chef salad, but instead of chicken, we do turkey cutlets. A big scoop of pimento cheese made with Swiss and Emmentaler instead of cheddar. A Southern twist on a classic."

"Hmmmm," Ross said noncommittally. "That might work."

"I love it," Aaron gushed, smile warm and friendly. Just what Ash had always remembered about Aaron—and really Ross too. Ross had always been the grump of the pair; never convinced by any idea, no matter how brilliant. But then, he *was* the one who usually had all the brilliant ideas. Ash remembered how his father, never someone who'd ever believed anyone could be as good as he was, had sparingly dished out praise to Ross. The miserly compliments would've been effusive accolades from anyone else.

Ash had always felt a little sorry for him, because he'd deserved better. And when they'd finally left Hook & Slope, Ash had been relieved, because both of them might actually find some freedom to set their creativity free.

And against the odds, they'd done that, taking Ross' Southern grandmother's recipes and modernizing them, adding a fresh California twist.

"What if we did a deep-fried stuffed deviled egg?" Ross suggested, proving yet again that Stephan Atkinson hadn't been wrong about him.

"Oh, I love that. And we could do a smoked, pulled turkey," Aaron added excitedly. "What do you think, Ash?"

"I think you leave the salad base to me," Ash said. "I'll do some pickled veg, I think, onions and cucumbers and carrots. Maybe even some beets. Maybe kind of a giardiniera mix?"

"I love it," Aaron said. "This is gonna kill."

"I'm trying to decide what to stuff in the deviled eggs," Ross said, who'd pulled out a pad and pencil from a drawer. "Goat cheese?"

"No, 'cause we've got the pimento cheese," Aaron said.

It was hard to remember, sometimes, why Aaron and Ross had decided to run this truck together, since they could be so different. Ross was the grump and Aaron could be confident bordering on cocky, but when he watched them together like this, heads bent together as Ross scribbled on the pad, everything clicked into place and made sense.

"Dill, I think," Ross said, "with garlic aioli mixed in, a true deviled egg, but elevated a bit. A touch of dijon mustard."

"What about the dressing?" Aaron asked.

"I've got it," Ash said, his own mind racing, pushing its boundaries in a way that he hadn't in some time. Tony had been so right; he'd been needing to do something like this. He'd been resting on his laurels, lost in the rut he'd created for himself. But Aaron and Ross would jolt him out of it. "I'm thinking a twist on a Thousand Island dressing, almost like an old-fashioned French dressing, red wine vinegar and a little chili sauce, maybe make it a little spicy, and a little sour, and a little sweet."

"God that sounds delicious. Sign me up," Aaron said.

"I'll work on it this afternoon."

Ross was already deep in thought about his deviled eggs, gesturing to himself, scribbling random words and pictures on his pad.

"Why don't we meet back tomorrow morning, with at least the start of the components begun, and we can do a taste test?" Aaron suggested.

"Sounds good to me," Ash said. "I can get here an hour early tomorrow."

"We should have at least some of it ready." Aaron gestured to where Ross was still muttering about freezing and frying and oil type. "God knows, this'll be a project he's occupied with for awhile, probably, but I'm sure we'll have a good enough prototype to test."

"Great," Ash said. "I really am glad you guys are here."

Aaron's smile was wry. "Probably because we're gonna bring a shit ton of business in?"

And there was Aaron's downside; always the ego, rearing its ugly head.

Ash was not surprised that if he'd talked like that anywhere near Tony, Tony would still be annoyed that he'd had his hand forced into letting Basket into the lot.

"We've done pretty good on our own," Ash pointed out. Kinder than Aaron's ego probably deserved. "You guys wanted in for a reason, right?"

"Right, right," Aaron said. "We did."

"Anyway, I *am* glad you're here, because yeah, you're popular and you'll bring people to the lot, but also because your food is awesome," Ash said.

"Thanks," Aaron said, patting Ash on the shoulder, which shouldn't have felt so patronizing, but it did anyway. Like Ash was still that kid, forced to hang around Hook & Slope while his father verbally demolished everyone in sight.

He almost asked then if either of them had talked to his father recently. If they had heard of anyone who might be angry with him, and had decided to take their frustration out on his son, instead. But he didn't, because Ash decided he really didn't want to know if either of them had talked to him lately.

He hadn't wanted anything to do with his father in years, and that hadn't changed.

"See you tomorrow," Ash said, and took off down the stairs, back to his own truck.

He met Lucas halfway. "Hey," he said, giving his friend a quick hug. "Congrats, by the way, we're all super proud of you."

Lucas rolled his eyes. "I think Tony only let me in to counteract the evil influence of the other newbies."

"They're really not so bad," Ash said, already accepting that he was going to spend a *lot* of time saying nearly this exact same phrase. "A little weird, socially, maybe, but not *bad*, not like Tony makes them out to be."

"It wouldn't be the first time Tony assumed someone was evil," Lucas said with a chuckle. "But I'll keep it in mind. You guys already hard at work on your new dish?"

"Yeah, we just talked it over," Ash said. "I think it's gonna kick ass."

Lucas shot him a warm smile. "If you're involved, it can't help itself," he said.

"I make salad," Ash deadpanned. "Which is less kickass than everyone seems to think."

"Yeah, but you can do more. You *should* do more," Lucas pointed out gently.

A thought that Ash had been having himself, more recently.

"I'm thinking about it," Ash said.

"Good," Lucas said. "Well, I'm off to say hello to Aaron and Ross. Wish me luck."

"They're . . ."

Lucas laughed. "They're really not so bad?"

Ash shrugged, almost embarrassed that he'd just said it *again*. "I've known them a long time," he said. "They *can* be weird, but I do think they mean well."

"Alright. I'm gonna try to keep an open mind," Lucas said.

"And try to convince Tony that it might not be bad for him to try it too," Ash added as he began to continue onto his own truck.

"I will, but you know Tony," Lucas said wryly.

Ash did know Tony. Knew he was unhappy that he'd been backed into a corner by Aaron and Ross, but also knew that Tony was a pretty decent businessman too. He'd make it work, in the end. Ash had faith.

The late afternoon between the lunch and dinner rush was always slow, especially with the heat of a late summer baking the lot with almost no shade. Ash knew Tony was looking into canopies and umbrellas to help, but for now, the lot was basically abandoned after two, and the crowds didn't pick up again until at least six.

Which gave him a few hours to work on his pickling, and on the new dressing for the salad he was doing with Aaron and Ross.

He'd just pulled out a measuring cup and some of the ingredients he hoped to use when there was a knock on his back door.

He'd propped it mostly open, and turned on the fan because it was *hot* today. Almost unbearably so, in the tight confines of his truck.

"Hey," Lennox said, appearing again without his trademark leather jacket, an unexpected smile on his face.

Ash thought of this morning, when his alarm had forced him to crawl out of Lennox's warm bed, of the peace and pleasure he'd found there, and understood why he was smiling.

He'd had a lot of sex with people and it almost never felt like that.

Scratch that, Ash thought, it *never* felt like that.

"Hey," Ash said, "I wondered if I'd see you today."

"I said I'd be by," Lennox said, climbing up the stairs and laying a quick kiss across Ash's upturned lips. "I know I did."

"I might have been a little distracted again," Ash said, grinning, as he gestured towards Lennox's body. It was a crime, an actual crime, to have it covered up.

"I can't imagine why," Lennox teased. "What are you up to?"

"Working on a new dressing. I stopped by Basket this morning," Ash said. "They're already here, getting prepped for opening this weekend. We started working on our dish together."

"And this is for the new dish?" Lennox asked, taking a few steps closer, examining the glass measuring cup like it might answer all his questions about who was after Ash.

"Yeah," Ash said.

"Can you tell me about it?" Lennox asked.

Ash shot him a look. "I know you don't care about the tarragon vinegar I want to use. *You* want to know if I learned anything today that might make me change my mind about Aaron and Ross."

Lennox leaned against the back counter and shrugged. "I want to get to the bottom of this," he said. "It's killing me that I'm not making any progress."

"You know what I learned today?" Ash asked. "That all Aaron and Ross want to do is cook their awesome food and develop a following here. That's it."

"Did you ask them if they'd been in touch with your father?"

Ash knew the question was coming and it still stung, a little. "No."

Lennox's gaze softened. "I get it," he said. "But . . . I need to talk to them. And I need to talk to your father, too."

Ash turned away, because he knew Lennox was telling the truth, and he also knew that it shouldn't have hurt this badly, after all this time. He'd gotten over his father's rejection and then his own subsequent rejection of him, hadn't he?

Did you ever really get over your own father calling you worthless and useless?

Ash didn't know. But he'd done everything he could to put that time behind him.

"What if I say no?"

"No to your father, or no to Aaron and Ross?" Lennox wanted to know.

It was a delicate balance; Ash knew that. He knew that he and Lennox were falling for each other, and that Lennox was also obligated to dig deeper into a situation that Ash didn't want him to dig into at all.

But he knew Lennox didn't have a choice. He wanted to get to the bottom of this. Ash even *wanted* him to, because a lot of this past history was shit he didn't want to get unearthed.

"You can talk to Aaron and Ross all you want to," Ash finally said, cautiously. "I don't think anything they say is going to help, because honestly, I still don't think it's either of them. Aaron can be a patronizing, egotistical asshole, and Ross is just a weird, grumpy asshole, but don't listen to Tony. They want to be here. They're not the villains in anyone's story."

"But someone is the villain in yours," Lennox said firmly. "And I intend to find out who it is."

"You know what?" Ash turned and put a hand on Lennox's t-shirt-clad chest. "Talk to them. Eliminate them. It'll make me happy I don't have to defend them anymore, and you'll sleep easier."

"And your father?"

Ash sighed.

"I know you don't want me to talk to him," Lennox said. "But . . ."

"You'll talk to him anyway, right?" Ash said, trying to keep the bitterness out of his voice and not really succeeding. "About other things. About the work you do for him."

"Sometimes, yeah," Lennox said.

"But what you want is permission to talk to him about *me*."

Lennox hesitated. "Yes," he finally said. "I do. I think he might be able to give me a direction to go here, because I'm gonna be honest here. I'm out of ideas."

"Nothing on the security footage?" Ash wondered.

"Seth and I are working on it, but nothing so far. And the paint's generic. The paper's generic. The interviews they copied were from magazines thousands of people could have access to." Lennox sighed. "I'm not asking because I *want* to, Ash. I'm asking because I *need* to know . . . well, you know how much I care about you, right?"

It was undeniable. Even before they had slept together, Ash had known that Lennox took their developing relationship seriously. He wouldn't be around otherwise. But after hearing about Lennox's past history and then the sex they'd shared? Ash *knew* they were falling for each other.

And Lennox would never, ever purposefully cause him pain, unless he knew it was for a good reason.

"Alright," Ash finally said. "You can talk to him about me."

Lennox closed his eyes briefly. "Thank you," he said, tugging Ash into a tight hug. "You're not going to regret this."

"I hope not," Ash said, tucking his face into Lennox's warm, soft chest. He trusted him, as much as he'd trust anyone, but his father was a different story. Had always been a different story.

"If I can avoid talking about you, I will," Lennox said, "but I'm going to have to tell him what's going on, or I don't think he's going to tell me much about what happened when Aaron and Ross left his restaurant."

Ash pulled back, even though he didn't really want to let go of Lennox. "You're still stuck on them? They're nothing, they're a non-issue, I *know* them."

"Do they know you're keeping your identity a secret?" Lennox wanted to know.

"Well, *yeah*," Ash said. "The last name I'm using kind of gives it away, don't you think?"

"So you told them at some point, that you'd broken with your father and you were not disclosing who you were?"

Ash groaned. "Really? We're back to this?" He turned back towards his dressing ingredients, and poured some of his tarragon vinegar into the glass measuring cup. "Yes, I think so, but it was years ago. When I first started this truck. I probably ran into them on the festival circuit, and we talked about it, probably for a few minutes, and that was it. There were no fireworks, they weren't angry, they weren't *anything*."

"You're very determined to believe they aren't involved." Lennox leaned against the back counter and crossed his arms over his chest.

"Probably because everyone else is determined to hate them," Ash said. "I don't like it when people judge."

"I'm not judging. I just don't believe that any employee just tells your father they're leaving and he lets them go, easy as that. Do you?"

Ash hesitated. Lennox had a point. *Had* his father been angry that they'd left? He hadn't seemed it, at the time, but then with Stephan Atkinson, there were only varying degrees of annoyance and outright anger. Had they just left and he'd let them go? That was the memory Ash remembered but maybe there *had* been more.

"I don't know," Ash said, "I guess we'll find out. Or *you'll* find out."

"I'm going to try," Lennox promised.

Ash reached for the honey and drizzled it into his measuring cup. "I guess I should wish you good luck," he said.

"Will I see you tonight?" Lennox asked.

Ash thought of all the work he had to do. Of the dread he felt when he thought about Lennox going to his father.

He'd known they worked together, but of all the things he and Lennox had talked about, they'd rarely discussed his father.

But tonight? It was inevitable.

Ash closed his eyes. "Yes," he said. Maybe it would be easier to just deal with it up front, instead of worrying about it.

To his surprise, Lennox wrapped his arms around him, his chest pressing warm and firm against Ash's back. "If you don't want to talk about him, we won't," he said, his voice low and serious, his breath brushing the sensitive skin of Ash's neck. "We can do whatever you like."

"Whatever I like?" Ash teased, finding the lightness came more easily when Lennox was touching him. *Loving* him.

You don't know that he loves you, Ash reminded himself firmly, *you're creating castles in the sky.*

"Whatever you like," Lennox said with certainty.

Lennox pressed a goodbye kiss to Ash's cheek, and then he was gone. Ash looked out the front window of his truck, mixing his dressing, and couldn't help but see the mirage of a castle there.

"We didn't have an appointment today," Stephan Atkinson said, leaning over a single plate on the wide stainless steel counter.

"No," Lennox said. But he'd known that Atkinson would be here, at his flagship Hook & Slope restaurant, because he was always here.

"Was there something you needed?" Atkinson's voice was clipped. "I'm busy."

"I met your son."

On the drive here, Lennox had invented and discarded half a dozen ways to bring up what had been happening to Ash.

"Oh?" Stephan did not seem particularly interested; barely even looked up from the dish he was meticulously plating, arranging light green pea sprouts one at a time with a pair of tweezers, fanning them out in a half-moon.

Personally, Lennox thought it was a fucking waste, but he wasn't going to say so. Not because he was working for Atkinson, but because he had information that Lennox knew he needed.

Ash might be quick to dismiss the two guys who owned Basket, but Lennox couldn't.

"I've been to his food truck lots of times," Lennox said. "It's great." He didn't suggest Stephan check it out, because he already knew he wouldn't, and if hell froze over, and he *did*, Ash would kill him. Slowly.

Stephan looked up. His eyes narrowed. "You don't seem like a guy who likes *salad*." The last word came out in a sneer.

Lennox didn't bother addressing the insult, but he had to re-mind himself that pointing out to Atkinson that he was a fucking piece of shit wasn't why he was here. "I've been to some of the other trucks, too," Lennox said. "I'm actually doing work for them."

"Is there a point to this conversation?" Atkinson snapped.

"Yes." Lennox moved around the front of the counter. Stephan finally looked up at him from the pea shoots. "There's some stuff happening at the food truck lot. Stuff that's targeting your son."

"What kind of 'stuff'?" Atkinson's voice was brusque. Not particularly concerned. But then Lennox hadn't really expected any differently.

There was a reason that Ash had left this man and had never looked back, not once.

"Someone wanted him to know they know you're related, and then they moved on to some vandalism," Lennox said. "It's getting nastier. I'm trying to get to the bottom of it. Do you remember Ross Stanton and Aaron Bolton?"

Stephan laughed, the edge tinged with unmistakable bitter-ness. "Yes," he said. "How could I forget my greatest proteges?"

There was an ironic lilt to the word *protege*, and it pinged Lennox's Spidey senses. There was something here, a story, and goddamn it, he would get to the bottom of it, and figure out if it had anything to do with what was happening to Ash now.

"Is that what they were? Your proteges?" Lennox asked casu-ally.

"What do they have to do with this?" Stephan's voice had gone defensive now, and that was all Lennox needed to confirm that there *was* something more to the story than the publicly circulated version.

"They just joined the same lot as Ash," Lennox said. "And they know who he is."

"What does that have to do with me?"

"It occurs to me that if they left your employment under . . . less than ideal circumstances . . . one or both of them might have an issue with you."

"And Oliver?" Stephan said. "Why would that have anything to do with him?"

"I'm not sure yet."

Lennox had known that Atkinson would dismiss his son. Ash hadn't told him explicitly that he would, but his behavior was enough of an indication. Still, Atkinson's total coldness surprised Lennox.

Made him want to punch him in the face for every time he'd broken and destroyed Ash's dreams. When Lennox was finished with him, he'd be a bloody mess.

You're not here to defend Ash's honor; he did that himself, when he broke away and started his own business, and made it a huge success.

"Then I'm still failing to see the point of this conversation," Atkinson said, returning his attention to the plate in front of him.

"I want to know what happened," Lennox said bluntly.

"I fired them." Atkinson's words were clipped.

"Then why did you let them tell everyone that they chose to leave?"

It was unlike Atkinson to not have the final word; to not destroy someone's career just because he could.

But Atkinson just shrugged. "They weren't worth my time or my attention. If they wanted to tell everyone who would listen that they were ruining their careers to start a *restaurant on wheels*, who was I to stop them?"

Lennox couldn't miss the disparaging tone Atkinson used when he said "restaurant on wheels." His opinion of food trucks was hardly a secret, but Lennox hoped that the fact that his son was doing the same thing, very successfully, ate Atkinson up inside.

"They didn't just say that though," Lennox said. "They said you supported them."

Atkinson waved a hand. "As if anyone actually *believed* that."

He decided it wasn't worth trying to tell the guy that *yes*, people had. There'd been countless media articles about it. People had talked about it for ages because it had been so unusual for Stephan Atkinson to let anyone go without a fight.

"So that's all to the story, then? You fired them? Why?"

"I don't even remember," Atkinson said.

Lennox was pretty sure it wasn't the first time he'd lied today, but it was definitely the most blatant lie. "You fired them, and they made up shit about you after the fact," he said, "why protect them now?"

Stephan huffed, clearly annoyed now. Well, *more* annoyed than his natural annoyed state. "I'm not," he said, enunciating each syllable distinctly. "What they do or do not doesn't concern me."

"Even when it concerns your son?"

"You haven't proved that it does concern Oliver," Atkinson pointed out. "And from what it sounds like, he's not in any real danger, anyway. Whoever's doing this will get bored, and it will end."

Lennox was not convinced.

"If you decide to tell me the rest," Lennox said, "you have my number."

"I don't . . ." Atkinson blustered, but Lennox had had just about enough of his bullshit for one morning.

"No," Lennox said, taking two steps over to where Atkinson was standing, looming over him. Not touching him, but making sure he knew, that even though their heights were almost equitable, that he could kick his ass into next week if he wanted to.

That the person in charge here was not him, but Lennox.

Atkinson *cowered*.

"You know what I mean," Lennox said, not stepping back, effectively pinning Stephan against the countertop. "You know what I'm asking about, and I'm fucking tired of listening to you act like your son's safety doesn't matter and you're clueless."

"I'm not . . ."

Lennox pressed harder, pushing Atkinson back. "You are," he said inexorably. "Stop fucking around."

"They were doing drugs, okay? Not a little, not like some do to work late or get up early or whatever, but a *lot* of drugs. It was a distraction, and I didn't want them fucking up my other employees, so I fired them."

"And why did you let them tell everyone that you were letting them go with your blessing?" Lennox asked archly. Pleased, though he wouldn't show it in front of this *worm*, that he was finally getting somewhere.

Men like Atkinson would only respond to strength and intimidation. He'd known it would come to this, even though he hadn't wanted it to.

"They said they'd smear me," Atkinson said, the words coming out in a rush. "Believe it or not, I don't want people thinking I'm an asshole."

"Really?"

"Fine, *fine*, they told me that if I told anyone the truth, they'd claim they got the drugs from me. I don't need . . ." Atkinson took a deep breath. "I didn't need any bullshit investigation slowing down my employees or digging into places where they didn't belong."

"Have some other secrets, do you?" Lennox asked.

Atkinson shrugged jerkily. "Don't we all? It's not like you're squeaky clean, Lennox. I'm sure you've got plenty of shit in your closet."

"Maybe," Lennox said. "But I do know that if I had a son like Ash, I sure as fuck wouldn't drive him away, and then when he was possibly in danger, not give a shit."

Atkinson opened his mouth and then snapped it closed. "Our relationship is more complicated than you know."

"No," Lennox said, and before he could stop himself, his arm was pushing against Atkinson's throat, his eyes going wide and panicked. "No. I know all about your intimidation and how you made him feel useless. Like a failure, just because he's not like you. Just because he's got a goddamned heart."

"Is that what he told you?" Atkinson swallowed hard. "I know he's going to come back. He's going to fail and then he's going to crawl back. It's inevitable."

"You don't know a goddamned thing about him," Lennox said, pushing away from Atkinson in disgust. "He's worth about a hundred of you, and you know it."

"That's what I told Stanton when he came here, anyway." Atkinson's voice had gone snide and patronizing again. Like he knew Lennox wouldn't be able to help himself. Like he knew Lennox would ask.

"He came here? Ross Stanton came here?"

"Thought I would hire him back." Atkinson sniffed. "It was a joke. Oliver? I'd consider taking him back, because I need a successor, and despite all his character flaws, he's at least potentially worthy. But Stanton? That drugged-out imbecile? Not likely."

Lennox felt his heartbeat accelerate. This was the first break he'd gotten. "Did you tell him that?"

"Tell him what?"

"Tell him that you'd hire Ash back, but not him," Lennox repeated, his patience wearing thin.

"Maybe. I honestly *don't* remember," Atkinson said. And this time, Lennox heard the ring of truth in his voice. But if he knew this worm at all, he knew he'd probably said it.

And maybe? Just maybe, that might have been enough to set Ross Stanton off.

At the very least, he'd have to talk to him and figure out why he'd come back, asking Atkinson for his old job.

He had a lead, and that was what he'd come here for.

Lennox turned and walked away, not even bothering to say goodbye.

The asshole didn't deserve it. Same way he didn't deserve a son like Ash.

CHAPTER ELEVEN

"Do I want to ask how it was?" Ash asked as soon as Lennox opened the door.

"Do you want to ask?" Lennox wondered as he pushed the door closed, hearing it click behind him.

Ash sighed. "Yes. And no. Did you get what you needed?"

"I have a lead," Lennox said. He knew Ash wasn't going to be happy about this. Not only was he continually trying to defend Ross and Aaron, he was working with them.

"So it was worth going, then," Ash said, collapsing onto Lennox's couch. "I'm glad."

"Are you?" Lennox wondered, coming to sit down next to him.

Ash sighed for a second time, longer and deeper than before. "I thought about it all day," he said, "and I realized you were right. I want this shit to end, and if you had to talk to him to get to the bottom of it, then it was the right thing to do. And if you got a lead . . ."

"How much do you know about Ross Stanton?" Lennox asked.

Ash shot him a look. "This, *again*?"

"Your father said that he fired them, both him and Bolton, for using drugs on the job. They threatened to get the authorities involved, so he let them go without a fight. Let them say whatever they wanted. And then a few months ago, Stanton came around, wanting his old job back."

"Really?" Ash looked skeptical.

"That's what he said."

"He could be lying."

"He wasn't," Lennox said. "I talked to Ross this afternoon. He did go ask for his job back. I'm not sure . . . I'm not sure things are quite happy in paradise for Ross and Aaron."

"They're not together, not like that anyway."

"But they're friends, and I think they've been having some difficulties." At least that was the impression Lennox had gotten when he'd pulled Ross Stanton aside and asked him why he'd gone back to his old boss, not exactly known for being the friendliest or the most welcoming employer on the planet, and asked for a job.

"Maybe," Ash said. "But they'll work through it. Obviously my father said no."

"He did. But he mentioned that during that conversation, you came up, and that made me wonder if that might be why our culprit is angry at you and is doing these things to you."

"Just because Aaron and Ross are fighting and Ross thought about leaving and going back to work for my father?"

Lennox clamped his lips together. He didn't want to tell Ash this but there was no way to convince him if he didn't confess everything. "Because your father said that if *you* came back, he'd welcome you. With open arms."

Ash rolled his eyes. "That is bullshit and you know it. I'd never . . ."

"I know you wouldn't, but we're not talking about you, and what you'd do, we're talking about *him* and what he went blabbing about to someone who's disgruntled and looking for a way out."

"Oh." Ash rubbed his hands on his shorts. "So you think Ross is doing all of this."

"I think he's a suspect," Lennox said. "He came clean, immediately, when I asked him about it. That makes me suspect him *less*, but I can't eliminate him. It'd be easy for him to resent you, if *he* wasn't allowed to return to your father's restaurant, but you would be."

"I really doubt he'd let me come back," Ash said. "Even if I wanted to. He's just talking. He's all fucking talk."

"I know," Lennox said dryly.

"So what's next?" Ash asked, taking a deep breath. "Should I . . . should I keep working with them? We had a taste test today; the dish is coming along really well. And I know Tony really wants to make this work."

"Keep working with them," Lennox said, even though he hated potentially exposing Ash if it really was Stanton that was behind everything. At the very least, whoever was doing this had yet to do anything violent. That was still a cold, bleak comfort.

Ash looked at him skeptically.

"I'm going to make sure you're safe," Lennox promised, reaching out and taking his hand, squeezing it. He wanted Ash to trust him, to *believe* him. And he was pretty sure he knew why, too.

Lennox hoped that this time it would be different, and he wouldn't end up loving someone who didn't love him the same way.

"I know you will," Ash said, sincerity shining out of his blue eyes. "I'm not worried about that at all."

"Well," Lennox chuckled, "maybe you should be a *little* bit worried." Worried enough, he thought, that he wouldn't do anything stupid or careless. Because even though the vandal had yet to turn violent, that didn't mean that they wouldn't.

"I'm not," Ash said, curling up closer to him. "I'm with you, remember?"

Lennox found himself relaxing into Ash's body, letting go of some of his worries, at least temporarily.

"So the dish is going good, then?" he asked.

"Oh yeah," Ash said enthusiastically. "So great. I have to adjust some seasonings in the dressing, but the pickled veggies turned out fantastic, and oh my God, just wait til you try Ross' deep-fried deviled eggs. They're to die for."

Lennox raised an eyebrow. "I hope not literally," he said, "because maybe I don't *want* to try them."

Ash laughed. "I don't think he's going to try to poison either of us."

"I'd hope not," Lennox said. "He didn't seem like a bad guy. Kind of . . . difficult?"

He hadn't been sure what to make of the tall, slender guy with the dark hair and even darker eyes who had seemed so antagonistic at first, bothered that he was being bothered, but who had, when Lennox explained who he was and what he was trying to do, calmed down pretty quickly and had answered every question that he'd asked.

Lennox knew what to look for when someone was lying, but none of the signs had been there with Ross.

Truthfully, his conversation with the guy had only created more questions than he'd found answers.

"He's got some issues, I think, and yeah, I do wonder if he and Aaron aren't getting along. Did you talk to Aaron too?"

"No," Lennox said, "but maybe I will, in a few days. Check Ross' story against his."

"So you still think it's Ross, then?" Ash wondered.

"I don't know what to think," Lennox said with a resigned sigh. "And that's a whole other problem."

Ash leaned in closer. "Let's not think about it. Not tonight, okay?"

Lennox could not agree more. He leaned in and brushed a kiss across Ash's mouth. "What do you want to do? We could watch a movie? Go grab a drink from the Funky Cup?"

"We could," Ash said, his expression mischievous. "Or we could stay in . . ."

"I'd like that," Lennox said, because now that he'd found this guy, he really didn't want to share.

"But first," Ash said, his eyes still gleaming with mischief, "could I take a shower?"

"I'll do you one better," Lennox said, rising off the couch and tugging Ash after him. "I'll take one with you."

Ash had seen Lennox's bathroom before, when he'd been here the other night, but after he flipped the light on, all the white tile gleaming, it seemed different. Bigger, for sure. Before, he'd been all wobbly and distracted by some of the best sex he'd ever had, but now, he was paying attention and he could see the enormous shower Lennox had built.

"Is all this for you?" Ash wondered as he tugged his shirt over his head.

Lennox followed suit and Ash was really glad he'd asked his question first, because the other night hadn't been nearly enough to immunize him against the sight of Lennox shirtless.

He was all rippling muscle, the smoothness of his skin punctuated with his history, and Ash wanted to fall to his knees and kiss every scar, every reminder that while Lennox might be dangerous, he'd never be dangerous to Ash. Press his lips to every single reminder that he'd been through hell and come through alive on the other side, and then Ash had been lucky enough to find him.

"Yes," Lennox said. "It's for me. Well, and for *you*, too, when I get lucky enough to convince you to join me."

Lennox reached over and flicked the shower on, the glass enclosure beginning to fill with steam.

"Why such a big shower though?" Ash wanted to know as he pushed down his shorts.

Lennox shrugged, but Ash knew him well enough by now to know there was a story there. He hadn't expected someone like Lennox to have a shower you could fit ten people in, easily, or a big, luxurious bathroom. His kitchen was small. His living room was decent sized, but nothing to write home about. But the bathroom? It was like a mini spa.

"When I got out of the Navy," Lennox said, leaning against the counter, gaze avidly taking in Ash's nakedness, "I was kind of a fucking mess. I ended up moving here, and Seth helped me a lot. At some point, he asked me to make a list of things that I *liked* doing. Not things I thought I should be doing, or things the world made me feel obligated to do, but actual genuine shit that I enjoyed. And first on the list was a nice, long, hot shower." He waved around the bathroom, suddenly breaking into a grin that made Ash's knees weak. "So I gave myself a really big fucking shower."

It was nothing like the story that Ash had expected to hear. He stared at the man in front of him, watching as he tugged his own jeans down, and then leaned down and pulled his socks off.

"You look surprised," Lennox said, clearly amused by it.

"I didn't expect to hear that kind of story," Ash said. He was also more than slightly distracted when Lennox's cock was revealed, already half-hard. Like Ash hadn't already known what was going to happen when they got wet and soapy and couldn't keep their hands off each other anyway.

"You thought I'd still be into taking two-minute cold showers?" Lennox chuckled. "I'm not . . . you can't ever really adjust completely, not after you've been in for as long as I was, but I'm getting there. I know I can want things—and have them."

"Good," Ash said, taking a step closer and fitting into Lennox's arms like he was made for them. Feeling Lennox's skin against his own was a rush, and his own cock grew even harder. "I know I want *you*."

Lennox smiled, a soft, sweet smile that Ash would never have guessed Lennox was even capable of, only a few weeks ago. "Even better, it's not just the shower I want now . . . it's *you*."

"Do you think . . ." Ash murmured, tilting his head up until his lips were only a breath away from Lennox's.

"Yes," Lennox said, and turning and pulling open the door, maneuvered them into the steam-filled enclosure without letting go of Ash for even a second.

There were two large rain-style showerheads, spilling hot water over them in a cascade, and Ash spluttered, pushing his suddenly wet hair back, smiling up at Lennox. "What do you want?" he asked.

Lennox, reaching for the soap, shrugged. "You, here, that's always enough," he said.

Ash watched as he soaped himself up with those big capable hands. Couldn't wait to have those hands on his own skin. But first, he wanted something else.

"I don't know, last time you were sorta particular . . ." he teased as Lennox washed the suds off.

"I'm not now," Lennox said. "If . . ."

But Ash didn't let him finish. If Lennox wasn't so particular, then Ash had something he wanted to do. Something he hadn't been able to do last time.

Something he'd been dying to do from practically the first moment their eyes had met, through the front window of Ash's truck.

Ash had seen Lennox's guarded gaze, the hunger that had fired through him, that he'd buried so swiftly and so deeply that Ash had been certain that he'd imagined it, at first. But then he'd seen it again and then again and then half a dozen times after that, and he'd known the truth. Lennox wanted him, but he didn't *want* to.

Now Ash knew why. He also knew that Lennox wasn't burying the desire now. He was swimming in it, willingly, and holding his hand out, asking Ash to trust him. To join him.

Ash was going to show just how much he'd wanted, all that fucking time.

Hands flat on Lennox's chest, Ash pushed him gently, back and back, until he hit the tiled wall of the shower.

The floor was, not surprisingly, hard, but it was *warm*, like the heat of the bathroom floor was radiating through it. And maybe, Ash realized with a start, it *was*.

"Is your . . ." was all he got out before Lennox smiled.

"Floor heated? Yes."

"God, we are gonna do this all the fucking time," Ash said, as he reached up and wrapped a wet hand around Lennox's dick, giving it an experimental stroke.

Lennox groaned, the back of his head hitting the tiled wall, as his eyes squeezed shut. Like he could barely take the view.

Ash understood how he felt, as he leaned in, it was a *lot*. Lennox's heavily muscled thighs, the shapely calves, the grooves of his abs, and then his perfectly sized cock, jutting out of its well-trimmed nest of dark hair.

Flicking his tongue out, Ash licked at the tip, humming to himself. He was delicious, and he was all Ash's.

"God," Lennox moaned, "that feels so goddamned good."

Ash thought he was just getting warmed up, and decided he might as well surprise Lennox if he thought a little licking was all he was getting tonight.

He slid his mouth around Lennox's cock, sucking as he went, curling his tongue around the head. Twisting his hand with the rhythm of his mouth, he felt himself grow harder and harder, pleasure sizzling through him as he gave Lennox every little bit that he could.

Lennox's hands drifted down, curling around his head, fingertips tucking into his wet hair, not to guide or to push, but to cherish. Like he was the most precious thing that Lennox had ever experienced and he never wanted to let him go.

And then those fingers twisted hard, and Ash nearly choked, it felt so good. How had Lennox known?

But he knew, because he never pushed Ash too hard, just gave him exactly the counterpoint he wanted, and he *needed*. His own hand slipped down to his cock, giving it a quick twist, sending a shock of pleasure rushing through him.

He wasn't even sure Lennox had been looking, but all of a sudden his hands jerked and Ash was held motionless in his grip. Proving once and for all that the man was strong as hell and yet knew how to be gentle all at the same time.

It was one thing to find the strength sexy, and another entirely for the gentleness to turn him on.

"No," Lennox said firmly. "That's all mine. Not yours." He relaxed his hand, as soon as Ash nodded in agreement.

If that was how he was going to play it, Ash rededicated himself to blowing Lennox's mind, taking his cock deeper and deeper, until he could feel Lennox's fingers trembling on his scalp. Overwhelmed with how much he wanted to let go. Trying to prolong the pleasure for a few more moments.

But a few more moments was all Lennox had; he rhythmically jerked on Ash's hair, warning him, and a second later, he was groaning and Ash was swallowing his come.

After he finished sucking him dry, Ash let Lennox's dick slip from his mouth and wiped the back of his mouth with a wet hand, breath coming in harsh, hard pants. He was so horny that if Lennox just *touched* him, he was probably going to explode. He'd always enjoyed giving a blowjob, but that had been on a whole different level.

Just like the sex they'd shared the other night had blown him apart and put him back together again.

Ash had been fairly sure that this was more than just lust, more than just a few hot hookups, but now he knew for sure.

This was the man for him.

He'd been waiting for him for a long time, dating some decent guys and even some losers in the interim, but now the waiting was over.

There was only one person that Ash was going to love after this, and it was Lennox.

"Get up here," Lennox said, the edge of his voice rough, but his tone kind and sweet, and he tugged Ash to his feet, bracing his wobbly knees with his own, hand reaching for his hard, leaking cock.

The moment his fingers closed around him, Ash moaned and buried his face in Lennox's broad chest, shuddering as the man's hand worked him to a fierce, electric orgasm.

The shower washed away the evidence, but Ash was fairly sure that he'd actually *cried* when he came, the feelings rushing through him in a dizzying burst of happiness and trust, and ultimately, relief.

He wasn't old, not by a long shot, but he'd dated so frequently that he'd really begun to wonder if he'd ever find the guy who would set him on fire and also tenderly put it out. Cuddle him afterwards.

For a long moment there was only the sound of the water falling around them, hitting the tile.

"Was that alright?" Lennox asked cautiously.

"Yes," Ash said. Maybe at another time, in another place, he might have teased or joked or said something about how it was more than alright. But he couldn't now. Everything was brimming inside him, too close to the surface.

"Good," Lennox said, and pulled him even closer. "Let's get you cleaned up."

He washed him as quickly and efficiently as if he'd been taking one of those cold military-style showers, but his fingertips were still gentle, still cautious, even as he scrubbed shampoo into Ash's hair.

It was nothing like before, but Ash could feel the echoing throb of it as Lennox washed away the suds.

Finally, he flipped the water off, and only opening the door a crack, grabbed two fluffy towels from the rack.

Ash plucked one of them from Lennox before he could do something like dry him, too. The shower had been nice—better than nice—from start to finish, and it had been especially nice to have Lennox clean him up, but he was feeling a bit more equilibrium than he had only a minute before.

They finished drying in silence and exited the shower.

"Maybe if I'd known what your mouth was like," Lennox said, wrapping the towel around his waist, and reaching out to flick Ash's swollen bottom lip with his thumb, "I'd have let you blow me before."

"No," Ash said, and wondered if the honesty in his gaze was too much, but he couldn't quite help it. "You needed that. Just like I needed that today."

"Yeah, I think so," Lennox agreed. He hesitated as he leaned back against the counter again. "This was not what I expected it was going to be."

"Me either," Ash said. They were clearly going to talk about it. Ash wasn't sure he was quite ready yet, but if Lennox could be brave and bare his heart, then Ash knew he could follow suit. "But then, if I think about it, it's not really all that surprising either."

Lennox raised an eyebrow.

"You've never dated much. You . . . you take it seriously. You took it seriously with your ex," Ash said. "And I've definitely dated around, but I've never . . ." He took a deep breath. "I've never felt about anyone the way I feel about you."

Lennox's gaze was thoughtful and penetrating. As needy as he probably ever allowed himself to be. "You really mean that."

"I do," Ash said.

Lennox didn't respond with words, but with actions. Pulled Ash tightly against him, wrapping his hands very firmly around his still-damp back. He didn't say anything for a long moment. "I do, too," he said quietly.

Ash wanted to ask what he was agreeing to, but deep down, he already knew.

Maybe they couldn't say it yet—it was still so early, that was hardly a bad thing—but they both knew they were on the same page, feeling the exact same thing.

Love.

The instant the phone rang, Lennox knew something terrible had happened.

One time waking him up way too fucking early was one thing.

The second time?

Lennox felt dread coalesce in his stomach as he fumbled for the phone, detaching Ash's arms from around his middle as he squinted in the darkness.

"Lennox," he answered.

He heard Ash stir next to him, and out of the corner of his eye, saw him sit up, eyes blinking sleepily.

"We're here at the lot," Adam said.

"Let me guess," Lennox said with a heavy sigh, "I'd better get down there."

"Yes," Adam agreed.

When Lennox hung up, he glanced at the clock. Well, at least it was after six.

"Who was that?" Ash asked quietly as Lennox slid out of bed and began to get dressed. This was definitely not the way he'd wanted to start the day—not with Ash in his bed.

"Adam. He's on the patrol that's stopping by the lot a few times every night," Lennox said.

"Something's happened," Ash said, perceptive even when he was half-asleep.

"Yes," Lennox said, and was just about to tell Ash that he could stay in bed as long as he liked, when Ash slid out and began gathering his clothes too.

"What are you doing?" he asked, instead.

Ash shot him a look, the heat of it evident even in the semi-dark of the room. "Coming with you," he said. "What else would I be doing?"

"You . . ." Lennox hesitated.

"No," Ash said, interrupting the silence. "No, you don't get to tell me I'm not coming."

"I don't know what we're going to find," Lennox said. Afraid, not necessarily for Ash's safety, but for his mental state. He knew that Ash still blamed himself for what had happened to Alexis' truck.

"They didn't tell you over the phone?" Ash said, the edge of his voice rough. He was already afraid too, Lennox could hear it in his voice.

"If it was bad, they would have said something," Lennox said. Adam was a good guy and an even better employee. But then Adam wouldn't have expected that the subject of all of these attacks would be sleeping in the bed next to Lennox.

He hesitated, and decided he wasn't so much warning Ash off as he was making sure that he understood the irrevocable step he was taking.

"If you show up with me, everyone will know," Lennox finally continued. "They'll know that you were here, with me."

"I live close," Ash argued.

"Ash," Lennox said simply, and Ash, after pulling on his t-shirt, sighed.

"Yeah, they will," Ash agreed. He turned towards Lennox, an unexpected challenge in his eyes. "Is that a problem for you?"

"No," Lennox said. He'd wondered if it would be. If, when the truth about their relationship finally came out, he'd feel nervous or upset or worried. That he'd feel unnecessarily exposed. That he'd experience remnants of all that anxiety that he'd endured over the course of his relationship with Marcus.

But he felt none of that.

"I'm surprised," Ash said, and Lennox had to nod in agreement.

"Me too," he said.

"I wouldn't have been upset if you had told me to show up ten minutes later or something," Ash said earnestly, and Lennox realized he meant it.

"But there's no need," Lennox said, reaching out and cupping his cheek. "I don't mind if people know."

Ash's smile was so bright that it felt like it lit the room.

"I'm going to call Tony, have him meet us there," Lennox said.

"Sounds good," Ash said with a nod. "I'm going to use the bathroom, if that's alright."

"Of course," Lennox said, dialing Tony's number. He'd had to call him too early two times too many.

Tony answered on the third ring. "What now?" he groaned.

"Ash and I are headed to the lot. There's been another problem."

Tony groaned again. "I'm getting real fucking sick of this," he said.

"Me too," Lennox said. He intended to get to the bottom of this, especially now that he had a lead. Maybe Ross Stanton wasn't to blame, but maybe he was. Lennox wasn't convinced yet, and at the very least, he could use Ross' help in figuring out what his next step might be.

"I want this to end," Tony said, his voice growing harder.

"It's going to," Lennox promised. "I'm gonna make sure of it."

"Alright. We can talk about it when I drag my tired ass out of bed." Tony yawned. "Lucas and I will be there in a few."

After hanging up with Tony, Lennox went into the bathroom, catching Ash just as he brushed his teeth. He followed suit, wiping a damp hand across his face and wiping it on a hand towel.

"Let's go," Lennox said, and he and Ash slipped on their shoes and headed out the door.

The walk to the lot was quiet, they didn't run into anyone other than a few random joggers, out for an early morning run.

Ash was quiet too, not even trying to make conversation. Lennox assumed that was because he was feeling apprehensive about what they'd find when they arrived at the lot.

When they did, Lennox was not surprised that Ash went immediately to his own truck, and he watched as he checked it over carefully.

There wasn't a thing out of place. Not a taped-up letter to be found or a scratch on the stainless steel.

Lennox watched as it hit Ash that whatever had happened, it had happened to someone else *again*. Watched the relief fade into something like dread.

"Where are your guys?" Ash said, turning towards Lennox.

Lennox pointed to where he could see them, over in the middle, by the stage, in the early morning light.

As they began to walk in that direction, Lennox immediately saw the problem, and the moment he heard Ash's breath exhale harshly, that he had as well.

On every single truck, except for Ash's, the stalker had drawn a big purple "X" on the front.

Every truck, vandalized, except for the one Ash owned.

"Why would they do this?" Ash whispered, sounding destroyed. "Why would they target me this way?" He sat down heavily on one of the picnic tables, and Lennox saw out of the corner of his eye that Adam and Daley were on their way over.

"Paint's still damp, but not wet," Adam said. They'd been set to do four patrols of the lot every night, but now that this had happened, Lennox already knew that he'd be making changes.

Whoever was doing this wasn't going to stop and there was something painfully ominous about the ghostly purple X's dotting every single truck, except for Ash's.

What did they mean? Were they a threat? Were they something else entirely?

Maybe Lennox had read these wrong the whole time and this wasn't really a threat directed at Ash but directed at the rest of the food truck owners.

He didn't know, but the one thing he knew was that he was going to get to the bottom of this if it took every piece of knowledge he'd ever gleaned in the Navy.

"I'm assuming you didn't see anyone," Lennox asked Adam.

"No," Adam said. "And I have to assume that was on purpose," he added, gesturing towards Ash's truck, which was currently missing the same X that was decorating every other one parked on the lot.

"Missing it?" Lennox nodded. "Seems a pretty pointed message."

"But *why*," Ash inserted angrily. "I can't even figure out who wants to do this to me."

"I'm going to," Lennox promised. Painfully aware that this was the second promise he'd made this morning alone.

Tony arrived then, Lucas following behind him.

"Oh God," Tony said, coming to stop in front of Ash. Lucas leaned in and gave him a quick hug. "How're you holding up?"

"Fine, I guess," Ash said reluctantly. "More confused and angry for you guys than anything else."

"Well, I guess we're gonna be scrubbing that shit off," Lucas said, turning to Lennox. "You okay with us getting started?"

"You take any pictures?" Lennox asked Adam and he nodded.

"Uploaded to the server, boss," Adam said. "Got several angles of every truck, maybe half a footprint at one of them, but it was hard to tell."

"Not like there isn't a ton of foot traffic here already," Lennox said with a sigh. "But I'll take a look, run it through some of my programs, see if I can narrow down the search parameters."

"I'll go grab the cleaning supplies," Lucas said.

Ash stood up. "I'll help you," he said.

When they'd headed off in the direction of the storage shed, Tony turned to Lennox.

"You come here with Ash?" Tony asked.

Lennox nodded.

"Ah," Tony said. The expression on his face was neutral, almost bordering on friendly, and so was his tone of his voice, but the threat was clear. "If you hurt him, I'll kill you. Or," he added with a sudden lopsided smile, "you'd probably—okay, *definitely*—get to me first, but if I didn't make sure you knew Ash was ours and we care about him, Lucas would probably kill *me*."

"I'm not what you need to worry about," Lennox said. "Trust me."

"I . . ." Tony hesitated. "I do, I actually do."

"Good," Lennox said. "Now what are we going to do about this guy?"

"You know it's a guy?"

"No," Lennox said, "though I'm leaning that direction, if only because so many males hang around here."

Tony shrugged. "We're a little bit of a gay mecca." He shot Lennox another one of those grins. "Lucky you moved in just down the street, huh?"

"Maybe *you're* the lucky one," Lennox said. "Because otherwise you'd end up with someone who wasn't going to do whatever it took to make sure Ash is safe."

"What are you gonna do?"

"Twenty-four-seven guard," Lennox answered without hesitation. He'd known, as soon as he got the call, that having Adam and Daley rotate through here a few times a night wasn't going to be enough. He'd probably known it when he'd set the schedule, but

God, he'd hoped that it would be enough, or maybe that they'd get lucky and catch the culprit in the act.

Of course they hadn't gotten lucky.

Lennox thought he hadn't gotten very lucky in his entire life, with one single exception.

That exception was headed towards him now, a wry smile on his face.

"I guess we should be glad that they're sticking to paint, huh?" Ash asked as he and Lucas walked up, loaded with cleaning supplies. "That's at least easy enough to clean."

Tony looked up from his phone. "I just sent a 911 message to all the owners," he said, "to get down here now and help."

"I wanted to do it," Ash said, frowning. "This is all my fault, I don't want to . . ."

"No," Tony said firmly, coming over to stand by him, putting his hands on Ash's shoulders. "It is absolutely *not* your fucking fault. Whoever is doing this is insane and fucked up in the head, but it's not your fault. That's one thing I know for goddamned sure. Nobody could have a problem like this with you. Not you. Ever."

"I can't imagine it," Lucas chimed in, agreeing with his boyfriend. "You're always so nice, Ash. To *everyone*."

"Even the people who don't really deserve it," Lennox added. Thinking of himself, thinking back to the time when he'd been brusque and uncomfortable every time he'd come to Ash's food truck, and yet Ash had smiled at him every single time. Like he knew with time, he'd eventually wear Lennox down.

And he *had*.

Surely Ash already knew Lennox was putty in his hands. Soft and malleable, like he'd never been before. He'd never even let Marcus in this close, this deep, and he'd been with him for almost six years. But Ash had burrowed in deep. Even Lennox wasn't sure how deep yet.

And the craziest part? Lennox wasn't even freaking out about it. It just felt *right*.

"You're practically a fucking saint," Tony said. "It's not your fault. Okay? Let us help. This is our lot. Our trucks. We want it to be nice. We want to protect it." He shot Lennox a sideways look.

"And it's gonna be," Lennox responded immediately. "I said it and I mean it. Twenty-four-seven coverage." He was already mentally sorting through the contractors he knew, who he could hire in a pinch, who would be trustworthy enough to actually monitor the lot, and not just go through the motions.

Lucas and Ash went to get started on Lucas' truck, and Tony walked over.

"You know," he said, a crease forming between his brows, "the lot really can't afford . . ."

"No," Lennox said. "This is on me."

Tony looked surprised. "Really?"

"I care about this place, too," he said. "This is . . . well, it's yours, of course. You guys built it. But I'm more me when I come here than any place I've ever been."

"I'm glad to hear it," Tony said, and patted him on the shoulder, his smile widening. "That's why we're here."

"And it's why *I'm* here," Lennox echoed.

He was going to do his job and catch this sonofabitch if it was the last thing he did.

CHAPTER TWELVE

It took most of the morning, but eventually they got the purple paint cleaned off the trucks.

Ash leaned against the back of his, washing his hands with the hose, trying to get the smell of the solvents out of his nose. But even when his hands felt clean, they still lingered.

He switched off the water with a frustrated motion.

He couldn't fucking believe that this asshole wouldn't leave him alone.

What had he ever done to them?

Ash knew Lennox still thought it could be Ross or Aaron—probably Ross, based on what he'd said the night before, but Ash still couldn't believe it.

As weird and antisocial as Ross could be, he wouldn't stoop this low. Wouldn't put a target on Ash's back like this.

"Hey."

Ash looked up and Lennox was standing there, a dark shadow of scruff on his cheeks, his eyes tired and his expression worried. It had been a long morning; Ash wasn't sure he looked any better than Lennox.

But no matter how long it was and how much it wasn't part of his job, Lennox had helped them clean every truck off. And Ash had heard Tony telling Lucas that Lennox wasn't going to be charging them a dime for the twenty-four-hour guard he was going to be posting at the lot. That he'd taken personal accountability and responsibility.

Ash had known he'd picked a good guy before that moment, but in that moment? A swell of certainty and something that felt a hell of a lot like love had rippled through him.

He was so goddamn *good*, and every time he thought about Lennox's steadfast heart or his unshakeable loyalty *and* the bulge of his biceps and the quiet sweetness of his smile and the way he'd tangled his fingers in Ash's hair last night and *pulled*? Well, it turned Ash to jelly.

"Hey," Ash said. "You heading out?"

Lennox nodded. "And you should too. Get a shower. Eat something. Drink some coffee. You've got a long day ahead of you, already."

Ash had already glanced at his watch. He was supposed to have been prepping an hour ago, but thankfully he could probably fit in some here or there during the day and it wouldn't be the end of the world.

"I may go grab something to eat," Ash said, his stomach grumbling. "Good thing I got a shower last night," he added with a grin.

Lennox's expression went soft. "Yeah, you did," he agreed. He paused. "I wanted to suggest something, something you might not like."

"What is it?"

"I think you should come stay with me for a little bit. Until this all dies down."

Ash was surprised. No. He was *shocked*.

"What?"

"I don't like how this is escalating and I'm still struggling for a lead to chase," Lennox said, and then added, with a bashful, boyish smile that set Ash's heart racing, "It's not like you wouldn't be around anyway, probably."

"I probably would be, but I . . ." Ash's independence, so hard-won, had always been important to him. It felt even more important now. "Why would I be in danger staying at my house? They haven't targeted me once there. Only here."

"It's a precaution," Lennox admitted. His voice dropped lower. "I care about you, Ash. I couldn't bear it if something happened and I could've prevented it."

"You can't fix everything," Ash said, feeling like he was being reasonable. Lennox couldn't shelter him forever. Couldn't wrap him up and put him in his pocket. They'd end up hating each other—and that was the very last thing he wanted.

"I know, but it's hard to resist the urge to try," Lennox said with a dry chuckle.

"Well, *try*," Ash said. "Listen, Tony already invited me to go out to the Funky Cup tonight, after work. He thinks we need to like . . . *celebrate life* or something, he's feeling awfully sentimental lately."

From the moment Tony had suggested it, Ash had wanted to go, because hiding had seemed indicative of guilt, and like Tony had said, and like Ash was trying to believe, *it wasn't his fault*. He'd only worried about telling Lennox. They'd spent so much time together recently, and this, Tony had reiterated, was *just* for the food truck guys. Not their boyfriends. Even Chase wasn't going to be there, even though it felt like Tate hardly ever went to the Funky Cup without him.

"I think you *should* go," Lennox said. "It's not like you're going to walk home alone. I trust Tony and Lucas to look after you." He paused. "Well, I trust Lucas anyway."

"I can also look after myself," Ash said.

To Lennox's credit, he didn't even sound the slightest bit patronizing. "Of course you can," he said, "there's just always more safety in numbers."

Ash whipped something out of his pocket that he hadn't carried around in years. Not since he'd used to go clubbing in his younger, wilder days. "I've got my pepper spray on me, don't worry."

"Good." Lennox nodded approvingly. "And don't be afraid to use it."

"I won't," Ash said. He'd used it before, when a guy had gotten a little handsier than he'd liked. He definitely wouldn't hesitate to use it now, not when whoever was targeting him had also started to target his friends.

"Are Ross and Aaron going?" Lennox wondered, and Ash could tell he was trying to be casual about the question.

"I don't think so," Ash said. "Tony didn't mention them, and they haven't opened officially yet. Not til Friday."

"Good," Lennox said, sounding more pleased about that than Ash had expected.

Ash stepped closer to him, letting Lennox fold him into his tight embrace. "Don't sound so pleased," he murmured into his shoulder.

"It works out with my plans," Lennox said softly.

"Plans?" Ash felt a thread of concern.

"You sound worried." And Lennox sounded amused. Which *wasn't* okay.

"So you're allowed to be worried about me, but I can't be worried about you?"

Lennox chuckled. "Point taken."

"Just . . . be safe, okay?" Ash didn't know what he'd do if he lost this man, just when he was beginning to realize exactly what he meant. What he might mean in the future.

"Ditto," Lennox echoed.

"You really think it's this Stanton guy, don't you?" Seth asked as Lennox stared through a pair of binoculars at Ross Stanton's apartment windows.

"Yes," Lennox said shortly. On the positive side, the apartment was fairly exposed, just on the third floor, the windows easily visible from the street, where he and Seth had parked an hour earlier. On the negative side, Ross Stanton appeared to be boring as hell. He'd come home from working about seven, and gone upstairs, and not left since then. Lennox had only seen him even cross in front of his windows a handful of times. Nobody had come in and nobody had left.

He sighed.

"I'll admit," Seth said, "when you said you were going to follow your main suspect, I thought you must be pretty desperate, but now it's obvious."

"Is it?" Lennox knew he sounded testy, but Seth would understand why. He was frustrated. He was stymied. He was more than a little lost, and it was driving him nuts.

"You don't have a clue what to do next," Seth said.

"Whoever this is, they're smart. And they're using the same paint. Cheap, generic paint. A disposable brush you could buy down the street at the hardware store. I asked there, and they said nobody had bought any in some time, which makes me think they bought more than one, which means they're thinking ahead.

They've planned a lot of this. Or at least the possibility of it, ahead of time."

"You found the brush this time, didn't you?"

"Yeah," Lennox said, "they'd tossed it in one of the garbage cans."

"And you've got nothing on the video footage."

"A dark figure, that's all," Lennox said. "He's covered his face and his head."

"He *is* smart, then." Seth paused. "Clever."

"It's pissing me off," Lennox admitted. He saw a flash of something in Stanton's windows and followed it but it turned out to be nothing. Just the edge of a person walking somewhere. Probably Stanton going to grab a beer or something equally, annoyingly inconsequential.

"Did you get anything else from Atkinson?" Seth asked, leaning back in the driver's seat and stretching his legs. As much as he loved Seth, Lennox wouldn't have invited him to ride along, but he didn't personally have a car. Just the bike. And it was a whole lot harder to do surveillance on a motorcycle.

"He mentioned that Stanton and Bolton were using when they left."

"Yeah, that's not unusual in the restaurant biz," Seth said. "Lots of uppers for those long shifts. But I can't imagine Atkinson tolerating that kind of shit in his places."

"He didn't. They were fired for it."

"So are they *still* using?" Seth wondered.

"I thought the same thing. But what would that have to do with Ash?"

"You sure he isn't using too?"

"I'm sure," Lennox said, grinding his teeth together. "Never been more sure about anything, ever."

Seth grinned at him. "Check him carefully, did you? I noticed his bike locked on the gate, the last few nights."

"Yes," Lennox said tightly. "Yes, he's stayed over."

"Good for you. Really, good for both of you," Seth said. "I'm a little jealous though."

"You could've done it with . . . what's that guy's name?" Lennox couldn't remember.

"You talkin' about Ren?"

"That's it," Lennox said with a nod. "You said he asked."

Seth rolled his eyes. "He's hot, but I'm way too old for the kind of shit he probably gets up to."

"Old?" Lennox scoffed. "You're just afraid." And he had been, too. Wanting someone as much as he wanted Ash was terrifying. But also, he'd discovered, freeing in a way he'd never imagined.

"A little," Seth admitted, laughing. "But it's not like that with Ren. He's just . . . well, he's just someone who likes a lot of variety. And I don't, not really."

"You could . . ."

But Seth just shrugged. "It's not a big deal. I'm glad you're happy. Really. It's been long enough."

Lennox wouldn't ever admit it, but Seth wasn't wrong.

"Now that Landon and Quentin's situation seems just about wrapped up, maybe I'll help you out," Seth said. "Go over everything, see if there's something you've overlooked."

Lennox shot his partner a look. "Something I've overlooked?"

"It's possible," Seth said. "Did you read that letter the stalker sent Landon?"

He had read it. Had tried very hard not to laugh at some of the more florid phrases.

"It seems he's very upset to be breaking up, but he hopes Landon understands."

"Landon didn't just understand, he was pretty fucking relieved," Seth said with a dry chuckle. "Imagine sending a breakup letter when you're done stalking someone. What a nutjob."

"It was pretty fucking strange," Lennox agreed. "And we've decided to trust this? You don't think he's going all out, claiming to move on when he's just waiting for us to let our guard down?"

Seth shook his head. "You read it. *And* he's been making some rounds of another neighborhood. I think it's the one Taylor Swift lives in."

"Oh great, he's just moving from Landon to someone else?" Lennox had believed when Seth had sent over the letter from Landon's stalker they'd finally caught a break. But if he was just moving on to someone else . . .

"I know some of her security team, from back in the day," Seth said. "I sent over what we had. They're prepped for his particular brand of crazy, and good news, she seems to take her safety a lot more seriously than Landon does."

"Than Landon *did*," Lennox corrected.

"Yeah, I will say, he's gotten a lot more observant. Careful, even."

"It's a silver lining." There'd been a time when Lennox had been sure that Landon would never think about it. But this stalker had changed that. And if the stalker had really moved on to Swift, maybe they could *all* breathe a little easier.

"I wonder if you could find a way to search that Basket truck," Seth said, dragging the conversation back to Ash's stalker. "I doubt they'd keep anything there, but they might, and at least it would give you a place to start."

Lennox made a noncommittal sound. He felt like he was walking such a fine line. He wanted to catch whoever this was. He wanted to keep Ash safe. But Ash was testy about his continued interest in Aaron and Ross as suspects.

"You could ask Ash to keep them distracted for a few minutes?" Seth suggested.

"No." It was bad enough that Ash was still working with them. That he wouldn't let Lennox protect him the way he wanted to. Asking him to assist? To put himself out there as possible bait. No way.

"Hey," Seth said, throwing his hands up in mock surrender, "it was just a suggestion."

"We'll have to come up with something else. Can you talk to your sergeant friend on the LAPD? The one who works in vice? See if they know anything about a drug ring in restaurants?"

"Yeah, I'll shoot him a text," Seth said. "But really, you don't have any other ideas?"

"The guy isn't really breaking any laws, except some minor vandalism ones," Lennox sighed. "I can't even get the police involved. And I'm not sure what they'd do anyway."

"Not any more than you're already doing."

"I just . . . I want to keep him safe," Lennox said quietly. Hating how vulnerable he sounded. "It's killing me that I can't."

"We'll stay, then," Seth said. "As long as we need to."

Lennox raised an eyebrow. "What if he never comes out?"

"Then he never comes out. You've got a guard on the lot. Daley and Adam will switch off. Make sure nothing happens down there. And we'll be here. In case Stanton decides to leave and pull some more shit."

"Thanks," Lennox said shortly. Not sure that anything he said would be enough to thank the man who had not only pulled him out of the dark hole he'd fallen into after his injury and his discharge—and after Marcus had abandoned him—but had helped him start the business that had come to mean so much to him.

The business that had eventually brought him to Ash.

"What *is* Ash up to tonight?" Seth wondered. "He's not gonna be wondering where you are and waiting for you, right?"

"Ash is with his friends. He couldn't be safer," Lennox said, and realized he meant it.

"Oh my God," Ash exclaimed, "you *cannot* keep following me around like this. I just gotta go take a piss and grab a refill."

Lucas shot him an amused glance. "I have been given very specific orders," he said.

"From Lennox?" If that was the case, then Ash was going to have to go over there after all, and kick his ass.

It would probably be a metaphorical ass kicking, but there were some lines that Lennox wasn't allowed to cross. Setting his friends to guard him, *officially*, was one of those.

"Nope. Tony," Lucas answered with a grin.

"Ugh," Ash complained. "Really?"

"He's worried. We're *all* worried," Lucas said, slinging an arm around Ash's shoulders. "Now I'll just watch the door while you pee, okay?"

"What, you think someone's going to come abduct me while I'm in the bathroom?" Ash asked incredulously. "Really?"

"I don't know. Abduct you, cover you in purple paint . . ." Lucas trailed off. "I just . . . *I* would feel better if I was watching, alright?"

"Aw," Ash said, tapping him affectionately on the shoulder. "You're sweet."

And Lucas was, Ash thought as he did his business in the bathroom, and then checked the mirror as he washed his hands, flicking a few strands of hair back in place. His friends *all* were, watching out for him like this. Even if they were driving him a little crazy.

Lucas, as promised, trailed him over to the bar, where Shaw was serving up drinks next to his brother, Jackson.

"Another gin and tonic?" Shaw asked, barely glancing up at Ash.

Ash nodded. "And a beer for my shadow here," he added, gesturing to Lucas.

"I hear you've had some real interesting shit going down at the lot," Shaw said as he started to make Ash's drink.

"Yeah, it's been weird," Ash said.

"And," Shaw added, "I heard you're related to Stephan Atkinson?"

Ash sighed. He supposed it was only a matter of time before people started to find out. He'd been lucky to keep it a secret for so long, and now, it seemed, the cat was officially out of the bag.

"He's my father," Ash said. "And he sucks."

Shaw's gaze was sympathetic as he set his gin and tonic on a Funky Cup coaster. "I'm sorry, dude, that blows. I've not heard good things, either, but I can't imagine growing up with him was much fun."

"Not so much," Ash admitted.

He was struck, suddenly, but not for the first time, by a desire to apologize. To say he was sorry he'd kept his famous family a secret.

"So your last name isn't really Powell?" Lucas said after they'd grabbed their drinks and headed back outside, where everyone was gathered around the firepit.

"Nope," Ash said.

Lucas looked very curious. A trait he must have picked up from Tony, who could've given cats a run for their money. "And?" he prompted as they sat down.

Ash sighed. "Oliver Ashton Atkinson. Powell is my mother's maiden name."

"That's your name?" Tony exclaimed. "That's a fucking mouthful. I don't blame you for going by Ash."

"I've always liked Ash," he said. "Feels like *me*."

"Ash fits you," Alexis said, nodding. "I've always thought so."

"Oliver feels like the guy I left behind when I struck out on my own," Ash said. "So I changed my name and left him behind."

"You and Lennox are sure two of a kind with the whole name thing," Tony said slyly.

"What?" Ash was confused. What name thing?

"You know, is Lennox his first name? His last name? Nobody knows. Surely he's told you," Gabriel chimed in. He glanced over at his cousin, Ren, who was poking the fire with one of the wrought iron tools. "Ren and I might have some money riding on it."

"What?" Ash couldn't believe this.

Actually, scratch that. He could *totally* believe this. The food truck guys could be awesome; they could also be more gossipy than a whole herd of Southern church-going grandmothers.

"He must have told you," Sean said.

Ash shot a look at his good friend. "Surely you're not in on the bet too."

Sean gave him a weak grin. "No? Of course not?"

"I can't believe you guys," Ash said.

"Yes, you can," Tony said. "We've got nothing better to do with our time than pry into everyone else's lives. Why do you think I spend so much of my life matchmaking?"

"Because you're not only so happy you want to foist that same bliss on everyone else you know, but also because you can't help meddling?" Ash asked pointedly.

Tony laughed.

"He can't," Lucas said. "I would tell you how many times I have told him to cut it out, but . . . you wouldn't actually believe me."

"I might, actually," Gabriel said. "But so far, Tony's batting average is pretty good. Sean and me, Tate and Chase, and now . . . well, I hear you're not sleeping at home much, recently, huh, Oliver Ashton?"

"I didn't tell you that so you could use it all the time," Ash said primly. Ignoring, pointedly, the other insinuation. Because it wasn't wrong. He *hadn't* spent the last few nights in his own bed.

And why should he, when Lennox's was not only so comfortable, but it contained *Lennox*?

"So you really don't know his name?" Gabriel wheedled.

"His name is Lennox," Ash said firmly.

"First? Last? Maybe his *middle* name?" Ren teased.

"I haven't asked." He hadn't. Because, Ash realized, he'd never cared. A name was just a name; he knew that better than anyone. What mattered the most was the person. The *man*. And Lennox was one of the finest he'd ever known.

"You should," Sean said.

"At least so we can clear this up," Tony said. "I even tried to find out when we formalized our contract but *nope*, no luck."

"Why does it matter?" Ash wanted to know. Feeling strangely protective of the man he'd gotten involved with. "Up til five minutes ago you didn't realize that Ash wasn't *my* real name."

"Well, we don't have a hundred bucks riding on your real name," Sean said, and at least *he* was slightly apologetic about it.

"You really want me to do this," Ash said. "I'll think about it."

"What could it hurt?" Gabriel pointed out. "It's just a name."

"If things get weird between us, it's going to be all your fault," Ash warned.

"Nothing's gonna get weird," Tony promised. "He's crazy about you. I bet you he didn't even want to leave your side today."

He hadn't. Ash had needed to persuade him to leave during the day, so he could work properly, and then there'd been that whole suggestion that he move into Lennox's loft.

"Yeah," Lucas teased. "Sounds like the *L* word."

"Who calls it that?" Tony asked, taking a long drink of his beer.

"*You*, only about a thousand times," Lucas said with a laugh.

Ash couldn't believe his friends actually cared so much about Lennox's name. But, at the same time, it had felt so good to be with his friends, to not, for once, be worrying about what was going to happen. Who was going to find out. Because finally, everyone who mattered to him knew the truth.

He was Oliver Ashton Atkinson. And he was still Ash.

No matter what Lennox told him, he'd always be just *Lennox* to him.

The man he might be feeling the *L* word for.

CHAPTER THIRTEEN

ASH WOKE UP THE next morning with the sun shining and a smile on his face.

After switching off his alarm, he lay there for a long moment, trying to balance the surge of joy he felt at his growing relationship with Lennox with the frustration and the guilt of this horrible stalking situation.

And then there's the fear, Ash's brain added, *you're afraid, even though you don't want to be.*

He hadn't really been afraid until yesterday morning, when he'd walked onto the food truck lot and felt, despite the lack of paint on his truck, like he'd been covered in it. Like he'd been observed, assessed, and then targeted.

Ash shivered even though the warmth of the sun was already streaming through the window, but he dismissed it. He wasn't going to focus on the fear. Lennox had already promised that he would protect him, and he trusted Lennox. He was pretty sure he might *love* Lennox.

Pushing the covers down, Ash slid out of bed and reached for his phone. There were two texts from Lennox. One, from last night, that Lennox must have sent after he'd fallen asleep.

Not much progress on this end, Lennox had written, **but I'm back at the loft and already missing you, too.**

Ash smiled. He'd missed Lennox too, and sent a message to that effect before he'd fallen asleep. Not really expecting much in return, because he'd learned that Lennox wasn't the most vocal or the most demonstrative guy he'd dated—so the message came as a pleasant surprise. One that Ash hugged to his chest as he scrolled to the next.

Morning report from the guard at the lot is clear. Didn't see a soul last night.

Even though Lennox had delivered this one in a more brisk, businesslike tone, Ash felt his heart (and his hope) swell a bit more at this message. Maybe this nightmare had finally ended.

He walked into the bathroom, took care of his morning business, and then headed towards the kitchen to start the coffee before taking a shower and heading to the lot, to work.

The first sign something was . . . *off* . . . was that he could feel the cool morning breeze on his bare chest as he left his bedroom.

"That's weird," Ash said to himself, even as his heart rate began to accelerate. "I swear I closed the windows . . ."

But he hadn't. Or *someone* hadn't, because the window in his little eating nook was wide open.

Ash's breath caught in his throat. Had someone been in his house last night? Was someone *still* in his house?

He wished that he'd brought his phone in with him, because he'd have called Lennox, even if he sounded like a paranoid nutcase. But he didn't have his phone, and instead of going back to get it, he grabbed the fire poker from the ornamental set his mother had given him for his fireplace that he had yet to actually *use*. Lennox had insisted a dozen times or more that the stalker wasn't violent, and Ash clung to that idea even as he clung to the poker, carefully edging around the corner of the living room, and into the kitchen.

Ash gasped.

The purple paint was back. This time it was slopped across his kitchen countertops in a massive spill, dripping down the sides of the counter, to the floor.

He could hear the sound of his heartbeat in his ears and the persistent drip of the paint, and nothing else.

For a long moment, he wasn't sure he could move. They had been *here*. In his house. While he was sleeping.

After the bar last night, he'd detoured into the kitchen for a glass of water before heading to bed. Then, just after eleven, the countertops had been pristine, like he'd just wiped them down.

Now, they were a mess.

His fingers tightened around the poker, numb and nerveless, but he didn't let go, even though there was nobody around.

The paint looked like it had just been spilled, but when Ash took a step closer, he saw that it had begun to crust over in spots. And that was when he saw it.

Written in the bright purple, in a finger-tipped scrawl, was a single phrase.

Poor little rich boy.

Ash dropped the poker. Didn't hear it hit the floor through the roaring in his ears.

He didn't know how long he stood there, staring at the letters, at the paint, as it destroyed his kitchen, but he knew his eyes grew dry, his nose burned unbearably from the chemical smell of the paint, but he couldn't turn away.

Someone hated him. Someone hated him so much that they would invade his home like this and stab him, right where it would hurt the most.

Yes, he'd been unbearably privileged in some ways. He'd grown up never having to question where his next meal was coming from. They'd lived in a huge house, at one of the most prestigious addresses in Los Angeles. He'd gone to the best private schools. He'd never lacked for a thing in his whole life.

Except parents who cared about him. People who loved him.

He'd been left on his own forever, and then, when he'd become a teenager, his father had suddenly and unpleasantly remembered that he not only existed, but that Ash would be the next generation of famous Atkinsons. He would mold Ash into a vision of himself.

But Ash, already resentful that he'd been left on his own for so long, had resisted.

He didn't want to be a narcissistic asshole like his father.

He didn't want to be obeyed and feared just because of who he was.

He'd never wanted to be feared at all.

It had never occurred to Ash that someone might actually resent *him*, when his father was *right there*, controlling and mean and self-serving, right down to his core.

None of this made sense.

It was that thought that finally pushed Ash away from the kitchen, back to his bedroom, to grab his phone.

His voice, when Lennox answered, was not quite as steady as he'd hoped it would be. But then, Ash reasoned, it wasn't like Lennox could blame him. Someone had broken *into his fucking house*.

"Someone was here," Ash said.

"What?" Lennox practically barked into the phone. "*What?*"

"Someone was here," Ash repeated. "In my house."

"Don't move," Lennox said. "I'm going to be there in five." He took a short, deep breath. "Less than five."

"It's alright," Ash said, even though it was very much *not* alright, at all, "they're gone."

Lennox didn't answer, just hung up.

Ash shivered, the cold air from the window blowing on his skin again, but the chill made him feel like he was actually here.

Was the only thing that felt real on this weirdly sun-drenched morning. Shouldn't it be raining? he thought absently. Gloomy? There should be different weather. Weather that might better fit the storm wailing inside of him.

He hugged his arms around his chest and waited by the door for Lennox.

He would make it alright. He'd make sure Ash was warm again. Protected. *Safe.* He'd sworn to catch the person who was doing this, and even though he hadn't yet, Ash had more faith in him than he'd ever had in anyone else, except himself.

The knock on the door came a spare five minutes later.

Might have even been four.

Ash unlocked the door, laughing a little inside because *the door was still fucking locked and what good had that done him.* The moment he opened it, Lennox was pushing it open further and gathering Ash, still shivering, into his arms.

He held him for a long moment, Ash soaking up his warmth and his safety. Something he'd never before thought he'd look for in a man, but with Lennox was not only an intrinsic part of who he was, but during a moment like this, felt bigger than anything else.

If Ash hadn't been so viscerally attracted to Lennox before the stalker had arrived, he'd have worried that the safety Lennox represented might have skewed his feelings.

But Ash, who'd always been forced to be painfully level-headed by an emotionally manipulative father, knew that wasn't why he loved his man.

The safety he represented was only a small part of it.

"Are you okay?" Lennox asked, finally pulling away.

Ash was still shivering. Lennox shed his hooded sweatshirt and draped it over Ash's shoulders.

"It's there," Ash said. "In the kitchen." He pointed, but Lennox didn't move.

"I asked if you were alright," he said gently.

"I'm . . ." Ash didn't know what he was. He felt violated. Someone had been in his house, while he slept. Had poked at the one wound that he'd always tried so carefully to hide. That he'd literally changed his name to avoid.

And that poking and prodding *hurt*. So much more than Ash had ever thought it would.

Lennox reached down and grasped his hand tightly, squeezing. "You're going to be alright," he said, his voice like a vow.

"I'm going to be alright," Ash said mechanically.

Lennox let go, and only then walked towards the kitchen, his fingers straying to the matte black metal of the gun resting in its shoulder holster.

Ash watched as he took in the open window. Then watched as he approached the destroyed countertop, the purple paint crusted over even further now. Saw as he took in the words.

Then to Ash's surprise, he went through every room of the house. Carefully, with purpose. Searching, Ash supposed, not just to confirm that the culprit had left, but probably to make sure they hadn't left any other surprises behind.

He pulled his phone out then, and Ash listened as he talked to someone in hushed tones. Probably someone he worked with, if Ash had to guess.

The next call he made was more obvious, and he cringed.

Only then did Lennox turn back to him. "They opened the window using an old-fashioned technique that worked because your windows are original to the house," he said.

"I'm . . . sorry . . ." Ash stuttered. It had never occurred to him that his house might not be secure. It had always felt secure to *him*.

"No, no, no," Lennox insisted, pulling him into another warm, comforting embrace. "No, don't blame yourself, *please*. It's all my fucking fault," he muttered.

"You didn't know they would do this," Ash said, the logic of the statement seeming to come from very far away, considering the emotional maelstrom coursing through him currently.

"I drove them away from the lot by posting the guard," Lennox said simply. "I should've known when their primary target was taken out, they'd attempt a secondary one. I never thought . . . I didn't dream it would be your house, or that they'd break in. Still, I should have done a cursory security sweep. I would've seen that your window locks had vulnerabilities. Put new ones on."

Lennox took a deep breath, and steered Ash towards the couch and set him down gently, and then continued, kneeling in front of him. "I still don't think they're violent. I think they hate you, but they don't want to hurt you."

"They had the perfect opportunity," Ash said in a voice that didn't even sound like his own.

"We should call the police," Lennox said. "I called Seth, asked him to talk to someone he knows at the department. And I talked to Tony."

"I know," Ash said, hearing the misery in his own voice. "I heard you."

"After we talk to the police, and hopefully file a report, I think you should talk to Tony."

"What for?" Ash was aware there was some fundamental connection he was missing, but under the layers of fog, he couldn't find it.

"I want you to come stay with me," Lennox said and held up a hand. "No, please don't protest. Please, *please* let me keep you safe."

Just yesterday, Lennox had made the suggestion and Ash had barely even considered it. No, Ash revised, he hadn't considered it at all. He'd immediately dismissed it as reactionary and unnecessary.

It didn't feel like that now.

"Okay," Ash said. "But why Tony?"

"My loft is secure. It's got the best security money can buy. I want you to stay there until I've found and dealt with this . . . *person*." Lennox spit the word out.

"You don't want me to open my truck," Ash said slowly. "You want me to lock myself away so I'm protected."

"I want you to take a few days off and let Tony cover your truck. I think he'd be willing to, don't you?"

Ash licked his lips. He swore he could still smell the chemicals from the paint. "He probably would." He hesitated. "Why wouldn't I be safe at the lot? What about the guard?"

Lennox considered this. "Do you really want to open today? Tomorrow? While this person is at large? While you don't know who it might be? There are hundreds of people that show up every day at the lot, sometimes thousands. The guard can't be everywhere. I can't protect you if you're out there, exposed in the open like that."

He'd always believed that the shit he'd gone through with his father had made him a strong person. A nearly indestructible person. But it turned out that wasn't quite true after all. All it took was someone who knew him, who knew the places to prod and poke, the sensitive spots he tried to hide. Ash knew it was pointless to claim that he wasn't afraid, because Lennox already knew he was.

"Okay, I'll pack a bag and talk to Tony," Ash said, taking a deep breath. "You get two days, but I want to be back by the weekend, okay?"

Lennox leaned in, brushing a quick, fierce kiss across his lips. "Okay," he said, sounding both relieved and grateful, "and thank you."

"Shouldn't I be thanking you?" Ash wondered.

"No," Lennox said, "you should be pissed as hell at me, but by some miracle, you actually trust me still. And I'm going to make absolutely fucking sure I don't fail you again."

"You haven't, and you won't," Ash said, standing up. Feeling a little stronger now. Still terrified. Still angry. Still violated. But *better*.

"You have a lot of faith," Lennox said. "Hope it's not misplaced."

"I know you're going to find this asshole, and I know he's going to be punished," Ash said simply. "And in the meantime, I trust that you're going to keep me safe."

Lennox's concerned expression melted into a hesitant smile. "You're better than I deserve."

"I think," Ash said, "I'm just exactly what you deserve."

Lennox's gaze softened, and he opened his mouth and Ash almost wanted to say, *no, no, please don't tell me like this. Not after this dickwad was just in my house and I'm so terrified that I'm voluntarily giving up everything that makes me* me.

But before Lennox could make any kind of heartfelt confession, there was a knock on the door and there was Seth, and only a few steps behind him was Tony.

Ash had never actually *met* Seth, Lennox's second-in-command, before. He'd seen him on the lot before, Sean had pointed him out once, had mentioned that he ordered from his truck a lot, and also from Gabriel's. But not Ash's.

He'd been forced to conclude that Seth was not a fan of salad. Frankly, he wasn't sure *Lennox* was a fan of salad, and the reason he'd always been stopping by hadn't been for Ash's mixed greens or his house-made salad dressings.

"Hey," Seth said, as Lennox let him in. "What do you need me to do?"

"Pictures of the damage in the kitchen and the open window," Lennox said. "Did you talk to Morales?"

"He's sending a team out. It might be drug related but it's not really a case for vice," Seth said. "But he still said he'd try to get some men on it. See if anyone saw anything. He definitely wants us to keep him looped in, especially if we find this bastard."

"I'll be reporting him . . . eventually," Lennox said with a grim smile that surprised Ash.

"What does that mean?" Ash asked, worried he'd look stupid. But this was *his* life, and really *his* stalker. He wanted to know what was going to happen to him.

"It means he might be a little roughed up when we turn him in," Seth said. He stuck out his hand. "Seth Abramson," he said. "Nice to meet you."

Ash shook his hand briefly, wishing that they'd met officially under better circumstances. Like under the lights at the Funky

Cup. Not in his house, with the chemical smell of paint pervading everything and Ash only wearing his boxer briefs and Lennox's sweatshirt.

"Ash," Tony said, his face creased with concern. He wrapped him up in a tight hug. "God, are you okay?"

For a split second, Ash considered lying. "No," he said, truthfully.

"Of course you aren't," Tony soothed. "We're gonna take care of everything, though. I've already been in touch with Harmony. She's going to open your truck, and I'll help her."

"I can write out some instructions…" Ash trailed off. It seemed *wrong* to put his business in Tony and Harmony's hands, even though he trusted both of them to do it justice.

"If you want," Tony said. "But Harmony seems to have a real good handle on what needs done."

She would. She was a great employee and even Ash could admit that it wasn't like any of his prep work was particularly difficult or complicated. "Okay. But if you guys get stuck or lost, just call me," Ash said.

"Perfect." Tony hugged him again, and then turned to Lennox. "Do you need me for anything?"

Lennox shook his head. "Just needed you and Ash to touch base, to make sure his truck is going to be alright."

"It will be," Tony promised.

"It's only going to be for *two* days," Ash reminded not just Tony and Lennox—but himself, too. Still, when he went to get his keys to give Tony what he needed to get into his truck, it hurt more than he'd thought it would.

"It's just for a few days," Tony said as Ash glumly handed the key over. "Maybe you can even do some development on your own. Lennox's place has got a kitchen, right?"

Ash thought back to the handful of times he'd been in the loft Lennox owned. He had the barest impression of some cabinets, a fairly small workspace, and some shiny stainless appliances. He'd worked in worse, anyway. His first apartment, after he'd broken away from his father, had been a shithole, the kitchen tiny and the appliances broken or useless. Anything Lennox had would at least be in perfect working order—he wasn't the kind of person to stand for anything else.

"Yeah, it does," Ash said. "Looks barely used, but . . . it exists."

"Well, you're just the person to break it in," Tony said. "What's the status on your dish with the Basket guys?"

"It's done," Ash said. "They're making a few final tweaks, but there's a list of ingredients pinned up in the truck. When I'm back, I'll make a batch of the dressing, and start more pickled veg. We should be fine, all set to go for their official opening this weekend."

Seth and Lennox had already gone into the kitchen, and Ash could hear them discussing the situation, the words indistinct.

"You sure it's just going to be for a couple of days?" Tony asked, glancing in the direction of the kitchen. "I'm not sure they're really all that close to catching this asshole."

Ash wasn't sure either. He still wasn't convinced that Ross or Aaron would do this to him. He'd known them so long. Surely if they had hated him all this time, he'd have known, right?

"It's just for a couple of days," Ash said firmly. He had no intention of staying away longer. If he kept himself locked up in Lennox's loft for any longer than that, he'd go crazy.

"You sure they can wrap this up in that amount of time?" Tony did not seem convinced. And frankly, neither was Ash. Lennox was so focused on the wrong set of suspects.

At least Ash *hoped* they were the wrong set of suspects. How fucked up was that?

"I don't care if it's not wrapped up or not, I'm going to be back by the weekend. Lennox can put a guard next to the truck if he's that worried."

Tony raised an eyebrow, not looking convinced, but he didn't say another word about it. "Alright," he said, jingling the key that Ash had given him. "I think I'm all set. You good here?"

Ash nodded. "I've still got to pack, and then there's the statement I'll be giving to the police."

"I'll send Lucas over with some food at lunch, alright?" Tony said as they headed towards the front door.

Ash smiled, maybe for the first time all day. "Really?"

Tony hesitated in the doorway. "We're all worried about you, you know? Lucas hated leaving you here last night, by yourself, and when I got the call this morning? He was really beating himself up."

"Why?" Ash couldn't quite believe it. He knew Lucas cared about him as a friend, and there'd been the way he'd followed him around at the Funky Cup last night, but he hadn't imagined that it went any further than that.

"Honestly," Tony said, "Lucas' family sucks. To him, you're part of our family. And he's not going to let anything happen to you."

Ash was touched. "Well, I consider him family, too. Both of you."

Tony patted him reassuringly on the shoulder. "We take care of each other, you know?"

"I know," Ash said. He'd known it, on some level, before all this shit had gone down, but now he knew it on a visceral, *ride or die,* level. "Thanks for doing this, Tony."

"Of course. Wouldn't dream of doing anything else." Tony grinned. "Maybe you'll come back and I'll have changed the whole menu."

"You wouldn't . . ." Ash trailed off.

"I wouldn't," Tony agreed. "But your face! Anyway, I'll see you soon, hopefully sooner rather than later?"

"Fingers crossed!" Ash said, though he knew it would probably take more than two days to find the culprit. He was sure that in two days, he'd be arguing with Lennox, trying to go back to work.

Deep down, as he watched Tony walk down the sidewalk, he knew that Lennox wouldn't stop him, not if he put his foot down.

The only question was if he was going to be back to his regular self enough to put it down.

Lennox was used to pretending patience, but it never really got any easier.

He waited around, forcing himself to not seem impatient, as the cops did their work, interviewing Ash—who did not know much—and then Lennox gave his own statement.

When they finally left, he didn't have much faith that anything would come of it, but then he'd known that when he'd told Seth to call them. But he'd done it anyway, because it was the right thing to do, now that Ash's house had been broken into, and the asshole behind everything had stepped right from annoying to *illegal*.

"Are you all packed?" Lennox asked as he stood in the doorway of Ash's bedroom. These were not the circumstances he'd wanted to come under, when he'd imagined being here.

Ash looked up from the duffel he'd just finished zipping up. He'd showered after his interview with the police, and changed into a pair of baggy shorts and a worn t-shirt. "Yeah," he said. "I just need to grab my laptop from the kitchen table."

Lennox watched Ash's face change as he realized that he'd not done a thing to deal with the mess currently crusting over on his countertops.

"I took care of it," Lennox said. "There's a cleaning crew coming this afternoon. Whatever they can't clean up, good as new, I'll get replaced."

"Wait," Ash said, holding up a hand as he lifted his duffel. "*You'll* get it replaced? I can replace my own goddamn countertops."

"Let me, please," Lennox said. He could hear the guilt bubbling up, until it was all through his voice. "It's the least I can do, considering that it's my fault this asshole is still out there."

Ash flashed him a look. "We'll talk about it," he said, "if they can't clean it up. Okay?"

That was not the agreement that Lennox wanted to make, but he'd already acknowledged to himself that he couldn't keep Ash locked away, no matter how much he might want to, and he couldn't fix every problem for him, either.

If they were going to be together, there were always going to be compromises to be made, and this was one of them.

Lennox already knew that when the two days were up, he was going to have a devil of a time convincing Ash not to go back to the food truck lot.

"Okay," Lennox agreed.

Ash looked suspicious of his easy agreement, but didn't say another word about it as they walked into the kitchen. Lennox watched as Ash packed up his laptop, flashing one more look full of confusion and frustration at the destroyed countertop as they walked out.

He didn't say anything about it until they were almost at Lennox's place.

"I don't get why this person would go after me," Ash said as Lennox unlocked the door to his loft, "when they had my father to go after. Isn't he a much more satisfying target?"

"Maybe," Lennox acknowledged as Ash tossed his duffel bag on the bed and set his laptop bag on top of the dresser. "But he's also a much more high-profile target. Much easier to break into your house than it is to break into his."

"Yeah, I get that," Ash said, running fingers through his still-damp hair, and collapsing onto the edge of the bed. "But *why*?"

"I'm going to get to the bottom of this," Lennox said, approaching the bed and reaching out for Ash, pulling him in, holding him close. "I can promise you that. And I can promise you that it *isn't* and it has *never* been your fault that this person is targeting you."

"That's not how it feels right now," Ash admitted, resting his head against Lennox's chest.

"It wouldn't," Lennox said softly.

Ash chuckled wryly. "The way it feels right now *sucks*. I'm so fucking angry. And after everything he put me through, I keep thinking, didn't I pay enough for him being my fucking father?"

"I think . . . I think it's a miracle you didn't become bitter and angry all the time. Instead, you always smiled at me, and not just because you wanted in my pants." Ash smiled. "I mean it,"

Lennox added, "it's not just your attitude that's the miracle, *you're* a fucking miracle."

Ash leaned in and kissed him, and Lennox knew that he'd meant every word he'd said, all the way down to his bones. *He* was the one who'd grown—perhaps understandably—bitter after his injury and then even more so after Marcus. Coming to LA and starting the business with Seth had helped, but there'd been a hard, uncompromising kernel, deep inside of him, that had resented the hell out of the hand he'd been dealt.

Instead of saving lives and watching his team's back, he'd been relegated to the sidelines, to installing security systems and protecting spoiled actors and too-rich pop stars. Even though he liked Landon and his husband, making sure he kept them safe from a man who apparently thought Landon could carry his children hadn't felt worth all that blood and sweat and pain.

But now a few years in, Lennox discovered that that hard place inside him had been shrinking, a little at a time.

Then he'd met Ash and his sunny smile had begun to melt it even faster.

Lennox tilted his head and let himself slide into the kiss. Let go of all the worries of the morning. Hoped as Ash groaned into his mouth that he was doing the same.

Maybe they could lose a little of their frustration in each other.

Reaching down, Lennox tugged on the hem of Ash's t-shirt, letting his hand graze over the front of his shorts, Ash hissing as his palm pressed against his hardening cock.

Ash *was* into this, then. Lennox hadn't been sure he would be, but he was now eagerly pressing into his hand and groaning into his mouth.

It was an easy decision to sink to his knees in front of Ash, who was still sitting on the edge of the bed. The only hard part about it was that he needed to stop kissing him, and it *was* tough to tear his lips off Ash's. But he could use his mouth so much better.

Gazing down with eyes already glazed with pleasure, Ash sank his teeth into his bottom lip, and as Lennox pulled his shorts down, he couldn't help but remember what *his* mouth had been like. The echo of it was still thrumming through his veins, and he'd do anything to show Ash that he could make him feel just as good.

He'd wanted to do this for so long, and it blew his mind that he *could* now.

"God, Lennox," Ash said, his voice unsteady as Lennox finished pulling his briefs off, and his cock bobbed, hard and already wet at the tip, between them.

He leaned in and curled his tongue around the head, the unique flavor that was *Ash* sliding across his tongue. Lemons and some kind of herb, probably from his soap, and underneath it all the man he'd fallen in love with.

He'd told himself that he'd never take that risk again, but with Ash, it wasn't even a risk. It was as natural and as easy as breathing.

Curling a hand around Ash's thigh, he felt the muscles tense as his mouth sank a little deeper. Lennox could feel his own dick, heavy and hard between his legs, but he ignored it, always more comfortable with giving than receiving. Ash probably had no idea, considering what he'd asked for the first night they'd been together, but he loved doing this. It was like he was writing his love, one letter, one lick, one long slick slide at a time.

Ash moaned above him, fingers reaching in and tangling in his short hair, tugging, not nearly as hard as he'd pulled Ash's the other night, but curling against his scalp, delicately encouraging him. Like his groans of pleasure weren't making Lennox hard as a rock. Weren't already spurring him to go further, to take him deeper.

He reached in and cupped Ash's balls in his palm, gently rolling them, feeling Ash tense even more, the muscles in his thighs flexing. Lennox could tell he was getting close, from the taste of precome on his tongue, and the way Ash's fingers flexed on his scalp.

He just needed to push him over that exhilarating edge. Reaching back, Lennox slipped a spit-slick finger behind his balls, and Ash gave a strangled yelp as he circled his hole, remembering what he'd asked for, the first time they'd had sex.

Ash's fingertips dug into his scalp and he let out a breathless giggle and that was all the warning Lennox got before Ash was coming down his throat. He swallowed, milking the last bit of pleasure out of him, letting him soften in his mouth as he gave one last suck before letting Ash's cock slip out.

"Oh my God," Ash said, collapsing back on the bed. "Oh my God. If I had known you could suck cock like that, I'd have propositioned you the first day."

Lennox chuckled dryly. "Practice makes perfect?" He knew a lot of guys—a lot of people, *period*—didn't like hearing about their new partner's past partners, and what they'd done with them, but Ash hadn't seemed jealous at all of Marcus before.

In fact, he'd seemed more angry on Lennox's behalf.

He didn't seem jealous now, either, just smiling dopily down at Lennox.

"Give me a minute," Ash said breathlessly. "I'm . . . I'm still trying to figure out which end is up after that."

"I can wait," Lennox said, even though his cock was so hard it was practically hurting. There'd been plenty of times when there'd been only enough snatched time to get one of them off, when he'd been with Marcus. He was used to depriving himself, sometimes.

But now? He really didn't *want* to.

And Ash didn't seem to want to, either, especially as he leaned over and kissed Lennox thoroughly, apparently not at all squeamish about the come that had just been in his mouth.

Ash reached down and palmed him through Lennox's jeans, and he groaned.

"You want my mouth?" Ash asked, breaking the kiss. The look in his eyes was mischievous. Definitely a little dangerous. "Or I could fuck you again, if you give me a little bit of time."

Lennox did want that. But he had things to do today, and right now, if he didn't come soon, he was never going to be able to concentrate.

"Just your hand," Lennox said, pulling down his jeans and Ash didn't waste any time, kissing him hard and deep as his hand curled around him.

Lennox had known he wouldn't last—giving Ash that kind of pleasure had wound him up so much—but it still only took a couple of strokes of his capable fingers, and he was coming in hard, abrupt pulses into Ash's palm.

"Fuck," Lennox exhaled. "I needed that."

"Me too," Ash said, standing up and heading to the bathroom. Lennox could hear the water running in the sink, and then he came back out, carrying a damp washcloth. Lennox expected him to hand it over, but instead Ash kneeled down and cleaned his cock off himself with quick, easy movements.

"Thanks," Lennox said, and Ash glanced up. Their eyes met, and Lennox felt the weight of the moment, the emotions brewing between them.

There was a lot he wanted to say, but it was so soon. Lennox had been buying salads from him for six months, and Ash had been flirting with him for just about as long, but they'd only been dating for a few weeks.

That was too soon to say that he didn't know what his life would be like, if Ash wasn't in it. Too soon to say that he'd fallen so hard and fast, it felt like maybe he'd been falling from the first moment Ash had smiled at him and asked him what kind of dressing he wanted.

"What are you going to do today?" Ash asked, after he'd risen to his feet, breaking the moment.

Lennox told himself he was relieved he hadn't confessed everything, but he didn't really *feel* all that relieved. He almost felt . . . disappointed. Like a moment had passed by that they might not get again.

But that was ridiculous. He was going to find the person who was doing all these shitty things to Ash, and he was going to make sure that whoever it was, never touched Ash again.

And after that? He had to believe they had all the time in the world.

"I'm going to go talk to Ross again," Lennox said. "Seth dug up some records, and I want to talk to him about his drug use."

Ash looked surprised. "Ross used?"

"Ross could *still* be using," Lennox said. "And Aaron too, for that matter. He'll be my second stop."

"Well, let me know what you find out," Ash said, picking up his t-shirt from the floor and tugging it over his head. "I'll be here." He chuckled dryly. "Not that you expected differently."

"Two days," Lennox said, brushing a quick kiss on his lips as he finished getting dressed. "I'll get him in two days and you can go back to your real life, again."

Ash nodded, but Lennox wasn't stupid enough to miss the shadow in his eyes.

Not even the best orgasm in the world could take away how terrible it felt to be ripped away from everything you loved.

CHAPTER FOURTEEN

THE MOMENT THAT LENNOX walked out the door, Ash was afraid he was going to be terribly bored. And he was.

At first he dragged out his laptop. Went over the monthly budget and even checked on his yearly budget. Despite the disruptions at the lot, it was thrilling to see that he was not only ahead for the month, but significantly ahead of where he'd projected he'd be for the year.

His father might not think salad sold, but Ash had done it. He'd taken the one thing that his father had said would never work, and had made good money off it and had found a lot of job satisfaction, as well.

"Job satisfaction," Ash said out loud to himself, "that's something that Stephan Atkinson wouldn't even understand."

Ash's personal theory had always been because his father was miserable, he wanted to make everyone else around him miserable too. And he'd *succeeded*.

It was disgusting.

After the budget, Ash went on Facebook, then almost immediately remembered why he rarely went on Facebook, and closed the browser as well as the laptop.

Next he tried the TV, clicking on the power button, and watching as Lennox's sophisticated audio system powered up and the screen turned on, the volume set down low, to ESPN.

There was a feature on the Riptide, and one of their upcoming games. Ash raised the volume, wondering if they'd say anything about Tate's boyfriend, Chase, who was a wide receiver for the Riptide.

The reporter mentioned him briefly, rhapsodizing about what a great season he could have, and also mentioning his contract extension, which would keep him in Los Angeles for many years to come.

It was great news, and even though Ash was sure that Tate knew, he pulled out his phone and more out of boredom than anything else, sent Tate a text that read, **hear your boyfriend is now SUPER rich instead of just regular rich.**

It was almost eleven, which meant that the lunch rush was about to begin at the lot, so Ash wasn't surprised when Tate didn't reply right away.

Leaning back on the couch, Ash watched with little interest as the segment on ESPN changed to something about baseball. He couldn't remember the last time he'd been home during the day. He had a day off every week, of course, but he usually planned those ahead, structuring his time so that he could get all his errands and other miscellaneous plans done in the short time he had.

This break? Totally unplanned. And Ash was feeling every bit of the complete uselessness of it.

It would still be a few hours until Lucas stopped by with lunch, as Tony had promised, so Ash pushed himself off the couch and went to go explore Lennox's kitchen.

It was, like he'd told Tony, *small*. It had only two abbreviated counters, one broken up with the sink, and the other cut short by the fridge on one side and the stove on the other.

Everything was, as Ash expected, painfully clean. The stove looked like it had been barely ever used, and the stainless steel sink shone. He pulled open the fridge door, and unsurprisingly, the fridge was both neat and fairly bare. There were a handful of Greek yogurt containers, all arranged neatly by flavor. Condiments were lined up in one of the side bins, and looked like they'd never been opened.

There was a water pitcher and a container of orange juice, and a six-pack of beer, as well as one of blue Gatorade.

Ash made a note to tease Lennox later about considering *blue* a flavor.

The cupboards were equally bare. He had a few bananas in a wire basket on the counter, joined by half a dozen tangerines. Ash picked one up and peeled it, eating it over the sink so the juice wouldn't dirty any of the shining marble countertops.

Clearly, the complete disuse of the kitchen was why Lennox seemed to get a lot of meals at the food truck lot. But he had the basic supplies. A good knife set. A decent set of pans, hiding in a cupboard. A blender. A good quality hand mixer. Spatulas and tongs and even a whisk, hidden in a drawer, and a handful of spices in another drawer.

Ash pulled out his phone and dialed the number of his favorite produce supplier. Explaining the situation, he got Mark on the other end to agree readily to send over a selection of things that he wasn't going to be using anyway. Then Ash opened the Amazon app and ordered the rest of what he'd need delivered in the next two hours.

He didn't often use big box stores for delivery, but he had almost nothing to work with here.

On his days off, he liked to do some recipe experimentation, always looking forward to the day when he might not just serve salads. He didn't know when that day would come, but he liked to prep for it, anyway, and today might not be a typical day off, but he could still accomplish something.

He'd been playing with the idea of empanadas for awhile, first perfecting the dough, until it was soft yet crisp after coming out of the hot oven, and then he'd moved on to fillings.

He'd played around with the typical fillings at first, and then he'd started experimenting. A few weeks ago, he'd put the finishing touches on an Argentinean-themed empanada, complete with a garlicky, herby chimichurri dipping sauce.

Today, he was craving comfort food, so he dug a frozen chicken breast out of Lennox's sparse freezer, and letting it begin to thaw in the sink, grabbed the produce that Mark had dropped off.

He had Lennox's biggest pot on when the doorbell rang again. He was hoping it would be the Amazon delivery, because his filling was going to be done before he'd even begun the dough.

But when he checked the security camera outside the door, as instructed by Lennox before he'd left, Ash saw Lucas instead.

He unlocked the door and pulled it open. "Tony let you out early?" he wondered. He didn't think it was much past one—which was much earlier than he'd expected Lucas, considering how busy the lot had been lately.

"I wanted to check in on you," Lucas said as he followed Ash into the kitchen. "You seem . . . not terrible?"

Ash shot his friend a look. "How would you be if you found out that someone broke into your house *while you were sleeping* and ruined your kitchen?"

"Not very good," Lucas said, setting a plastic bag on the counter. "I brought you Sean and Gabe's Thai chicken crunch wrap. Thought you could use something to eat to break up the boredom, but . . ." He glanced around. "You're cooking."

"Not for me," Ash said, waving a hand. "I'm working on this new recipe."

"For your truck?"

Ash reached over and grabbed the wrap out of the bag. "No," he said. Then corrected himself. "Well, not really. It's not a salad."

Lucas raised an eyebrow. "You don't have to serve salad, forever, you know. Or you could, if you wanted to. Everyone loves your truck. It's always up to you."

Ash knew it. But he'd worked his ass off to establish a brand and an identity, and to change it now seemed foolish. He shrugged. "We'll see," he said, even though he knew he'd probably never put any of the empanada recipes on the menu. But then, why was he collecting them? To keep his hand in? To prove he could still be a damn cook?

He thought of his father, and the derogatory way he'd responded the one time they'd met after Ash had left, and Stephan had found out that his new food truck would only serve salad, with a limited number of protein options.

Ash had expanded over the years, but that was still the foundation of his menu.

Had he kept at it *because* of how his father looked down at it, or had he kept at it because he loved it? Ash was annoyed that he wasn't sure.

"Is this about your dad?" Lucas asked.

It was still weird that the rest of them knew the truth. Ash hadn't quite adjusted yet to the fact that his best friends knew the very worst part of him. The part of him that he couldn't ever change, no matter how much he wanted to.

"No," Ash said, not sure if he was lying or not. "He doesn't have anything to do with what I'm doing."

"Right," Lucas said, detouring to the fridge and pulling it open. Ash watched as his friend made a face. "How does Lennox *live*?"

"Sparsely, and much augmented by our delicious offerings," Ash said.

"I guess." Lucas sounded unimpressed. He pulled out one of the blue Gatorades.

"Not you, too," Ash said. "Blue is not a flavor."

Lucas grinned. "It is when it's delicious."

There was a knock on the door, and Ash glanced up. "I think that's my Amazon delivery," he said, "can you grab it?"

"Sure," Lucas said, and went to the front door, grabbing the box and closing the door with his hip. "Where do you want this?"

Ash waved to the end of the counter. "There is fine," he said. "I've got to get my dough made."

"You want some help?" Lucas asked.

For a second, Ash wanted to say yes. He was bored. He was lonely. He was still a little freaked out, his nerves still alight with the remembered shock and fear.

But Lucas had work. He couldn't sit here all day and babysit Ash; Ash didn't even *want* him to.

"No, I'm good, thanks," Ash said. "I know you've got shit to do."

"Yeah," Lucas said, picking up his Gatorade. "I left Tony manning the vegan truck. God only knows what he's going to do while I'm gone."

"Start serving meat? Sneak in some cheese somewhere?"

Lucas smiled, and there was over a year of love, life, frustration, and adoration in his eyes. Ash would have never imagined last summer that Tony and Lucas would end up being hashtag-couple goals.

Or that he would look at the bright, imperfectly perfect love shining in Lucas' eyes and think, *I want that, and I want that with Lennox.*

"He knows better," Lucas said. And he did, but this was Tony. You never quite knew what he'd do.

"Thanks for lunch, though," Ash said, gesturing to the wrap that he still hadn't touched yet. "And it was good to see a friendly face."

Lucas detoured around the counter and gave him a hard, quick hug. "I wouldn't be surprised if you see a lot more of them," he said.

Before Ash could ask what he meant, he'd already headed to the front door and it was closing behind him.

Ash shrugged and went to start his empanada dough.

It was still early enough when Lennox left the loft that instead of heading directly to the food truck lot, he detoured and went by Ross' apartment first.

Seth had sent over some old arrest records—all drug-based—from a couple of years back. He wanted to talk to Ross about them. Feel him out for an alibi for Ash's break-in, even though he and Seth had been here for hours last night.

Whoever had broken into Ash's house had done it *very* late or *very* early.

Almost like they'd somehow spotted Lennox and Seth, and waited until they'd given up on the stakeout.

Lennox approached the door to Ross' apartment, making a note of the exit down the hall to the stairs, and also the elevator, three doors down and behind him. He didn't really expect Ross to run, but it never hurt to be prepared.

He knocked on the door briskly, standing to the side of the peephole, just enough that his face would be obscured. There were noises in the apartment, almost like someone dropped something, and then Lennox heard footsteps as Ross approached the door.

A second later, it was opened, and Ross was framed in the crack. Lennox wasted no time shoving his steel-toed boot into the gap between the door and the doorframe. Ross hadn't been particularly reticent before, but Lennox was half-convinced he was guilty, and this conversation was going to end on *his* terms.

"You again," Ross said, not sounding particularly pleased to see him. His gaze dropped momentarily to Lennox's boot, wedged in the doorway, then back up. He frowned.

"Me again," Lennox said casually.

"What do you want?"

"Just wanted to talk," Lennox said. He gestured at the door. "You gonna let me in?"

"I don't have to," Ross said.

"No," Lennox said. "We can always talk right here, too. No sweat off my back."

"I don't have to talk to you *at all*," Ross said. He was still frowning, and there was a closed-off look in his eyes. Was he afraid? For himself? Lennox felt adrenaline begin to spike, like a shark scenting blood for the first time.

"No, but you should, because at least for now, it's me, and not the cops."

"Why would the cops even give a shit?" Ross wanted to know. "There's been some vandalism, and some flyers. Who cares."

"Not last night," Lennox said.

Ross' brows shot up. "What happened last night?"

Lennox leaned a bit harder into the door, pushing it open further. "Yeah, let's talk about what happened last night," he agreed. "Why don't you tell me where you were."

"Here," Ross said. "I was here." He frowned harder. "Which you *know* because I spotted you." He crossed his arms over his chest. "I didn't appreciate that, by the way. I haven't done anything wrong."

"You know about Ash. You know Ash's father. You tried to get Ash's father to hire you back, and he said no."

"What does that have to do with Ash?"

"I know Atkinson said that he wouldn't hire *you*, but that he'd hire Ash. Did that piss you off?"

"No?" Ross said. "I was pissed off at Atkinson. I . . . I don't have an issue with Ash. He's a good kid."

"What about the threats you made to Atkinson?"

"The threats?" Ross sounded genuinely confused. "I didn't . . ." Suddenly his brows shot up. "No, *no*."

"What is it?"

Ross let out a defeated sigh. "I think we should talk," he said, and he finally opened the door.

Lennox felt a thread of suspicion wind through him, despite Ross' easy acquiescence. "You do?"

"I know I look real fucking suspicious, because I tried to get that job," Ross said, leading him into his apartment. It was sparsely furnished, and it didn't look like he spent much time in it. He gestured to the couch, and Lennox sat, but still stayed alert. He wasn't convinced this was going to be an easy solution to any of their problems.

"It doesn't look good," Lennox agreed.

"But it's not me," Ross said, sitting opposite him on a club chair, upholstered in a wildly patterned fabric. He sighed. "I wasn't going to tell you this, but you said it's gotten worse . . . for a little bit I thought it wasn't him, because of the vandalism on all the trucks. But it sounds like something bad happened last night."

"Whoever is stalking Ash broke into his house and poured paint all over his fucking kitchen," Lennox said in a hard voice.

"What?" Ross looked genuinely shocked.

Lennox knew a lot about how to spot a lie. It seemed impossible, but he was pretty sure that Ross wasn't lying right now. His surprise hadn't been faked. He hadn't known what happened.

"That's why the police have gotten involved, though I still want to take care of this myself," Lennox said.

"I can understand that," Ross said. He was picking at the frayed threads of his cutoff jeans. "I . . . there's something you need to know. About Aaron."

Lennox leaned forward, excited, because he felt like he might finally be hearing the truth. "What about Aaron?"

"He's got a weird hang-up about Ash," Ross said. "I didn't want to say anything before, because I didn't think he could . . . and also because if it was him, he wasn't really hurting anyone."

"What about Alexis' truck?" Lennox asked.

"Alexis' truck?"

"Someone vandalized it with paint. He's probably going to have it re-covered with a new wrap. Is that nothing? And then the other night, someone did it to *all* the trucks. Including yours. That you own with Aaron."

"You don't get him," Ross said. "He wouldn't hesitate to fuck me or our truck over, because he hates Atkinson that much. And to an extent, Ash."

"Really?" Lennox had heard and seen situations before when personnel would deliberately hurt themselves or destroy something they owned, just to deflect suspicion. But he hadn't thought whoever was doing this would go that far.

"We haven't been getting along for awhile. I mean . . . for longer than that," Ross said with a heavy sigh. "He's a hard person to deal with. And well . . . I guess I am too, when it comes down to it. I get so focused. I want things to be perfect, I get lost in my own fucking head."

"And?"

"We fight sometimes. Sometimes Aaron does shit I don't like when my head's down. Like . . ." Ross threw him a suspicious look. "Don't tell Tony this, but Aaron's the one who stole his stupid fucking onion dip recipe. The one he's been worked up about forever."

Tony had described every part of the incident about the onion dip recipe and how it had related to his ex-employee, Jeremy, and how he had been convinced that Jeremy had been hired by one or both of the Basket owners to steal it.

Honestly, considering that Jeremy had gone back to Napa, and that it was a *recipe*, Lennox hadn't given the story much weight or consideration.

"Aaron doesn't like to work at shit," Ross continued. "He wants it handed to him, like a fucking gift. And that recipe is a perfect example. He wanted it, so he got that guy to take it."

"And you?"

"What about me?"

"You let him put it on the menu?"

"Well, it *was* until Tony wouldn't let us join the lot with it on our menu." Ross frowned. "But yeah, sometimes, it was just easier to . . . go along with Aaron's bullshit, instead of fighting it."

"So you think it's him," Lennox said. "You think it's Aaron."

Lennox ignored the pulse of guilt that he'd somehow overlooked Aaron. Focusing on the man in front of him instead. And it wasn't like Ross' hands were perfectly clean, but Lennox believed him when he said he didn't bear any grudges towards Ash.

Ross didn't say anything for a long time, just stared at the fraying hem of his shorts. "I don't want you to think I'm a shitty friend, or whatever," Ross said, "but yeah. I don't blame him for being pissed as hell at Atkinson. He *sucks*. But that's not Ash's fault."

"It's not," Lennox agreed. "Why do you think it's him? Besides how much he hates Atkinson?"

"When he found out that I'd asked Atkinson for my job back, he was furious." Ross looked regretful. "I shouldn't have told him; he did not take it well. Ranting and screaming. I really thought he might hit me, and I thought I could distract him by telling him what Atkinson had said about Ash. How he still thought he'd come crawling back, and how he'd never be able to hack it out on his own. Of course, he's wrong, but that's Atkinson for you. Totally fucking delusional."

"So you tried to deflect Aaron's anger with you onto Atkinson," Lennox said, tapping his fingers on his knee. "And it backfired."

Ross looked miserable. "I guess so," he said.

"Fuck," Lennox swore. He stood and began to pace in Ross' living room, which was pretty easy, because it was so empty. Just the couch, the chair, and a bare-bones coffee table that looked like it was the cheapest kind from IKEA. Not the kind of living arrangement he'd have expected to see from a guy who'd been lauded as the next big thing in the Los Angeles culinary community. Who had a bestselling food truck.

He turned towards Ross again. "It's not doing very well, is it?"

"What? Basket?" Ross hesitated. "Yes and no."

"You really wanted to join Food Truck Warriors," Lennox pointed out.

"I thought Aaron might stop doing stupid shit if we had more structure," Ross confessed. "And yeah, it kinda pissed me off that Tony thought he was such hot shit." He hesitated. "I mean, he kinda *is*, the place is packed. And that was even worse."

At first, Lennox hadn't known what to make of Tony either. He'd been cocky and unbearably sure of his own charm. Lennox, who was definitely not that comfortable in his own skin, hadn't handled Tony well, at first. But then as he'd come to the food truck lot more often, he'd begun to see another side of Tony. The caring side. The one who'd created a safe place for his friends—friends who'd rapidly become more like *family*. And Lennox knew now that he'd do anything to ensure that safety wasn't compromised. Tony might have originated the concept, but Lennox knew, the more he'd experienced it, the more committed he was to it.

"So you convinced Tony's brother-in-law to let you in," Lennox said. "What did Aaron think of that?"

Ross smiled wryly. "He liked the idea. He said that anything that was good enough for an Atkinson was good enough for him. I should've known then. But I'd gotten good at ignoring Aaron. He was so fucking crazy, it was easier."

"It's not your fault," Lennox said, surprising himself. "We'll get him now."

"What's going to happen to him?"

"I'm going to go talk to him," Lennox said. "And I'm sure the police are also going to want to have a chat."

"And Tony will want his own pound of flesh," Ross said with resignation. "And I don't blame him . . . if I'd known . . . I thought it was just stupid pranks and Aaron would get over it."

"He doesn't seem like he will," Lennox said.

"No," Ross agreed. "The drugs . . . well, the drugs probably aren't helping."

"He's still using?" Lennox was surprised.

"He wasn't, for a long time. We both quit when we started Basket, it was something we agreed on. I didn't . . . I didn't want to be that kind of person. And I wanted Basket to be a success. A big middle finger to Atkinson. But a few months back, I think Aaron started again. He tried to hide it from me."

"That's why you went back to ask Atkinson for your old job," Lennox guessed.

Suddenly, Ross' dark eyes looked very tired. "Yes."

Everything had fallen into place.

Lennox was pretty damn pleased. He told Ross to stay in his apartment, and that he'd call him after he talked to Aaron, who was already at the food truck, based on a text he'd sent Ross about an hour earlier.

He called Seth, and Seth offered to meet him down at the lot.

"No," Lennox said as he took the stairs down to the ground floor. "No, I've got this."

"Are you sure?" Seth wondered. "I could at least be there in a supervisory aspect. Keep you from kicking the guy's ass."

Lennox chuckled. "Funny that you think you could stop me if I decided to teach him a lesson."

"Hey, I can still take you," Seth argued. Lennox could hear his friend's smile over the phone.

"One in five, old man," Lennox teased. "I'll let you know when it's done. Gonna call the LAPD after. Want to talk to him on my own first."

"You don't think he's gonna run?"

"He's a fucked-up asshole," Lennox said, "but no. He's not that fucking smart."

"If you're sure," Seth said, and Lennox knew he thought he was being cocky. Well, he *was* being cocky. He'd figured out how to nail this dick, in *less* than half the remaining time he had agreed on with Ash.

When he reached the lot, Lennox was relieved to see that there weren't many people milling around yet. Even if he was convinced that Aaron wasn't going to run or fight, he still had a feeling that it wasn't going to be the quietest confrontation he'd ever had.

The back door of the Basket truck was wide open, music filtering out of the open space. Lennox put a hand on his weapon, not pulling it out of its holster, but reminding himself that it was there, if in some extreme situation he was forced to use it.

He rapped sharply on the side of the truck, to the right of the open doorway. After a moment, the music turned down and Aaron poked his head out.

"What is it?" he asked. "I'm busy."

Busy tormenting Ash.

"Need to talk," Lennox said.

"I said I was busy," Aaron retorted, but with an easy, carefree grin on his face. Like he knew what Lennox was about, and knew he couldn't prove it.

Lennox felt his resolve harden. He was going to take care of this asshole, once and for all. Even his smile didn't sit right on his face, now that Lennox really *looked*. How had he missed that there was something fundamentally *off* about this guy.

Ross had been weird and standoffish, and he hadn't been a bad suspect.

"I could always go get Tony, suggest he have you drug tested," Lennox said, equally casually, even though he was fairly certain that Tony didn't have that kind of power. Technically, he wasn't Aaron's employer. He was Aaron's landlord.

Aaron stared at him, the smile melting right off his face like ice cream on a boiling hot day. "What the fuck," he said.

Lennox had told Ross that he wouldn't bring him into it. He figured things were probably going to be rough enough as it was; with Ross' friend and business partner going more than a little nuts.

There was no saying how long Aaron would stay in custody, or if he'd even go to jail at all. The last thing Ross needed was his partner coming for him.

Especially if it was anything like the way Aaron had come for Ash.

"I just want to talk," Lennox reiterated. "Let me come in."

"No." Aaron's voice grew harsh. "No way. You've got no fucking proof."

He didn't, but if he got into the truck, and pushed the right buttons, he thought he might. Might even do a quick surreptitious search and confirm that Aaron was keeping the drugs in there, hidden from Ross.

"Proof of what? I just said I wanted to talk."

Aaron was smart though. Lennox had known it, from the way he'd dodged identification on the security cameras. From the methodical way he'd gone about fucking with Ash's head. He just smiled again, fake and making no pretense about it, as he leaned a hip against the side of the doorway.

"But I don't want to talk to you."

The hard, inexorable edge of Aaron's voice was the only clue in advance of what he was going to do.

With a flash, Lennox saw the frying pan swooping through the air at the last second, and he ducked instinctively, just enough that it glanced off his head. The metal lip caught his ear and for a split second everything went still, the blow ringing in his brain, disorienting him.

It was just enough, despite Lennox's exceptional reflexes, for Aaron to take off, jumping down the stairs, elbowing Lennox hard in the ribs. It took him a second too long to shake off the searing pain in his head and his side, but then he straightened and took off after Aaron, who was running full out, dodging in between people, and then the trucks.

Lennox thought he saw Tony crossing across the lot, mouth dropped as he saw Aaron running and Lennox chasing after him, but he wasn't going to stop to explain. Especially not that he'd totally misjudged how fucking crazy Aaron was.

And that he'd apparently misjudged how fucking *fast* Aaron was. He was already in the street, running down the sidewalk, shoving people out of the way.

Lennox still worked hard to stay fit and ready. He jogged multiple times a week. Sparred religiously with Seth and some other ex-military buddies. Lifted weights, because that was what he'd always done.

But Aaron, propelled by fear and likely chemicals too, was fast as fuck, and instead of closing the distance as they ran down the sidewalk parallel to the food truck lot, it felt like Aaron was pulling away.

Lennox dug down deep and pushed aside the pain still radiating from his head, and the stiffness of his knee, and as they rounded a corner, felt like he was finally beginning to gain on him.

But then Aaron ran by a sidewalk cafe where they'd just put out the wrought iron tables and chairs for the day, and he picked up a chair and literally fucking *threw* it at Lennox.

He dodged it, because at least by now he'd figured out that Aaron was insane, and he'd had just enough time to register that was his move when he leaned down to pick up the chair, but it still slowed him down just a fraction.

Just enough for Aaron to make up the distance and pull a little further ahead.

Lennox mentally gnashed his teeth in frustration and decided that maybe if he couldn't run faster than this asshole, at least he'd be able to out-maneuver him. There was no way he could keep going like this longer than a couple of minutes, at *most*.

But it turned out that didn't matter, because suddenly, Aaron ducked down an alley, and by the time, a few important seconds later, Lennox ducked in, he was gone, like he'd just fucking evaporated. There was a high gate on the other side of the alley, and it was locked. Lennox almost climbed it, but there was no sign that Aaron had done it.

No matter how fast he was, Lennox wasn't convinced he could've climbed it. When he rattled it, it didn't move, a serious lock that looked like it hadn't been touched holding it closed.

Lennox stopped, abruptly, panting and swearing under his breath. He couldn't have lost him. He'd been *elite*, one of the best SEALs on his team, one of the best in the whole fucking Navy.

And this asshole had just evaded him.

There were no doors to the buildings on either side.

There was no explanation except that he *must* have gone over the fence, but by now, Lennox realized, he would be long gone.

Aaron was in the wind.

CHAPTER FIFTEEN

Lennox called Seth, who called his detective friend, and after conferencing in with Ash, they put out an APB for Aaron Bolton. The police would send a car to his apartment, and to his friends and family. Lennox also texted Ross, warning him, who said that he'd stay in his apartment today, and would let them know if he heard anything about Aaron's whereabouts. Also texted Lennox a list of places that he thought Aaron could hide.

Finally, when it was over, there was nothing to do but give up and go back home.

And face Ash.

Ash had seemed surprised on the phone that the culprit was Aaron, but he'd not offered any other thoughts when he'd discovered that Lennox had lost him.

Probably because Seth and his detective friend had been on the line at the time, and Ash wasn't going to expose their personal relationship that way.

But it didn't matter that he hadn't said a word, Lennox could feel the weight of his guilt bearing down on him.

He'd promised Ash that he would keep him safe, and instead of keeping his promise, he'd let Aaron slip through his fingers.

Trudging up the stairs, ignoring the twinge of his knee, Lennox was surprised to find three boxes sitting right by his doorway.

From the first glance, they looked like standard Amazon boxes, but he hadn't ordered anything.

He'd underestimated Aaron once before, and he wasn't going to do it again. Not with Ash's safety at risk.

Leaning down, Lennox examined the boxes carefully, noting the labels, and that every one of them was addressed to Ash Powell. No powdery substances on the cardboard, no evidence that they were anything other than what they seemed—packages full of stuff Ash had ordered and had delivered.

He picked them up, surprised at the weight, and typed in his door code, which disarmed the security system. When he pushed the door open with his hip, he was immediately struck by the comforting scent of . . . *chicken pot pie?* Yeah, that was definitely it. He could smell the pastry, and the distinctive chicken smell.

"Oh hey," Ash said, not a trace of anger or resentment in his voice.

In fact, Lennox would've sworn that he was happy to see him.

Not exactly the reaction he'd anticipated.

"Hey," Lennox said, setting the boxes down on the coffee table. "You order these?"

"Oh, did they come? They didn't ring the bell when they dropped them off." Ash was over by the boxes in a flash, brushing a quick, brief kiss across Lennox's cheek before leaning down to rip them open with his bare hands.

"Wait," Lennox exclaimed before he could get the first one opened. "That might . . . let me do it."

Ash shot him a look that said very clearly, *you're being ridiculous*, and maybe he was, a little, but then he hadn't expected Aaron to run either. Never had expected him to hit him with the frying pan. He'd grown soft after he'd left the Navy, and he didn't need any other proof than the fact that the side of his head was bandaged, because it wouldn't stop bleeding, and he felt a hitch in his side every time he took a breath.

Aaron had been dangerous, and he'd never even seen it coming.

He wasn't going to let anything else happen.

Pulling out his knife, he carefully cut the tape, while Ash watched, huffing every few seconds. When the flaps of the box opened, there was a set of metal mixing bowls, a whisk, and two small sheet pans with curled metal sides.

"You're welcome," Ash said, shooting another, far fonder look.

"For?" Lennox was still feeling the rush of relief that Aaron hadn't planted a bomb in front of his building. Not that he'd ever in a thousand years imagined that he was capable of that kind of violence or destruction—but Lennox wasn't taking any more chances.

"Stocking your kitchen," Ash said as he pulled the bowls and whisk out of the box. "Cooking here is practically impossible."

Lennox laughed, the warmth flooding him suddenly and unexpectedly. "I can imagine. As you probably discovered, I don't cook here much."

"No," Ash said, juggling the pans with his other hand, heading into the kitchen. He set everything in the sink with a metallic clatter and flicked on the faucet. "So, he ran away, eh?"

There was still no accusation in the statement.

"Yes." Lennox felt not only guilt swamp him but humiliation, too. He was *good*. He'd been *great*. And that dick had totally gotten the jump on him.

When Lennox approached, Ash reached up with one wet soapy hand and grazed the bandage. "He hit you?" Ash said.

"With a frying pan," Lennox said, making a face. "We were talking in the doorway of his food truck, and he was hiding it. Whipped it out and I only saw it at the last second." Made a frustrated noise. "Barely ducked in time."

"Doesn't really look like you did."

"It just grazed me," Lennox said. "But it was just enough to buy him a few seconds."

"It's not your fault." Ash glanced over at him, affection and worry warring in his gaze. "You figured out that it wasn't Ross after all."

"After Ross told me it wasn't, and gave me a few good reasons why it had to be his partner," Lennox explained.

"I never imagined it could be either of them," Ash said, rinsing a bowl. "But I really never imagined that it could be Aaron. He was . . . not nice precisely, because he was always so disgustingly cocky, but he didn't seem crazy enough to do all this stuff."

"He's on drugs," Lennox said shortly. The last thing he wanted was for Ash to blame himself for not seeing it earlier.

"Again?"

"Again," Lennox confirmed. When the police had arrived at the food truck lot, they'd searched Ross and Aaron's truck, and found the pills. Lots of different kinds of uppers. The kinds, Ross had confirmed, that they had used before. The kinds that Stephan Atkinson had subtly suggested they try, so many years ago, to help keep up with the insane workload he'd forced on them.

Lennox still didn't know if he was going to tell Ash that part.

Ash shook his head. "They both should've known better."

"Ross did. He got clean. They both got clean for awhile, but then Aaron started taking again, and well, you know how that turned out."

"Yeah, apparently he hates me now," Ash said, and there was the barest edge of bitterness there. "Hates my father enough that he can't even contain it to him."

Lennox wrapped an arm around Ash's waist and tugged him closer. "It's not you," he said, pressing his lips into Ash's hair. "It's never been you."

"I know," Ash said, his voice muffled. "Except it *feels* like it might be."

"I talked to him for only a little bit before he fucking hit me, and I'm telling you, the guy's crazy," Lennox said. "It's *not* you."

Ash pulled back, a smile back on his face. "You got any leads on him?"

"There's a few," Lennox allowed. "Ross was really helpful, in the end."

"He's a good guy. Weird, but his heart's in the right place," Ash said, turning back towards the sink. He rinsed the last bowl and set it out on a towel to drip dry. A *bathroom* towel. Lennox did a double take.

"Yes," Ash said, grinning brightly now, "you are *poorly* stocked. No kitchen towels! I had to make do."

"Feel free to use whatever you want, but . . ." Lennox hesitated, looking around at the organized chaos in his kitchen. He heard the oven click and realized that this was probably the first time it had ever been used.

"Yes," Ash said, following his gaze, "I am finally using your oven. How long have you been living here? I had to take the sticker inside off."

Lennox blushed. "A year? Two?"

Ash *tsked*.

"What are you cooking anyway?" Lennox wondered. His stomach growled again. He'd meant to stop to grab something to eat at lunch, but then he'd ended up meeting the cops at Aaron's apartment, which, *naturally*, had been empty.

"Empanadas," Ash said absently, turning towards the oven. "This batch is chicken pot pie. I keep trying to get it right."

"*This* batch?" Lennox noticed the plastic storage containers that he'd only ever used for re-housing his takeout leftovers were stacked up in the corner, and full.

"Here," Ash said, gesturing to the stack. "Try one. Try as many as you like."

"I think I will," Lennox said, popping open a lid and the smell of freshly baked dough and chicken wafting towards his nose. Making his stomach growl again. "I missed lunch."

"Lucas stopped by with a wrap," Ash said.

"Did you actually eat it?"

Ash shot him a look. "*Yes,*" he said. "I hope the grocery delivery gets here sooner rather than later. Tony said this is the one his brother and his husband use, and it's the most reliable."

"You're getting a grocery delivery?" Lennox knew his kitchen wasn't exactly stocked—either with tools and supplies *or* food—but what else could Ash need? They had enough empanadas to feed an army, already.

"Yeah, I want to try this cheesesteak idea," Ash said with a lopsided smile. "And you didn't have any steak in your freezer. Besides, I thought if I didn't restock what I'd taken, you'd probably starve."

Lennox demolished the empanada in two bites, moaning a little as the creamy chicken filling hit his tongue, and took another one. "We're hardly going to starve," he said.

"Lucas got me thinking," Ash said. "What if I've only stuck to salads because it's a big middle finger to my father?"

"Are they?"

Ash pursed his lips. "I'm not sure," he said, "but it pissed me off. I wasn't mad at Lucas, but at *me*. And I thought, there's plenty of things I can make. I don't have to always stick to salad."

"You can do whatever you set your mind to," Lennox said, and meant it.

"I think . . . I think you might be right."

Lennox grabbed a third empanada, and leaned in to brush a kiss across Ash's lips. "These are delicious and I *know* I'm right. But feel free to keep cooking. It's not going to go to waste."

"No?"

"No," Lennox said. "I knew you couldn't go out tonight, even though the rest of your friends are, so I invited them here."

Ash's eyes went wide. "You invited . . ."

"Yes," Lennox said. "I'm gonna go grab a quick shower."

"Tony and Lucas? And Tate? And Gabe? And Sean?"

"Everyone," Lennox said. "I even invited Ross, I hope that doesn't bother you."

"It . . . it doesn't," Ash said, still looking a bit shell-shocked. "*Everyone?*"

Lennox raised an eyebrow. "Is that alright?"

"Yes," Ash said. Sounding flustered. "I just didn't expect . . . you're not really the party-hosting type?"

"I can pick up beer and some bottles of wine just as well as anyone else," Lennox said, even though he'd already asked Seth to do it. "And there's plenty of food."

"That's true," Ash said wryly.

Lennox detoured back through the kitchen to give Ash a long, deep kiss. A reassuring kiss. He didn't want to say, *we're hosting this party together*, but he was pretty sure it was unspoken between them. *And* to grab another empanada.

"These are really damn good," Lennox said after he'd stuffed it in his mouth.

Ash rolled his eyes. "Those are the rejects."

"Damn good rejects, then," Lennox said, finally heading towards the bathroom.

The last thing Ash had expected Lennox to announce when he got home was that they were hosting all his friends and co-workers at the loft *that night*.

He *had* expected Lennox to come home and beat himself up about losing Aaron, right when he'd discovered that he was the asshole who'd broken into his house.

Who'd been baiting him with the knowledge that Ash was Stephan Atkinson's son.

Ash still couldn't quite believe that the guy who he'd looked up to for so many years, the one he'd always considered at least a friendly acquaintance, had hated him all this time.

It hurt more than Ash had expected it to.

"You okay?" Ash looked up from piling empanadas onto a plate to see Sean standing there, holding a beer in one hand.

He hadn't even heard anyone come in, but along with Sean, Gabriel and Ren had also arrived. Gabe and Ren were over by where Lennox had set up the temporary bar, chatting with him and Seth. Clearly, he'd been pretty lost in his own head.

Ash took a deep breath, trying to clear out the negative thoughts. The guilty thoughts, the self-recriminating thoughts, even the thoughts that weren't unfair in the least—Aaron *did* suck, big-time, and Ash wasn't going to argue with that one, even though he already knew he shouldn't be dwelling on that.

"I'm fine," he said.

Sean grinned, and tipped his beer in Ash's direction. "That's what Gabe likes to say when he's annoyed with me but doesn't want to argue about it."

"Well, I'm not annoyed at *you*," Ash said. "At least pretty sure I'm not."

"Nobody would blame you for being really fucking pissed," Sean said.

Ash knew it. He had a lot of reasons to be justifiably angry.

But he'd already come to the conclusion that he didn't want to focus on it.

It seemed silly to do that when he had so many great things in his life: his friends, his business, and now Lennox. He had everything he'd ever wanted, back when he'd been a miserable fif-teen-year-old, stuck under his father's brutal, unrelenting thumb.

"But I don't want to be," Ash said. "Not tonight. So tell me, was everyone surprised to be smack-dab in the center of a chase and then a manhunt?"

"Surprised and excited," Sean said, rolling his eyes. "You'd think that it was the most epic thing that ever happened at the lot. I heard someone was even patrolling with a rolling pin."

From the way Sean glanced over at his boyfriend, his look full of fond exasperation, Ash knew who'd been guilty of doing that.

"Lennox said everyone's safe," Ash said, snapping the empty container shut. "That he doesn't think Aaron will come back to the lot."

Lennox opened and closed the front door, and Ross was standing there, an uncertain expression on his face, like he wasn't sure he belonged there.

Ash hadn't been a hundred percent sure about Lennox's idea to invite Ross; after all, he'd known *something* before today, and not only had he kept his mouth shut, he hadn't exactly been all that nice to anyone.

But seeing him now? And realizing that, with Aaron's betrayal, not only was his future at the food truck lot now up in the air, his whole business had potentially been destroyed? Ash felt a wave of sympathy for the guy.

He picked up the plate of empanadas and went over to where Ross was standing with Lennox. Lennox, bless his heart, was doing his best to make small talk, but Ash felt a warm swell of affection as he realized that the two worst people at chatter were actually *trying* to chat.

"Hey," Ash said, "it's great to see you, Ross. How you hanging in there?"

Ross gaped at him. Probably not expecting that Ash would be happy to see him at all.

But Ash already knew that he wasn't going to let bitterness consume him.

You get to make the choice, and you're going to choose something else, he thought. *You're not going to be your father. You're Ash, not Oliver. And you haven't been, not for a very long time.*

Ross still hadn't said a word, so Ash kept going. "I hope you can still open tomorrow," he said. "I would hate for our collaboration dish to not see the light of day, because it's fucking delicious." He lifted the plate he was holding. "Empanada?"

Ross shot him a look full of disbelief, but picked one of the crispy, doughy bundles from the plate. He took a bite, chewed, and swallowed. "Chicken pot pie?" he asked, still sounding full of doubt. No doubt he'd been sure that even though Lennox had invited him, he wouldn't really be welcome.

"Yep," Ash said. "Cures all ills, doesn't it?"

"I don't suppose . . ." Ross took a deep breath. "You know, Basket's known for its comfort food, I don't suppose . . ."

"I'll give you the recipe," Ash said.

God forbid if Tony ever found out, but Ash felt it was time to turn the other cheek. And it wasn't like he was going to use the recipe anyway. He sold *salad.*

"Wow, okay, well, I really didn't expect you to say that."

"I know," Ash said.

Lennox reached over, and tucked his arm around Ash's waist. "Do you want a beer?" he asked.

"Sure," Ash said. "And make sure to get one for Ross too." He smiled. "He looks thirsty."

"He *is* thirsty," Ross inserted, his mouth turning up in what Ash thought might actually be a smile. "Thanks." He hesitated. "And yes, I want to open tomorrow, though . . ."

His eyes widened as a knock sounded on the door and then it pushed open to reveal Tony and Lucas.

"Well, I *did*," Ross said, under his breath, "but I guess it depends on how pissed Tony is."

Ash patted him on the shoulder. "It doesn't matter how pissed Tony is," he said. "*I'm* not pissed, and I'm the only one who gets to be pissed here."

Ross did not look quite as convinced as Ash felt, but Ash knew that he could work Tony around to the conclusion that it was better to embrace Ross than reject him.

"Hey," Tony said, coming up towards them, Lucas trailing half a step behind. He looked over at Lennox first. "Nice of you to host tonight, since Ash is stuck here."

"Of course," Lennox said. "I'm grabbing some beers. You two want one?"

Tony nodded, and then turned all his attention to Ross.

Ash felt the weight of the moment, and the way everyone held their breath, not sure what Tony would do or say. He loved Tony, considered the guy to be one of his best friends, but Tony could be petty and difficult and hold a grudge forever.

He'd never wanted Ross and Aaron to move to the lot, and when he'd had his hand forced, Ash had been sure that he'd never really forgive them. Now this?

But the one thing he'd forgotten about Tony was that he never quite did what you might expect him to do.

Tony smiled, and clapped Ross on the back. "I sure hope you're still able to open tomorrow," he said. "Do you need any help?"

Ross looked just about as shell-shocked as Ash—and the rest of the friends in their group—looked. Even Lucas looked astonished. The person closest to Tony hadn't even anticipated his reaction.

"Uh, I have a friend I can call," Ross said. "But thanks. I'll let you know if I need any. I know . . ." He took a deep breath. "I know you're still covering Ash's truck."

"Yes," Tony said, "but we've got resources. And we can use them. You're part of us now."

Ash grinned. "For better or worse, Stanton," he said, tipping his bottle against Ross'.

The relief in Ross' expression melted into gratitude. "I'm thinking it's the *better* half," he said.

"I mixed up a big batch of the vinaigrette," Ash said. "Remind me before you leave to grab it. And Harmony should have made all the pickled veggies that you should need."

"Yeah, she dropped some off this afternoon," Ross said. "Honestly . . ." He looked awkward again. "That's why I came. I wasn't sure if you'd still wanted her to, and I wanted to check with you myself."

"I wanted her to," Ash said confidently. "Tomorrow's a big day for the lot. We can't be slacking."

"Are you coming back tomorrow?" Tony asked, even though he probably should have known the truth.

Ash already knew the truth, even though he and Lennox had yet to discuss it.

"No," Ash said. "Not yet." He glanced over at Lennox, who had a bit of surprise of his own in his eyes, like he'd expected to have to fight Ash on this. "Not with Aaron still missing."

"He won't be for long," Lennox said, his voice hard and determined.

"Yeah, if anyone's capable of finding that asshole, it's you," Tony said.

"Thanks," Lennox said shortly.

Ash snuggled further into his side, wishing he could take away some of his boyfriend's guilt. It wasn't his fault he'd lost Aaron.

Aaron was not only crazy, he was on all kinds of drugs that made him even crazier. And faster, too, if what Lennox had said was to be believed—and Ash did. He'd never believed in or trust-ed anyone as much as he did Lennox.

He would have been scared, of feeling so much, so fast, but it wasn't really all that fast, was it?

They'd been flirting for months. Ash had known he'd wanted him forever. And he knew, more certain of anything he'd ever been in his life, that the feelings he was experiencing were mutual.

It was just before midnight when the final person left—Tony, more than a little drunk, with his arm around Ross.

Lennox had hoped that when he'd invited the guy, things would work out, but then he also acknowledged he wasn't always a good judge of these things. Interpersonal relationships often tended to escape him. Hadn't he misjudged Marcus so complete-ly?

But he was happy that this time, he'd been right.

Ross had needed friends, and Tony had been more than ready to forgive.

"You did good," Ash said, coming up behind him, and wrap-ping his arms around him.

"Really?" Lennox asked, feeling pleased at Ash's approval.

"Yeah," Ash said, tugging Lennox around to face him. He lifted up on his tiptoes and pressed a quick, hot kiss to Lennox's mouth.

But Lennox had been dying to kiss him all fucking day, and that wasn't enough.

He leaned down and pulled Ash in closer, enjoying the feeling of his guy in his arms again, after the shitty-ass day he'd had. Tipping Ash's head back with his fingers, he kissed him again. Thoroughly this time, and long enough that he could feel his desire, always barely leashed, beginning to overcome its bonds.

Ash groaned into his mouth, his hands slipping across his shoulders, his back, his neck, then dropping down to his chest, curling into his pectoral muscles.

"I thought they'd never leave," Ash confessed softly when the kiss finally ended.

"Me too," Lennox confessed, even though he'd been the one who invited them. And he'd do it again, because the smile on Ash's face, more hesitant earlier in the evening and growing brighter as he was surrounded by his friends, had absolutely been worth it.

But now they were all gone, and he could finally show Ash just how much he cared about him.

That smile, the one he loved more than any other, was back on Ash's face now.

"I was just thinking," Ash said, "that this is the way it could be."

"Me having to protect you from crazed stalkers?" Lennox said, raising an eyebrow. It would be good for his blood pressure if Ash was never in danger ever again.

"No," Ash said, shaking his head. There was a hint of mischief in his eyes, but more than that, his expression was unbelievably tender.

Lennox couldn't quite believe that he could be so lucky Ash meant that look for him, but there was nobody else here, and they were pressed together, like they couldn't bear to let go of each other.

Instead of answering, Ash kissed him again, both fiercer and softer than their last kiss. Lennox felt his cock growing harder, and wondered if he could maneuver Ash to the couch. It was the closest horizontal surface and he wanted—no, *needed*—Ash right now. Truthfully, he'd been burning up for hours now, and Ash's lips, always perfect, felt so goddamned amazing on his own that he wasn't sure he could wait any longer.

But then Ash pulled back, the most gorgeous flush on his cheeks. "I meant that it could be this way with us, with my friends, all the time," he said.

They had not really discussed the future. Lennox had been wondering for a few days now if he should bring it up, but there'd been a small, worrisome concern, buried deeply, that if he asked, Ash would sound just like Marcus when he'd told Lennox that they could keep fooling around if he wanted to.

Six years, and that was all it had meant to Marcus: a convenient way to get off.

He couldn't bear it if that was all Ash wanted.

"Do you want that?" Lennox asked, hearing that deep, inner fear reflected in his voice. Hoped that Ash didn't hear it, too.

"Yes," Ash said. "Yes. More than anything. I . . ." He licked his lips. Looked just about as nervous as Lennox felt. "I love you, you know. I know it's soon but . . ."

"It's not too soon," Lennox said, feeling his heart soaring. Ash wasn't ever going to tell him they were just fooling around. He *loved* him. And he . . . well, it was undeniable that he was in love with Ash. "I'm . . . I . . ."

"It's alright," Ash said, smiling, "I know."

He pressed his mouth against Lennox's before he could respond, could finish his sentence and tell him the truth—that he loved him, that he'd saved him from a lifetime of bitter regret.

It just about killed him, but Lennox pulled back an inch. He was *this* close to devouring Ash completely, from showing him every single way that he adored him, but Ash *needed* to know how he felt, *first*.

"You don't have to . . ." Ash said, before Lennox could marshal all his thoughts.

"Yes," Lennox said firmly, pressing a fingertip to Ash's lips, already slightly swollen from kissing his own. "Yes, I do. Love you, that is. I . . . I couldn't believe that I could be good for anyone, not again, but you made me believe again."

Ash reached up, and cupped his cheek. "Believe in?"

"So many things. You, love, the happily ever after thing that I was convinced was total bullshit," Lennox said with a wry chuckle. "But it's not bullshit. Not with you."

"Never with me," Ash said steadily.

"God, I love you," Lennox said, and swore he heard, deep down, that last little part of Marcus die completely.

He'd never let him back in. Not now. Not when there was so much happiness in his life to focus on instead.

"Come on," Ash said, reaching down and tangling their fingers together. "Let's go to bed."

Lennox wanted nothing more. Definitely nothing less. He let Ash tug him through the living room, and into the bedroom. Ash didn't flip the light on, just pushed Lennox onto the bed, and climbed on top of him. Lennox couldn't help his groan as Ash fitted their hips together and began to thrust slowly.

"You want that?" Ash asked teasingly, his voice disembodied, as the light from the kitchen was barely visible, all the way in here.

He'd thought about it. There was a certain kind of mood he could get into where he wanted nothing more than to be fucked into oblivion, but he didn't want that tonight.

Tonight? He wanted to show Ash just how precious, how miraculous, he was.

Tensing his muscles, he reached up, fingers digging into Ash's hips, and flipped him over. Ash let out a little surprised gasp but clearly was into it, because he was already straining against his body, pressing up, his hands scrabbling to pull off Lennox's t-shirt.

"God," Ash said, mumbling into his bare shoulder when he finally got the shirt off, "I guess you don't. I guess . . ." He gasped as Lennox slid a hand between them, palming at his hard cock, pushing up into the pressure of his palm. "I guess you want to fuck me, huh?"

"It would be a privilege," Lennox said, and meant it.

Ash's teeth dug a bit into the ridge of shoulder muscle he was kissing, and Lennox couldn't help the shudder that went through him.

"Like that, huh?" Ash asked, his nimble fingers already tracing lines down Lennox's chest, heading down to the fly of his jeans.

"I love it." Lennox paused, still experiencing disbelief that he could say those words and that Ash would look so lovestruck by them. "I love you."

Ash's smile brought light to the gloom of the room. "God, I love you, too." He grinned wildly. "Let's get naked."

Lennox had never heard a better idea in his whole fucking life. He slid off Ash, and made quick work of his jeans, and then his boxers, shoving them off as fast as he could. Ash was doing the same, and when they turned back to each other, it felt like every nerve in Lennox's body was electrified by the feel of them together, skin to skin.

"Get on the bed," Lennox said, before Ash could distract him any further with kissing or touching. He had a goal, and goddamn it, he was going to achieve it, even though every time Ash even trailed a finger across his body, it felt like he was going to go to his knees and just *beg* for any little scrap, any little crumb.

But tonight, there would be more than scraps, and way more than crumbs.

For once, Ash did what he was told, climbing up and giving Lennox a heart-stopping view of his backside, teasingly glancing behind to make sure Lennox hadn't missed it.

He hadn't, and his cock was hard as a rock as a result.

Grabbing some supplies from the drawer by the bed, Lennox then knelt next to Ash, trailing his lips down his spine. He had the most beautiful back, supple and graceful, with the kind of line that made Lennox appreciate beauty in a way that he wasn't sure he had before.

Ash moaned into the comforter, the sound of his voice growing louder as Lennox cupped his hip with one hand and used the other to press a thumb, damp with lube, into his waiting hole.

"God, you don't know how long," Ash murmured in broken words. "So fucking long."

Lennox got it. He'd wanted Ash too, practically from the first moment he'd ever seen him.

There was a reason he'd been binge-eating salad for months.

But he was also glad, in a way, that they hadn't acted on their attraction right away, and that they'd waited.

Because now? Now it wasn't just really great sex, it was *love*.

"More, more," Ash begged as Lennox rotated his thumb, marveling at how hot and tight he was inside. He would give him whatever he asked for, especially when he felt like *that*.

Lennox slid in another finger alongside his thumb, feeling Ash push back, desperate for more.

"Can't wait til you're squeezing my cock like this," Lennox ground out, his voice guttural. He swore he'd never been so hard in his whole life—except maybe when Ash had fucked *him*.

He loved that he could have that, could trust Ash completely with desires that others had never quite understood, and that he could have Ash horny and pliant underneath his hands.

"Want you bad," Ash panted as Lennox slid his fingers in and out, stretching him out just enough.

He wanted Ash to feel no pain when he was inside, only pleasure.

When he was finally satisfied, he grabbed the condoms and slid one on, climbing onto the bed behind Ash, blanketing his body with his much larger one. Gripping his hips, he began to press inside of him, his heart beating so fast, so hard, he could feel it in his cock.

Ash groaned, arms collapsing beneath him, pressing up his tight, perfect ass even higher for Lennox. Pressing in further, he reached around, grasping Ash's dick with a loose circle of fingers, letting it slip through them as he began to fuck Ash in earnest.

"You like that, baby?" Lennox crooned as he felt his own pleasure begin to wash over him. Ash felt better than anything he'd ever experienced. Maybe because he wasn't just a body, but so much more. He held Lennox's heart in his hands and Lennox already knew he was going to treat it right.

"More, *please*," Ash begged, and Lennox was putty in his hands, too. Wanted to give him everything he wanted, even though he felt his knees begin to buckle a little—not necessarily from the exertion of his thrusts, but the overwhelming pressure and pleasure squeezing around him. And, he had to admit, seeing Ash like this? It was a whole different kind of euphoria.

Suddenly, Ash tightened around him, and gave a long wail as he came hard, with long, jerking spurts that Lennox mostly managed to catch in his hand. But then he felt his own control slipping, and finally, with one last deep thrust, he let go, letting his own orgasm wash over him.

"Goddamn," Lennox exhaled as he let his cock slip out of Ash, and he unsteadily made his way to the bathroom.

When he came back, Ash was curled on his side, smiling sleepily, with a secretive tilt to his lips.

Lennox helped him clean up and then he slid into bed next to him.

"I really want this to be how it is all the time," Lennox said softly, bringing up the subject Ash had started earlier. "If this was what we could have together, I'd be the happiest man in the world."

Ash pressed his lips to his bicep. "Second happiest," he claimed. "Because I believe that first spot is already taken. By me."

CHAPTER SIXTEEN

Ash woke up with the warmth of Lennox still in the sheets, but as he stretched out, he realized the bed was empty. Sitting on his pillow was a bright yellow sticky note. Something about going to check up on a phone call he'd received about one of the clubs downtown he managed the security for.

Ash wished that Lennox had woken him up to tell him himself, but he understood that Lennox probably hadn't wanted him to wake at all. But he got out of bed anyway and went to the bathroom, and then when he came back, he detoured into the living room to find his phone.

They had agreed he wasn't going in today, but he wanted to send a text to Harmony, to make sure everything was ready for the new collaboration dish with Ross.

But to Ash's surprise, there was a message from an unknown number sitting in his inbox.

Ash sat down on the edge of the bed

It was from someone who claimed he was his father. And he wanted to meet up. To talk. To make sure Ash was alright.

They hadn't spoken in years. It was completely and totally possible that his father had changed his phone number and hadn't told him. When Ash had been growing up, he'd done it the way most celebrities do—once or twice a year, to prevent the "wrong kind of people" from getting it.

At the time, Ash had thought this was just another of his father's snobby quirks, but then a few months back, Tate had complained one night at the Funky Cup that Chase had had to change his phone number *again*.

Ash had almost forgotten about his father complaining about that, too—but Tate's comments brought it all back.

And now, staring at the unknown number, with its stiff message, so like Stephan, unable to actually *ask*. Instead, he'd demanded, *telling* Ash to meet him at the food truck lot, at his own truck, at seven.

It was just past six thirty now.

He could call Lennox and ask him what he should do. Lennox would want to do some digging. He would want to go in prepared. By the time he felt they'd vetted the message and the sender, the meeting time would be long past, and Ash would have lost out on the opportunity to know if his father actually meant any of this.

He'd told himself—and in the last week, everyone who asked—that he had no interest in mending the relationship.

And he *didn't*.

But he'd have to be made of stone, or maybe of ice, to not give a fuck that his own father didn't care that he'd been in danger.

Maybe he wouldn't be as receptive to what his father was going to say as he surely wanted him to be, but there was a part of him that still wanted to hear it.

He wanted to hear it, and then make his own decision. It had been a long time. Maybe, despite all his experience to the contrary, his father had mellowed. Maybe he'd come to regret how things had ended between them.

Ash couldn't say he *regretted* it exactly, because at the time, he'd done it for so many fantastic reasons, the most important being his own fucking sanity.

But it *had* been years. Things could have changed, for both of them.

He would be exactly like his father, a fate he'd worked so goddamned hard to avoid, if he ignored this message. If he refused to ever bend or even *listen*.

Ash stood up, his mind made up. But first, he should at least let Lennox know where he was going. But after he dialed his number, there were a dozen rings, and then it went to his voicemail. He left a quick message, explaining that he was going to talk to his father, at the food truck lot, but . . .

Ash sighed in frustration. He knew it was probably a mistake to go—this might not even *be* his father. It could be Aaron. But he felt like he didn't have a choice.

Maybe he'd even be back before Lennox even returned. Knowing his father, he would want to say his piece and then go back to the work he believed was more important than anything else.

No doubt he would be furious that Ash went out, alone, but there was the twenty-four-seven guard at the food truck lot, anyway. Nothing was going to happen to him there.

He threw on one of Lennox's big dark hooded sweatshirts, brushed his teeth, and pulled on a pair of loose sweats. It was early enough that there would still be a chill in the air.

Quietly, he walked through the living room and twisted the front door handle, letting himself out.

The walk to the lot was quick.

It was still early enough that he didn't see almost anybody.

He'd fully expected to see the guard that Lennox had hired as soon as he walked onto the lot. But not only was it still quiet, they were nowhere to be found.

Lennox, Ash knew, was not going to be very happy about that when he found out.

He headed to his own truck, which is where his father had suggested they meet.

Everything was dark. Even though it had only been a few days since Ash had been here, it had still been the longest amount of time since he'd started his truck, four years ago, that he'd gone without working.

He took a day or two off sometimes, but never three days. It had been interminable.

Ash pressed a hand to the stainless steel side. "Hey there, baby," he said in a low voice. "Good to see you again."

"And people think *I'm* the crazy one."

Ash heard the voice behind him, and he froze, the blood in his veins and every single muscle turning to solid ice.

That was *not* his father's voice.

"No, I'm not Atkinson, that fucker," Aaron said, all casually, like he hadn't just lured Ash here under false pretenses. "But isn't that sweet? I wasn't sure you'd even give a shit about him anymore, but here you are, still desperate for daddy's approval."

Ash took a short breath, wishing his lungs felt bigger. But they felt cramped and small, like he couldn't get enough air in them. *Panic*, he thought dimly, *I'm totally panicking.*

"Aaron," Ash said, finally turning around. The sight in front of him made his throat close up. There, in the early morning sunlight, stood Aaron, casually pointing a gun at Ash like he did it every single day.

There'd been plenty of times that Ash had been afraid in his life, but all of them paled in comparison to this one.

"I actually thought it would be hard to get you here." Aaron laughed, like Ash had heard him do a hundred times before. A thousand. It didn't sound any different than it had all those other times, which made Ash wonder, just how long Aaron had been like this.

For as long as he'd known him? Had the imagined slights been festering all this time, waiting for the right moment to explode?

Ash shuddered.

"Why are you doing this?" he asked. "I've never . . . we've always been friends, Aaron. I . . ." Ash swallowed hard. "I even looked up to you. The way you left Hook & Slope, and went out on your own. That inspired me to do the same. And now I find out that you . . .” Ash didn't know how to finish the sentence. He hadn't understood Aaron's enmity before, and he still didn't understand it.

He wondered if he actually *wanted* to understand it.

“Do you know,” Aaron said, still pleasant and conversational, despite the gun he was pointing at Ash, “that Ross tried to leave me? Tried to go back to your dad? I couldn't fucking believe it. And even despite whining and groveling, he wouldn't hire him back. But you know what? He'd hire *you*.”

“I don't want to work for him,” Ash said, holding his hands up, trying to reason with him. But Aaron seemed lost in his own world, and Ash wasn't sure there was a way to reason with him.

“And that,” Aaron snarled, suddenly angry, the hatred and resentment blooming on his face, “*that* is the fucking worst thing of all. He still wants you back, desperately, and yet you just waltz around here, fucking oblivious. Like you don't give a shit.”

“If you want to work for him again, if Ross wants to work for him again, I can talk to him for you,” Ash said, feeling his own kind of desperation wash through him.

“Of course you'd do that,” Aaron said with a sneer. “So sweet and giving and kind. Aren't you just Saint fucking Ash?”

Ash stared at the gun pointed at him, mesmerized.

He felt so stupid. How had everything gotten so out of control? How had everything gone so wrong?

He wished he'd never left the peace and safety of Lennox's bed.

Oh God, Lennox.

If Aaron didn't kill him, then Lennox was going to.

"Why would you even want to give up your food truck and go back to work for my father?" Ash thought he'd heard someone say, a long time ago, in some barely remembered safety presentation, that if you were ever threatened, it was good to keep them talking. And, Ash was certain, if anyone was going to want to give a hard-core villain soliloquy, it was going to be Aaron. He seemed just the type to want to brag about how smart and awesome he was. How good he was at being bad.

"I didn't want to give up and go back to work for him," Aaron snarled. "But fucking Ross. *He* wanted to. He wanted to leave me."

"I'm real sorry to hear that," Ash said with as much sympathy as he could muster. Frankly, he didn't mean any of it. He couldn't blame Ross one bit for wanting to escape this crazy asshole. Even if it meant going back to work for his father.

"No, you're not," Aaron said. "If you were sorry, you'd have never left him to begin with."

"You know how terrible he was," Ash said, "I couldn't stay there."

Aaron stared at him. It was unnerving and Ash wished he'd peed before leaving the house. Because he was so fucking terrified, the possibility of him peeing his pants was more of an option than he wanted to admit.

"You had *everything*," Aaron said, walking closer. Ash swallowed convulsively, eyeing the gun as it came nearer and nearer. "You had fucking everything and you gave it up. To make *salad*."

Ash hated, *hated*, the way Aaron was questioning him, but also making him question his own decisions. It was one thing to be really happy with how your life had turned out, and it was another to be really happy with how your life had turned out when you had a fucking gun pointed to your head.

He also remembered that the safety course had suggested that disagreements were bad—that you should do whatever you could to diffuse the situation, not enrage the person who was threatening you.

But Ash couldn't let Aaron's words stand.

"I'm actually happy making my salads, thanks," he said. He backed up another step, and felt the stainless steel against his back, the chill evident even through the heavy sweatshirt material.

Aaron kept coming, though, and there was nowhere else for Ash to go.

"It's fucking offensive that you keep clinging to this stupid idea that what you do is worthwhile. You could be working for your dad. Going places. Doing important shit. And you keep wanting to *slum it*." Aaron had gotten so close that the black matte metal of the gun barrel felt it was practically pressed to Ash's forehead. His knees felt weak and panic kept rising in him in desperate, horrified waves. He needed to do something, but he didn't know what.

He wished, more than anything, that he'd listened to Lennox. That he hadn't gone out on his own. That he'd been *smart*, and not cared if his father had actually ever given a shit about him.

"You know what? We're gonna make sure you can't fucking do it again," Aaron continued, like he didn't even care that Ash hadn't replied. Ash didn't *have* a reply. His tongue felt swollen and heavy in his mouth and his throat had closed over. He could barely huff out a breath. Anything else, with the gun that fucking close to him, was impossible.

"Do what?" Ash finally managed to speak. It was hard. Even harder was the deranged delight blooming across Aaron's features.

"We're gonna make sure you're done here." Aaron's fingers closed around Ash's upper arm with a firm, unrelenting grip, and Ash, for a split second, considered doing something crazy and insane, like kneeing Aaron in the balls and trying to run away. But the gun, the barrel practically resting on his forehead now, stopped him.

"Come here," Aaron said, dragging him along with him until they reached the back of the truck. The door was standing ajar, which probably meant that Aaron had broken in long before Ash had showed up.

Where was that fucking guard? Had he not been here after all? Maybe he'd just gone for coffee and he would be back soon?

Aaron must have seen the panic and the slight glimmer of hope in Ash's eyes because he just laughed. It was just like his normal laugh that Ash had heard so much, but now that he was truly listening, Ash could hear the ugliness underneath it.

"You think that security guard that your asshole boyfriend posted is gonna come save you?"

"No," Ash said. Except he had been.

"He's not going anywhere," Aaron said.

Ash felt an additional, nauseating wave of panic wash over him. "What did you do with him?"

"Nothing you need to worry about. He'll recover . . . eventually." Aaron's smile—just like his laugh—was something that Ash had seen so many times he'd barely even noticed it anymore. But he looked today, and it was impossible to miss the nastiness lurking in it.

How had he never noticed before? Ash was kicking himself now, for never really looking. For trusting that someone who appeared friendly on the outside was who they presented themselves to be.

"Now"—Aaron gave him a shove—"get in the truck."

Ash felt chilled. What if he got into his beloved food truck and then never left it again? Aaron had said that the guard would eventually recover, so at least he wasn't dead, but then he hadn't hated the guard the way he clearly hated Ash.

Who *knew* what he would do to Ash, if he gave him the opportunity.

"And don't even think about trying anything," Aaron continued, gesturing with the hand holding the gun. He seemed confident with it in his hand. Ash hesitated. "I know lots of places where a bullet won't kill you."

"Your Google search must be a real treasure trove," Ash said under his breath.

Aaron frowned. "You think I'm some kind of amateur, don't you?"

Ash watched as the fingers holding the gun tightened, going white at the joints. The gun never wavered, not one tiny bit. And Ash knew, deep down in his gut, that not only was Aaron *not* an amateur, he was not kidding around. He would, absolutely, without question shoot Ash. Not in his heart or his head, where he might die quickly. But somewhere horrible, that would cause unspeakable pain. And Ash began to shake, freezing despite the warmth of Lennox's sweatshirt.

He climbed up the stairs, Aaron following close behind. Too close. There was no way to escape.

"No, no, of course not," he said, his teeth chattering so hard he couldn't make them stop. He stopped, and turned, the edge of the front counter digging into his back. "God, please don't hurt me."

He hadn't intended to beg; he had his pride, didn't he? But in the end, it slipped out before he could stop it.

Aaron smiled, slow and satisfied. "If you do what I want, nobody has to get hurt."

"What do you want?" Ash was terrified to find out.

He gestured to an unmarked white plastic container that Ash knew he hadn't seen before, but that he'd missed in his general panic.

"I want you to take that and dump it out, everywhere," Aaron said.

"What?" It was nothing like what Ash had expected.

"Dump. It. Out." Aaron's tone turned inexorable.

"What is it?" Ash hated the way his voice shook as he reached for it. Wondered if maybe he could throw it in Aaron's eyes and disrupt him for just long enough to escape.

But Aaron moved back, down the stairs, just out of reach. Like he'd already considered the implications. Ash thought of what Lennox had said about whoever had been tormenting him. That he was scarily eerily smart. Always one step ahead.

Ash thought of the way his father had always praised Aaron's analytical brain, while, at the same time, maligning it for being *too* rational. "No art in you," Stephan Atkinson had always told Aaron. And seeing Aaron now, Ash could see it too.

Too much coldly terrifying logic.

"Lighter fluid."

Ash's fingers grasped numbly for the container. "What?" he exclaimed.

"I told you," Aaron said, so reasonable, "I was going to make sure you couldn't slum it anymore." He waved around at Ash's food truck. The one he'd slaved for. Dealt with every shitty hand he'd ever been dealt, just so he could have this and his independence.

"You want me to burn my truck."

Aaron grinned. "Big explosion. Maybe pull another few trucks in, too, with their propane tanks." He sighed. "Too bad Tony's truck is on the other side of the lot. I'd have loved for him to be collateral damage."

"You hate him, too," Ash stated. Hoping, without any real chance of success, that he might delay or distract Aaron long enough to forestall him. Maybe Lennox would get his voicemail. Maybe someone else would show up and unnerve Aaron just long enough to save Ash and his truck.

But Aaron's nerves seemed to be made of iron—unlike Ash's.

Still, he couldn't just let Aaron force him to do this.

"He's a smug asshole," Aaron said. "But *you* wasted everything I ever wanted. You had it all. And you took it from me."

Ash considered telling him that wasn't true. That it had been a poisoned gift, from the very beginning, and even if Aaron had eventually supplanted him, it wouldn't have been enough. Because nothing was ever enough for Stephan Atkinson.

"But Tony?" Aaron continued ranting. "Tony *thought* he was hot shit, from the beginning, even though he wasn't. Even though he didn't have jack shit."

Ash gulped. Maybe he *could* keep Aaron going like this. Anything would be better than dumping this lighter fluid out and then lighting the match.

"Come on, then," Aaron said. "What are you waiting for? Do you want to lose a kneecap forever? Maybe they can reconstruct those? I can't imagine you want to find out."

Ash didn't. With shaking fingers, he opened the top of the container, and feeling his heart fall painfully to the floor, he started pouring the lighter fluid everywhere. He tried to keep it away from the propane tank, though he was afraid that it wouldn't matter anyway.

Aaron made a tsking sound. "Get it everywhere," he said, gesturing with the gun. "Especially right over by the tank. Do you think you could possibly be smarter than me?"

"I guess not," Ash retorted, angry and terrified and really fucking sick to his stomach. He did what Aaron said, because what else could he do?

"Enough," Aaron finally said. He pulled a lighter out of his pocket, and tossed it. Ash barely caught it. "Drop it," he instructed. "And then we'll go have a nice little chat outside, warm our hands by the fire."

Ash took one last look at the truck he'd bought used, and remodeled and altered to exactly his specifications with his own two hands. It had been everything he'd wanted, four years ago. Everything he'd ever worked for.

It had meant everything. A chance for freedom, for independence. An opportunity to do things that *he* found valuable.

His truck had ended up being all of that, and more. It had brought him to Tony and his circle of friends—friends that had ended up supplanting the family that he'd rejected.

As Ash flicked the lighter on, he decided he had to believe that this was just a collection of stainless steel parts. It wasn't worth Ash's life.

Especially not the life he'd built now.

He dropped the lighter.

When he'd finally gotten out of the meeting at the club, Lennox had checked his phone, and as he'd listened to the message, his heart had just about stopped beating in his chest. Ash had left? Ash had walked, willingly, into a trap. He'd driven like a maniac on the way back to the lot, hoping that by the time he arrived, the worst hadn't come to pass.

He was off his bike and already running towards the lot, panic streaking through him, when the explosion rocked him back on his heels.

He was only a few hundred feet away, but later he wouldn't remember sprinting the last bit of distance, desperation and terror warring inside of him, that he'd just lost the most important person in his life, right when he'd found him, because he hadn't been there to protect him.

When he crossed onto the lot, he ducked behind Alexis' truck, feeling intense relief at seeing Ash and Aaron standing in front of the truck, flames shooting out of the windows. The explosion had probably been from the propane tank blowing.

Aaron had a gun trained on Ash, and even from across the lot, Lennox could hear Ash begging him to let him go, over the crackling sound of the flames and the sound of glass crunching in the heat of the fire.

He was smart, Lennox thought with annoyance. Aaron had deliberately not put his back to the rest of the lot. It would be almost impossible to sneak up on him.

"Please," Ash said, and it gutted Lennox to hear the tears in Ash's voice. "Please, you've destroyed my truck and my business. Just let me go. Surely this is enough."

Lennox wished that he could somehow grab Ash's attention without attracting Aaron's too, but he was too far away. And he didn't want to let Ash out of his sight now, not when Aaron had that gun and seemed totally comfortable with it in his hand.

He was kicking himself now, for all the times he'd insisted that the stalker hadn't been violent.

He was plenty violent. He'd just been biding his time, lulling them all into a sense of safety before striking.

Aaron tilted his head. "No, not yet," he said. "I'm not done with you yet."

Oh, Lennox thought, but you *are*.

First, he pulled out his phone, and sent Seth a quick text, asking him to notify the police and get a fire truck here, so the blaze didn't ignite any of the other food trucks.

Then, he crept out of his hiding place, trying to keep to the very edge of Aaron's peripheral vision, hoping that he wouldn't notice him approach.

He was about twenty feet away when Ash's eyes widened and Lennox realized that he'd spotted him, instead.

And Ash, his brilliant, brave, incredible guy, recklessly grabbed Aaron's arm. Not the one holding the gun, but the other one, launching into a new set of pleading demands, all while turning Aaron just enough away from Lennox's approach that he would probably miss it completely.

Lennox covered that last twenty feet impossibly faster than he had when he was eighteen. He raised his gun, and checking his own periphery one last time, announced his presence.

"Put the gun down," Lennox said in a hard voice. "And step away from Ash."

Aaron turned around, slowly, shaking Ash's grip off his arm. "You backstabbing asshole," he hissed to Ash, glaring at him.

Ash shot him a disbelieving look. "You made me burn my own truck!" he exclaimed.

Aaron still hadn't put the gun down. Lennox waited a second, and then another one. The gun in Aaron's hand didn't waver, and so Lennox made a decision.

He wasn't going to let this dick hurt the man he loved.

Shifting his own gun down in a single smooth motion, he aimed and fired, already moving to put himself between Ash and the gun, when Aaron's knee buckled underneath him, blood seeping through his jeans into the dry dirt below.

Two steps in, and Lennox had his gun wrenched out of his hand, flicking the safety back on.

He could feel Ash quivering behind him, and he put a hand out, steadying the man he loved.

"You're good, you're safe," Lennox murmured, not wanting to turn his back even for a minute, even though the blood pumping out of the ruins of Aaron's knee probably meant that he wouldn't be doing much walking. Not for awhile, he thought with a savage satisfaction.

He'd have to answer far more questions from the cops than he would have if he hadn't discharged his weapon and shot Aaron, but truthfully, he was glad he'd done it, and it didn't matter if he had to face more paperwork. Given the same set of circumstances, he'd do the same thing again.

Ash walked around him, staring intently at Aaron, who was moaning on the ground.

He spat on the ground in front of Aaron, his face a mask of anger and pain. Lennox wished he could take some of it away but he knew, from his own past history, that this was something that Ash was going to have to work through on his own. Lennox could support him—and he would, as long as Ash would let him—but he couldn't make it stop.

Ash turned to Lennox, but just then, the sound of a fire truck horn blaring cut through the morning quiet. "I guess you called them," Ash said, glancing over at the ruins of his truck.

Lennox pulled Ash into his arms. "It'll be a blessing if yours is the only one that's lost," he said.

"I know," Ash said, but Lennox could already hear the tears clogging his throat. The undeniably acute pain of the loss.

"You can start over," Lennox said. "We'll help. I can't imagine that everyone won't be eager to do their part."

Ash didn't say a word. Just hugged Lennox tighter, and he swore to himself that not only would *he* do what he could to help rebuild Ash's business—he'd do whatever he could to convince the others, too.

Not that he actually believed they *would* need convincing. Everything he'd seen of Ash's friends and fellow food truck own-ers led him to believe that he'd probably have to get in line to help behind *them*. They were generous and giving and absolutely loyal to a fault. Lennox wouldn't trust the man he loved with many people, but he'd trust these guys.

The sound of water rushing through the big fire hose and hitting the truck with a metallic crash interrupted Lennox's thoughts.

Ash stepped away as one of the firemen approached them. He waved at Aaron on the ground, who was currently being tended to by an EMT. "He the guy who started the fire?" the man asked.

Lennox nodded.

"Thought so," the man said. "Saw your handiwork. Pretty sweet shot."

"He wouldn't quit," Lennox said, "so I made him quit."

"Is it your food truck, too?" the firefighter asked.

"No, it's mine," Ash said, answering. He wiped his eyes and the brave tenacity in his expression was enough to make Lennox love him even more.

"We're doin' what we can," the man said, addressing Ash, respect etched across his face. "Not sure what we can save, but we'll save as much as we can."

"I appreciate anything you can do."

"You know what the accelerant was?" the firefighter asked.

"Yes." Ash's voice went hard and flinty at the edges. "Lighter fluid. And then the propane tank."

"Yep. Good thing it didn't spread." The guy looked relieved at that, but not as relieved as Lennox felt. He couldn't imagine the guilt Ash would've felt if the destruction of his own truck had caused the destruction of anyone else's.

Ash nodded. He didn't look like he trusted himself to say much more, and Lennox wrapped an arm around his shoulders.

The EMT approached then. "You hurt anywhere?" he asked. "Any burns?"

"No, I'm fine," Ash said wryly. "Not a scratch on me. But what about the security guard? He said he'd 'taken care of him,' whatever that means."

"We found him," the EMT said. "Just a bruise on his head from getting knocked out and then tied up."

"I'm going to suggest you go sit down though," Lennox said, tugging him towards one of the picnic tables. "If I know Seth, he called Tony, and he should be here soon. But while you wait, you should sit. You've been through a nasty shock."

"Yes," Ash said uncertainly. He went where Lennox led though, taking a seat. Lennox turned to go, to speak to the police who had just arrived, but Ash caught his hand at the last second.

"I'm so fucking sorry," he said, guilt written across his handsome face. "I shouldn't have come."

"He lured you out," Lennox said. "He did, right? With that text you mentioned in your message."

"I should've known it wasn't him. That he wouldn't give a shit," Ash said bitterly. "But I *wanted* him to give a shit."

Lennox couldn't help it. He leaned down, and wrapped Ash up in his arms. "It's not your fault. You don't need to apologize for that. I wish he did, too. You deserve way fucking better than him."

"But I *know* better," Ash said. "I really know better." He looked down, picking at a loose thread on the sweatshirt he wore. *My sweatshirt,* Lennox thought, with a wave of protective, possessive love. "I thought you'd be angry."

"I'm just fucking relieved that the rat bastard didn't hurt you," Lennox said.

Ash's gaze when he looked up was painful. "He did hurt me," he said, "he made me destroy something I love. But," he added, "he didn't think it through, because it's not the only thing I love. Not anymore."

"I love you so goddamn much," Lennox said, feeling the wave wash over him in a single polarizing wave. He'd never imagined that he'd feel this way again. That he'd ever *let* himself feel this way again, not after Marcus. But with Ash, it had felt so natural and right. Like they belonged together. Like once they'd finally stopped chasing each other around, and fallen in together, they'd both known this was the end of the line.

"And you saved me. You weren't pissed, and you saved me." A tear dripped down Ash's cheek. "What did I ever do to deserve you?"

"You were just your own goddamned perfect self," Lennox said roughly.

A glimmer of a smile emerged on Ash's face. "I guess I'll have to keep being myself," he said.

Lennox found himself smiling back, against all the odds. "I guess so."

"Oh my God," Tony exclaimed, and Lennox looked up and there he and Lucas were, expressions shocked as they stared at the charred, blackened, currently soaked remains of Ash's truck. "What the *fuck* is going on?"

CHAPTER SEVENTEEN

LENNOX NEVER SHOULD'VE WORRIED.

The moment Tony arrived on the scene, he'd absorbed the situation, and then immediately started texting people.

By the time the police came over to take Ash's statement, Tony had been on and off the phone for an hour. Already arguing with Ash's insurance. It seemed, Tony had reported, that they were willing to give him *some* recompense for the damage, but they wouldn't replace everything. *But,* Tony had said, *we're gonna take care of it.*

Now, a week later, the fundraiser that he'd started arranging way back on that horrible morning, was finally happening.

At first, when Tony had told him about the destruction of Ash's truck, Chase, Tate's rich football player boyfriend, had offered to replace it, without any strings. Lennox wasn't surprised at all when Ash turned down his offer, grateful, but determined that he wasn't going to take any free handouts.

"What would that make me except my father's son?" he'd asked Lennox that night, when they were curled up in bed together.

"It would make you a pragmatist," Lennox said wryly.

But Ash had just shaken his head. "I can't accept that kind of charity," he said.

"What about this big fundraiser that Tony is planning?" Lennox had asked the next day, when it had become clear that this fundraiser was growing exponentially, that everyone they knew wanted to be involved. So many food truck owners, even ones that Ash said he hadn't spoken to in years, had volunteered. All of the trucks at the Food Truck Warriors lot would be involved. Tony had shifted the time to make sure it didn't happen when the Dodgers had a night game, and Lennox had been pretty sure he expected Ryan to bring the whole team—which he had.

And Chase? Chase might not have bought Ash a new food truck outright, but a good portion of the Riptide was there, all of them stuffing what had to be hundred-dollar bills into the plastic bins set out on each of the food trucks' front counters. And Lennox wasn't even counting the check that Landon and Quentin, his clients, who had recently dealt with a stalker of their own, had sent over when they'd heard about what happened.

"You should've just let him buy you a new truck," Lennox said to Ash, who was tucked into his side, as they sat near the front of the lot, at the glittery table that still read, where Aaron had painted it months before in big scrawling purple letters, *Suck a dick*.

Funny how something that had terrified them at first had now taken on the gloss of the highest honor.

The band, one that often played at the lot, had just finished a set, and their friends had taken a break from the dance floor to come chat with them. Or, more accurately, to tease Ash about the insane amount of cash that had been donated tonight. Enough, Lennox was pretty sure, to buy half a dozen food trucks.

"I know," Ash said regretfully, but he was smiling, his face glowing in the light of the firepits set around the lot. "I really should have just let him."

"You're gonna have enough capital to start a whole fleet," Lucas pointed out.

"Probably," Ash said, laughing now. "But I'm just going to keep what I need to get the new truck off the ground. Anything extra I'll donate to the local LGBT center."

That was the kind of man Ash was.

Giving. Generous. Selfless to a fault.

Someone like Aaron, who only cared about himself, could never comprehend someone who refused to use his father's connections to better himself. That was what it had come down to, anyway. An unbelievable amount of bitter resentment and anger over Ash rejecting the position he'd been born into, the silver spoon he'd chosen to remove from his mouth.

"That spoon? It had sharp edges," Ash had said, that first day. "Aaron never got that."

"He's incapable of getting it," Lennox had said. Which was probably the nicest way to say Aaron was fucking insane.

The good news about that was that after he underwent surgery to repair his knee, he'd be spending a number of years in prison, as part of the plea deal he'd signed.

Ash wouldn't have to worry about him for a very long time—if he ever had to worry about him again.

"Still, you can do anything you want, now," Lucas said. "You gonna stick to salad?"

"I think . . ." Ash had talked about this a lot with Lennox, and Lennox already knew that he was still unsure what the right path forward was. "I think I'm gonna take my time," he said. "I've got the capital. And for right now, I'm actually really enjoying working with Ross."

Tony, who'd come up behind his boyfriend, wrapping his arms around his shoulders, raised an eyebrow. "You really want to keep working at Basket?"

"It's nice to do something different," Ash said. "And I *like* Ross."

"*You* even like Ross now," Lucas said, elbowing his boyfriend in the side. "Be nice."

"I'm always nice," Tony insisted, and even Lennox joined in the chuckle that went around the table at that particular lie.

"No, you're not, but we love you anyway," Gabe chimed in, then turned to Ash. "Well, I can hardly fault you for wanting to work at Basket. I think their sales have doubled since you added that salad to their menu."

"'Cause it's fucking delicious," Sean said. "Best salad I've ever eaten."

Gabriel shot a look at his boyfriend. "Yeah, that's what I *meant*. And yeah, for *salad*, it's pretty damn good."

Sean just grinned.

Lennox still couldn't believe that he'd ended up here, in the middle of this family—a family they had not only created themselves, but that was more than a little choosy about who they welcomed into the fold—after so long of feeling like he was on the fringe, unable to get any closer.

He'd missed his team so much—but now, he realized, he had a *new* team now.

New people to love and care for and protect.

He'd ended up right in the thick of things, and while Ash certainly had a lot to do with that, Lennox liked to think it was more than that. He'd opened himself up, and instead of the derision he'd expected, he'd gotten only love and acceptance in return.

He'd been calling Ash his miracle, but maybe it went deeper than that.

Maybe he'd created his own goddamned miracle.

It had started with Seth, then they'd added the business that had given him an unexpected sense of accomplishment, and then, the food truck lot had opened, he'd met Ash, and it felt like everything had fallen right into place. Just like it was meant to be.

Ash leaned in and brushed a kiss across his lips. "I'm so happy you're here tonight," he said.

Like he could ever be anywhere else. "Me, too," he said.

"Get a room," Tate teased, leaning on the opposite end of the table.

Lennox had already found himself, more than once tonight, regretting that he'd so systematically gone through and lit every single dark corner in the lot. There was nowhere to hide, nowhere to sneak off and trade a few of the kisses he'd become so addicted to.

"Wish we could," Ash said, shooting a look at Lennox that made it clear he was *also* regretting Lennox's dedication to lighting up every good make-out spot.

"Well, we *can* go grab another drink," Lennox said, formulating a plan that might work. He'd told himself, when his relationship with Marcus had imploded, that he'd never search out another dark spot, but this was different. What he had with Ash could survive the strongest light, but some things were always better in private, in the dark.

"Sure." Ash smiled. "I guess we're celebrating."

"We are," Tate said encouragingly. "You're alive, and the guy is in jail, with a busted knee, thanks to Lennox. And you have the freedom to make any choices you want. I think all of that is worth celebrating."

"And," Ash said, his eyes meeting Lennox's as he took his hand, letting Lennox pull him upright, "I fell in love."

"Yeah, you did," Tony teased. "We all saw it coming."

Lennox decided that their love wouldn't just *survive* the light, but it would bloom in it. A circumstance that he'd never expected, and definitely hadn't anticipated. But he should have known, because the first day when Ash had smiled at him, it had felt like the sun coming into his shadows, for the very first time.

"Doesn't mean it's any less amazing," Lucas said, grinning up at his boyfriend. "They're good for each other."

Ash tangled his hand with Lennox's, and they walked off towards where Jackson and Shaw had set up a makeshift bar, the voices of their friends talking about how much they liked their relationship echoing behind them.

"I never thought it was inevitable," Ash said softly. "I wanted to be that sure, but real life . . . real life can be a bitch. But I wished for it to turn out this way."

"I never thought I'd get this lucky," Lennox admitted.

Ash squeezed his hand. "But you did. Though I'm not sure luck had anything to do with it. You won me over, one salad, and one cautious smile, at a time."

"They weren't always so cautious."

"No," Ash agreed, "but every time you *really* smiled, I felt like we had a chance."

"I like this much better," Lennox said. He'd never imagined he'd be comfortable walking hand in hand with a guy, never mind a boyfriend, but Ash had revolutionized everything.

He felt made new again. Like he wasn't just some washed-up, ex-military guy with a bum knee and a bad romantic history.

"You want another beer?" Ash asked as they approached the bar. Alexis was with Jackson, a possessive hand on the other man's hip, and Shaw had disappeared.

"Two more beers, please," Ash said, digging some money out of his pocket before Lennox could stop him.

"You got it," Jackson said, walking over to the cooler and digging two bottles out of the ice.

"Your brother take off?" Lennox asked.

It had always been his rule of thumb to keep an eye on people, but after the events of the last few weeks? Lennox wasn't going to let a thing happen to anyone he cared about—or anyone Ash cared about.

"Nah, he's grabbing some food," Jackson said. "I think Ross is just closing up."

"That salad," Alexis said, coming up to stand next to his boyfriend. "It's so good, that's why."

"Thanks," Ash said, stuffing the tip money into the jar. "High praise, coming from you. Your Greek salad is one of my favorites. You know that."

Alexis nodded.

"You should tell them," Jackson said, nudging his boyfriend with his hip.

"No, it's Ash's day," Alexis said staunchly.

"Seriously, if it's good news, I want to hear it," Ash said.

"I'm getting a second truck," Alexis said. "It was time to expand and . . . well, I'm a little sad because I'm gonna miss being so involved in the day-to-day, but I think it's the right call."

Lennox knew that during a lot of shifts, Alexis ran out of his most popular dishes. It seemed like he was prime for an expansion and he was glad for the man that he was taking it.

"That's amazing," Ash gushed. He reached over the makeshift bar and gave Alexis a quick hug. "I'm so happy for you."

"It seems like good news is in the air," Alexis said, with a slight flush to his cheeks, like he was embarrassed at how successful he'd been. And knowing Alexis, he probably was, because from what Lennox had observed, he was always downplaying his own achievements and celebrating everyone else's. But it was time that he got his day in the spotlight, and Lennox was glad he was finally taking it.

"Sure feels like it," Ash said. "Congrats again."

"And you, you're going to end up with a fleet of your own," Jackson teased Ash.

"Nope, I just want my own little corner," Ash said. "Whatever it ends up being."

"Whatever you do," Alexis said seriously, "it is sure to be a huge success. You are such a wonderful cook."

It was Ash's turn to flush. "Thank you," he said, "it's . . ." He swallowed, Lennox watching as his throat worked. "It means so much to me." He tilted his head up, and there was a plea in his eyes. *Get me out of here before I break down,* it said, and Lennox knew he couldn't do anything but step in.

"Great to see you two again," Lennox said, and wrapped his free hand around Ash's waist, and led him away.

Lennox had originally wanted to seek out this *one* area that he'd been needing to try to re-light for an entirely different reason, but as Ash leaned against the back of Tate's truck and wiped his damp eyes, he was glad he'd thought of it at all.

"Thanks," Ash said, reaching out and tugging Lennox closer. "I needed a minute."

"It's a lot to have all this, just for you," Lennox said.

Because he never stopped looking at Ash—didn't think he was capable of stopping, honestly—he'd seen more than once tonight, when the emotions of what was happening had threatened to overwhelm Ash.

He couldn't blame him; it was a lot to have this many people not only be willing to help, and wanting to help, but to go to these lengths to do it.

"Yeah, I just . . . it's hard to shake the feeling that I don't deserve this," Ash said.

Lennox gently grasped his chin with his fingertips and pulled his gaze upwards so it met his own. "You do," he said, "don't ever doubt it, okay?"

Ash smiled. "Thank you for saying that, and for meaning it. Even though it'd be easy for you to say it just because you love me, I don't think you are."

"You're the strongest person I know. You survived something a week ago that would've brought anyone else to their knees."

"I'm still a little bit of a mess," Ash admitted. He sighed. "But," he continued a moment later, "I can't say the future doesn't look really bright."

"It does," Lennox said, thinking that it looked that way not just because Ash could do whatever he wanted moving forward.

Ash leaned against him for a long moment, Lennox's arm going around him instinctively. They heard the band start up, even from where they were standing.

"I love you," Ash said quietly.

"I love you too," Lennox said, his own voice equally soft. He'd enjoyed this whole night—watching everyone celebrate the man he loved would never get old—but there was something about this, an inescapable permanency in the air, that made him like this moment the very best.

The whole night, Ash felt he was about five seconds away from bursting into tears. Happy tears. Sad tears. Tears of regret and longing and yet also, *belonging*.

His friends had seen his despair—and he'd been genuinely in pain, at the thought that he'd burned his own truck down—and turned it around, giving him the opportunity to do *anything* he wanted.

The sky, it felt pretty literally, was the limit.

Then he almost *had* cried, but Lennox, like the goddamned savior he was, had known and had whisked him away for the quiet that he hadn't realized he'd needed until the moment had arrived.

"Hey," Ash said, leaning in to murmur into Lennox's ear, "let's go dance."

Lennox shot him a look. "How do you know I dance?" he asked very sternly.

But Ash wasn't fooled. Not for a moment. Lennox's walls might still be up, though not as high and not as fortified as they'd been in the past, but he'd let Ash in. And now Ash knew just how much of a softy he was. How he'd do anything, if it would just make Ash smile.

Ash knew that he'd do the exact same thing.

"You'll dance, for me," Ash said, feeling confident that he was right.

Lennox sighed, and shot him a very affectionate look. "Only for you," he said.

They were stopped a handful of times on the way to the dance floor. Sean and Gabe, heading, it seemed, to the dark area they'd just vacated. Tate and Chase were on their way out—along with all the football players that Chase had brought. "There's always time for an after-party," Chase had said with a bright, happy grin. "We'll be at my place til dawn."

Tate had rolled his eyes, and Ash had known they'd be happily settled in bed together by midnight.

When they finally hit the dance floor, Ash could spy several of their friends, already moving to the music, and when they joined them, it turned out that Lennox was a surprisingly good dancer.

"You're good at this," Ash said, surprised, because it was something he'd never anticipated from his boyfriend.

Lennox grinned. "You didn't think I would be," he said.

"No," Ash said, moving closer, feeling Lennox's fingers dig into his hips. Remembering a few nights ago, when they'd been digging in the same way, when Lennox had been moving deep inside of him.

For a long moment, they were quiet, hearing just the music, and the sound of laughter around them. It was hard for Ash to drag his eyes off Lennox—he was captivating in the firelight, all rough edges and flawless lines, those dark eyes that he'd once found so mysterious staring at him with so much love and adoration, Ash thought he could drown in them and never complain.

"You hiding any more secrets from me?" Ash said, as the band switched up the song to something a bit quicker in tempo.

To his credit, Lennox didn't bat an eyelash. "Me?" he asked.

"Yeah," Ash said. "*You*. Apparently there's some real big mystery about your name."

"My name?"

Ash laughed. "Yeah, apparently it's driving some people crazy that they don't know whether Lennox is your first name or your last. I think Ren put money on it being your *middle* name."

"*Some people* but not you?" Lennox wanted to know, surprise in his voice.

"Nah," Ash said, "it's not like a name really means anything, right? It's *you* I fell in love with, not your name. If you want me to call you Lennox, then I'm cool calling you Lennox. After all, you've never tried to call me Oliver."

"Probably because you'd try to chop my fingers—or my balls—off for doing it," Lennox said, smiling.

"Try?"

Lennox tilted his head as they swayed to the music. "I've got pretty good reflexes. Quick on my feet. You could try, but I'm pretty sure I'd get away."

"I guess that's true." Ash paused, for maximum dramatic effect. "Levi."

The shock on Lennox's face was genuine. "How did you know? How long have you known?"

"For a week," Ash said, sliding his hands up over Lennox's shoulders, pulling him in closer, until their lips were almost touching. "One of the police officers who interviewed me referred to a statement given by a 'Levi Lennox' and I assumed that had to be you."

"Damn it," Lennox said, but those dark eyes were twinkling now. He wasn't mad; and Ash hadn't really anticipated that he would be. He knew what it was to feel like a different person than the name you'd been born with. He'd never, not from the very beginning, felt like Oliver Ashton, and when he'd finally broken with his father, he'd finally begun to grow into the Ash that he'd always known he was inside.

"You're not upset that I know?"

Lennox leaned in even closer, their lips touching just barely. Just enough that Ash knew he'd never get enough, never stop craving *more*. "As long as you don't tell Tony," he said.

"My lips are sealed," Ash said, seriously.

"They are now," Lennox said, and leaned him back, finally kissing him thoroughly. Perfectly. Exactly the way that Ash had wanted to be kissed that first day, when he'd looked up and Lennox had been standing in front of his truck.

Everything, the good, the bad, the absolutely fucking terrible, had been leading to this, and right now? Ash wouldn't trade what he'd found for anything.

Because this moment in time, his friends and his family, dancing under the Los Angeles stars, with the love he shared with Lennox shining as brightly as anything overhead, had been worth it.

To read a bonus scene about Tony and the Opening Day of Food Truck Warriors, click here.
To continue the Food Truck Warriors series with *Wheels Down*, Shaw and Ross' story, click here.

INTERESTED IN READING MORE OF
BETH'S BOOKS?

CHECK OUT A FULL LIST OF TILES
BY SCANNING THE QR CODE
OR VISITING HER WEBSITE

WWW.BETHBOLDEN.COM/BOOKLIST

WANT TO FOLLOW BETH?

MAKE SURE YOU NEVER
MISS A RELEASE?

SCAN THE QR CODE BELOW
OR VISIT HER WEBSITE
FOR A SOCIAL MEDIA LIST,
NEWSLETTER SIGNUP,
AND SO MUCH MORE!

WWW.BETHBOLDEN.COM/ABOUT